Ambrose Bierce
AND THE
Queen of Spades

A MYSTERY NOVEL

OAKLEY HALL

UNIVERSITY OF
CALIFORNIA PRESS

BERKELEY
LOS ANGELES
LONDON

University of California Press
Berkeley and Los Angeles, California

University of California Press, Ltd.
London, England

Library of Congress Cataloging-in-Publication Data

Hall, Oakley M.
    Ambrose Bierce and the queen of spades : a mystery novel / Oakley Hall.
    p. cm.
  ISBN 0-520-21555-9 (alk. paper)
    1. Bierce, Ambrose, 1842–1914?—Fiction. I. Title.
PS3558.A373A84 1998
813'.54—DC21   98-22719
                                                                            CIP

FOR EMMA

HOMICIDE, *n.*
The slaying of one human being by another.
There are four kinds of homicide: felonious,
excusable, justifiable and praiseworthy, but it
makes no great difference to the person slain
whether he fell by one kind or another—the
classification is for advantage of the lawyers.
—THE DEVIL'S DICTIONARY

When Ambrose Bierce heard of the first Morton Street Slasher murder, he said, "It appears there is a fellow who dislikes women more than I do."

On certain subjects he was so sarcastic that it was plain mean. His eyes got small under shaggy eyebrows and his mouth twisted beneath his fair mustache, and he would say something scurrilous about women or women poets or preachers or the SP Railroad.

He was my hero then. I'd always had to wince when I heard people carry on in a manner that seemed a fraud to me, on the subjects of religion, or the pure goodness of poor folk, or their sainted mother, or someone hailed a hero on not much grounds. Bierce hated fraud right to the bone. When I'd quit the Fire Department for a job assisting Dutch John, the printer of *The Hornet,* I had in mind becoming a journalist like Bierce. I'd had a good education from the Christian Brothers in Sacramento, and I'd read a library of books. What other training could be necessary? Being a famous journalist seemed a fine way to make a living, and there was some tone to it, too: people greeting you on the street and calling out they'd liked your last piece or go-it after the Railroad some more.

Bierce was the editor of *The Hornet* and columnist of "Tattle." I worked up the nerve to bring him pieces of local interest I had written, one on the SP, which he hated especially—the Railroad, that is. He was courteous enough with me, since I wasn't a female poet who had offended him by publishing a volume of poetry he had to review in Tattle.

In fact when he wasn't abominating one humbug or another, Bierce was a generous gentleman.

The Hornet was a satirical weekly, with offices on California Street, right next to the Bank of California with its soaring columns. The new owner and publisher was Mr. Robert Macgowan. There were a couple of boozy reporters who hung around the police station at Old City Hall, a lady typewriter, a caricaturist named Fats Chubb, Dutch John the printer and his assistant Frank Grief, a couple of typesetters and Bierce.

Sometimes Bierce and I left the *Hornet* offices together in the evening, dodging through the traffic of buggies, carriages, hacks, wagons, horsecars, horsemen and bicyclists on California Street, and under the broad green awning into Dinkins's Saloon. The traffic on the downtown streets was so fierce that it was worth your life to cross over one of them, and almost every day, it seemed, in the *Chronicle,* the *Examiner* or the *Alta California,* there'd be a news piece on another bad accident, people killed and broken legs, and Something Must Be Done. But nothing was done except for things to get worse.

In Dinkins's with a lager before him, Bierce liked to talk about writing. He was the famous Almighty God Bierce for A. G. Bierce, Bitter Bierce, with his Tattle read all over the City, and I was a lowly printer's assistant and sometime reporter, who wasn't sure Mr. Macgowan was going to keep on paying my wages, but Bierce was pleased to give me advice.

"Check it sentence by sentence and word by word. Get the rubbish out! If you can't find the right adjective for a noun, leave it alone. A noun needs only one adjective, the choicest. Take out all the participles and adverbs you can. Participles grate like wheel rims on gravel.

Three participles in a sentence will ruin it. Too many adverbs makes language spineless.''

Dinkins's had a long bar solid with drinkers' backs, behind them a gleaming clutter of mahogany and mirrors and moony gaslight globes. Dick Dinkins laid out eats on the bar for the drinkers to dip into and kept the liquor flowing.

Bierce and I sat where we could see a broad slash of California Street through the door, with the traffic jammed up or moving fast and, on the sidewalk, gents in derbies and plug hats flipping canes in greeting to each other, and sometimes fine ladies or whores in pairs passing. Inside there was a pleasing stink of cigar smoke, beer, whiskey, sardines and cheese, and outside one of horse droppings, dust and busyness.

An old fellow with a billy-goat beard came over to ask Bierce if he'd heard the latest about Senator Sharon. Sharon had asked the famous French painter Meissonier if he was an Old Master, because Sharon wasn't dealing with any painters that "wasn't Old Masters.''

Bierce said he had heard it thirty-one times now by actual count. And added, "Served in the Senate, for our sins, his time / Each word a folly and each vote a crime." And he had something to say about the "Rose of Sharon,'' for one of Sharon's mistresses was presently in court claiming the King of the Comstock had married her, and she was divorcing him for adultery with a demand for alimony and her share of his millions.

So the old-timer didn't go off in a huff because though Bierce would scarify any kind of pretension that raised his ire in Tattle, when he was with fellows in a saloon there was an edge left off, or a joke added to soften his invective.

Bierce was in his forties at this time, a handsome figure of a man, just under six feet with sandy hair, a tangle of eyebrows and a full mustache. He had a smooth pink complexion and smelled of cologne, and he had a military way of carrying himself for he had been a major in the War. He was said to be the best-dressed journalist in San Francisco, with his tweed suit and high collar and fancy neckties with a diamond pin. I thought he was pretty much cock-of-the-walk, leaning back in his chair rubbing his glass against one side of his mustache and looking reflective, probably planning some verbal devilment.

Sergeant Nix stalked inside in his blue double-breasted nine-button uniform and sat down with his policeman's helmet on the table, one of the corps of folks who kept Bierce apprised of what was going on in the City. " 'Lo, Bierce," he said, and " 'lo, Tom," to me.

Nix and I had been baseball pals when the police team played the firemen, before I took the job on *The Hornet*.

Dinkins brought Nix a beer with a creamy head on it, and Nix told us about the messy murder last night in Morton Street, which was an alley running off Union Square bounded on both sides by red-light houses.

"Frenchy name of Marie Gar," Nix said. "Strangled her and slashed her open. Guts spilled out like a trout."

"It appears there is a fellow that hates women more than I do," Bierce said then.

"These cunt-hating lunatics," Nix said. "Their mother run off with a gambler when they was little tykes. Or some whore gave them a dose of Little Casino, and they can't wait to carve up a female."

"Any clues?" Bierce wanted to know.

Nix had a face like a hatchet and a black mustache that halfway wrapped around it. He nodded, licking foam from his mustache. "Ace of spades," he said. "Perpetrator left a playing card on the victim."

"Interesting," Bierce said. "Left how, if you please?"

"Stuck in her mouth like a letter in a postbox."

Bierce made a clucking sound.

"Ace of spades," I said. "Means death?"

They both looked at me.

"Anything a sterling young journalist like Tom Redmond ought to look into?" Bierce said.

"Ames from the *Alta* and that fat fellow from the *Chronicle* is all over it," Nix said. He scratched his fingers through his coarse hair.

"You could come down to the Morgue and look her over," he said to me with a bleak grin, and he said to Bierce, "If you are going to make a reporter of this young fellow, he is going to have to spend some time at the Morgue."

"I will make a prediction," Bierce said. "It has got to do with the Railroad."

Nix snorted. Bierce had an obsession about the Southern Pacific, the "Railrogues" as he called the Big Four, Leland Stanford, Collis B. Huntington, Charles Crocker and company.

"Simple deduction," Bierce said. "The Southern Pacific is behind 90 percent of the corruption in the State of California. A strangled and slashed dove is an eruption of corruption. Ergo."

Nix and I gaped at him.

"When a monopoly controls the state legislature—both houses and both political parties—and runs the state from their offices at Fourth and Townsend, it is a state of disgrace. The SP is the monopoly on transportation in the State of California, and the monopoly on corruption."

"They don't control the Democrat party in the City," I said. "The San Francisco Democracy is Antimonopoly."

Bierce said scornfully, "Do not be too sure of that, Tom."

What Bierce said of the SP was true enough. The transcontinental railroad had been completed in 1869 and since then the Big Four's Monopoly had covered the state like knee-deep muck. The Railroad not only owned the Republican legislature, they hired bullyboys and enforcers and, in the Mussel Slough Massacre, gunmen. And my father worked for them.

But Bierce also denounced the Democrat machine that ran the City government—Chris Buckley, the Blind Boss, and Mayor Washington Bartlett and the Supervisors—in what he called the "hauls of power."

I was a member of a Democrat club called the True Blue Democracy. Sometimes we had brawls with Railroad toughs who liked to break up our meetings.

Nix finished his beer, clapped on his helmet and rose. "Come along then, Tom," he said to me.

So I went along with him to the City Morgue in Dunbar Alley, to view my first corpse.

I was born and raised in Sacramento, where my mother and father still lived on M Street, my mother with her children grown and gone, sitting on the porch to smoke a cigar when one came her way, watching the wagons pass. My father, the Gent, was apt to troop off after the latest bonanza. He'd never got the gold fever out of his blood. Between jaunts he worked for the SP at one job or another. In his time, I knew, he had chased women as well as silver strikes.

I left home to move down the Sacramento River to San Francisco as soon as I finished my schooling. I was a fireman for four years. After that I worked at the *Chronicle* for six months as a printer's devil. There I began writing pieces and showing them to an editor who recommended me to Bierce at *The Hornet*.

And I attended Policemen's and Firemen's and Charity Balls, in the hopes of meeting my True Love, in San Francisco where there were not enough women to go around.

I roomed with a family named Barnacle, on Pine Street, and made my ablutions at the Pine Street Baths. Jonas Barnacle was a carpenter who suffered from "the weakness" and did not work much, except to make repairs on his house and sit on the stoop observing street passages. Mrs. B. was the harried keeper of a boardinghouse with four male boarders who shared dinners with her and Mr. Barnacle and the young Barnacles aged five to thirteen, the oldest being pretty Belinda, whom I'd promised to marry when she was eighteen.

My room was the third-floor loft, with bed, desk, washbasin and pitcher, three shelves of books and a slice of view out a bay window down Pine to Kearny. An outside rickety staircase gave me more privacy than any of the other tenants, though I had less headroom. Boarders were forbidden to bring women to their rooms.

There was an outhouse in the backyard, with its path obstructed by Mrs. B.'s washing on the clotheslines Mondays. I had nailed a buggy seat to the cellar wall, and went down there to practice boxing maneuvers and straight lefts and right hooks, to help protect the True Blue Democracy Antimonopolies from the Monopoly bullies.

Belinda Barnacle sat on the stoop with a book hugged to her chest, watching me thump up the wooden steps. She was a bright-haired, small-featured, skinny child with no figure to her yet. "Good evening, Tom!"

"Good evening, Belinda." I was not feeling much like our usual evening literary conversation because of what I had seen at the Morgue. But I asked what she was reading.

She showed me the cover of one of the books I had lent her: *Ivanhoe*.

"Good book!"

"Is a Jewess like Mr. Cohen?"

"Just like."

"They wrote things on his store. 'Jews must go!' Like 'Chinese must go!' "

"People write things like that about Irishers too, Belinda. It is just low-tone people trying to make somebody else lower still." The ignorant persecuting the helpless, as Bierce might have said. Belinda had asked to read *The Adventures of Huckleberry Finn*, which had nothing but low-tone characters, but I didn't think she was ready for it yet. The novel had come out to a lot of criticism from readers who had liked *The Adventures of Tom Sawyer*. Bierce had praised its plain style of narrative, though I suspected him of being jealous of Mark Twain's successes. Bierce was the only famous writer other than Sidney Lanier who had actually served in the War between the States.

I had to wash off the morgue stink. The sight of that poor, chalk-pale, torn-apart body had laid a pall over me. It was beyond comprehension why anyone would want to do such a thing. I hadn't been shown the ace of spades.

"I've got to get a bath," I said.

"Are you going to the Firemen's Ball?"

"Yes!"

Belinda hugged *Ivanhoe* to her chest. Tight braids hung down the back of her checked gingham dress. Her feet were pigeon-toed in scuffed shoes.

"Will you dance with ladies there?"

"I hope to."

"Will you dance the waltz?"

"Indeed we will!"

"Father Kennedy says it is very sinful."

"I don't believe Father Kennedy has ever seen a waltz waltzed."

She grinned, showing outsize front teeth, which gave her a charming raffish air. "Will you take me waltzing some day, Tom?"

"With Father Kennedy's permission!" I said and trotted up the steps that Jonas Barnacle ought to spend some time strengthening with his hammer and a pocketful of nails.

It was to be the night I met my True Love.

MISS, *n.*
A title with which we brand unmarried women
to indicate that they are in the market.
—THE DEVIL'S DICTIONARY

Her name was Amelia Brittain, and she had come to the Firemen's Ball accompanied by her brother, who was home from Yale. I was fortunate to be granted a dance with a young lady whose father was at least minor nobility of what Bierce called the "instant aristocrats" of Nob Hill. She was tall and graceful-gawky with a heart-shaped high-color face and light brown hair frizzed around her forehead like a halo. She weighed no more than an ounce of lace in my arms as we swept around the gleaming floor. I breathed her flower scent and took notice of the engagement ring on the hand I held in mine. The ring cast expensive glints as we circled under the heat of the gaslights.

Yes, she was engaged; to Beaumont McNair. I knew who Beau McNair was, all right. She was Nob Hill, and he was to Nob Hill what Nob Hill was to South of the Slot. His mother, the widow of one of the Comstock kings, had gone to England and married a title so that she was Lady Caroline Stearns. Beau McNair was only recently back in San Francisco. Amelia Brittain was his childhood sweetheart. Some of this I learned around the punch bowl from the socially interested firemen there and other young bachelors working in the City like myself, and some from Amelia herself.

I waltzed sinfully with Amelia past the band of music on its dais, sweat damp on my forehead from the July heat, and a gleam on hers as well. She smiled at me with her pink lips. Her dark stripes of eyebrows were raised as though she was always pleasantly surprised. I may have led her to believe I was a more important journalist than was actually the case and did not mention that I turned into a printer's helper and general tote-and-lift on Thursday nights when *The Hornet* went to press.

She said she didn't think she had ever danced with a Democrat before.

We compared educations. I had received my sums, grammar and Latin from the Christian Brothers in Sacramento, she had "finished" at Miss Cooley's Institute in San Francisco.

I steered her outside onto the balcony that overlooked the Tenderloin and, down to the left, the broad swath of Market Street cocooned in light. To the west the city lights spread out over the hills and ganged together in the valleys, disappearing into the fog bank. We stood at the railing in the cool air off the Bay. I pretended to be intent on admiring the views beneath us. I was unused to women who were almost as tall as I.

"It is so beautiful at night," Amelia said. "But think of the evil events that may be happening down there even as we stand here."

"Earlier this evening I viewed the remains of a poor young woman who had been slaughtered by a madman."

"My father read of it in the *Alta,*" Amelia said. "A terrible murder. And she was a—*low* woman?"

"On Morton Street." I pointed. Between Nob Hill and Market Street was Union Square, fronting on it the fancy parlorhouses of the Upper Tenderloin. Running off Union Square toward Market Street were the red-tinted lights of Morton Street. Out of our sight was Portsmouth Square, another rabbit hutch of cribs and whorehouses and, in between, the warrens of Chinatown where the slave girls shrilled their invitations.

It was shameful, with this young lady at my side, to be thinking of the City as a palpitating mass of fornication.

"It is difficult for a young person to understand—" she said in a low voice. "All these women—"

"They say there are three men for every woman in San Francisco," I said. "Not so many years ago it was ten to one."

"But it is not merely young men, I understand. Married men as well." So we had been thinking of the same thing.

"A relief to their wives," I said.

"I don't understand that, Mr. Redmond."

"The gratification of the husband often endangers the health of his wife."

Her silence indicated that she didn't understand that either, and I was digging myself deeper into this matter than was proper.

"Wives who already have six or eight children," I added. "Or ten or twelve."

"Yes, I understand," she said quickly.

I turned to see the breeze riffling the curls that wisped around her face, which was set and intense as she gazed down on Morton Street. I glanced away so as not to be caught admiring her.

"Was she pretty, the murdered woman?" she asked.

"She was French. She had a bit of mustache, but she was pretty, yes." I could feel the expression on my face, like mud drying.

"Very young?"

"Not very young."

She rubbed her hands over her forearms as though she was chilled and said, "Mr. Redmond, young women of my station are very innocent of the life that goes on around them. We were speaking of our educations just now. I would like to take advantage of your more comprehensive education."

This time it was I who didn't know what she meant. I found my own hands smoothing the sleeves of my jacket, in imitation of her gesture.

"Will you escort me down to Union Square and Morton Street, Mr. Redmond?" she said. "So I may see something of these—*stews* with my own eyes."

"*Tonight?*"

She giggled suddenly. "My brother will be shocked. May I tell him you will escort me home?"

"Certainly!" I said, shivering.

So I accompanied Amelia Brittain down off Nob Hill, she in her cloak and bonnet, I wearing my derby and pretending more command of the evening than I actually felt. Her hand rested lightly on my arm. We turned down Bush Street in the darkness between the illuminated corners and passed men in groups of two and three. Some tipped their hats to Amelia.

The Alhambra Saloon, Boss Chris Buckley's headquarters, wore a crown of balls of light. Just as we were passing, a group of drinkers pushed their way outside, boisterously laughing and compounding my nervousness.

Among his consort of cronies was the Blind Boss himself. His fat white eyeballs stared straight ahead, his hat was cocked on his head. Amelia and I were surrounded by his bunch.

"Good evening, Mr. Buckley," I said. He would recognize my voice, for the magic of his hearing was that he could identify people by voice or even, some said, by footstep.

"Good evening indeed, Tom Redmond!" His face was wreathed in the ripples of his famous smile. "And how are you this pleasant evening, my friend?"

I introduced Miss Brittain.

Buckley doffed his hat and hunched his shoulders in a half bow. "And would this be the daughter of James M. Brittain?"

"Yes, he is my father," Amelia said in a strong voice.

"The highly regarded mining engineer," Buckley said, nodding. "Good evening to you, Miss Brittain. Your companion is a very fine young man, as I am sure you know. You must take trustful care of her, Tom. Good night, Miss Brittain! Good night, Tom!"

And he was swept away in his clutch of courtiers, who had, all, tipped their hats properly.

"That was the infamous Blind Boss!" Amelia whispered. Her hand had tightened on my arm.

"That was the famous Chris Buckley," I said, and turned us to cross Bush headed for Morton Street.

It was no place for a lady, and I was sorry I'd ever contracted for this tour before we even reached Union Square. The streetlights here burned more brightly while the shadows between were denser and alive with the movement of hatted men passing every which way, and restlessly grouping together. They generated a deep rustle of conversations. The fog was blowing down the streets with shivery air that seemed to touch my face like fingers.

"I don't believe I should take you any further along here, Miss Brittain," I said.

"It is by my request that we are here, Mr. Redmond. Is there danger?"

"I don't know," I said.

"Are you concerned that I will be insulted?"

"Yes."

"I believe I can tolerate that. Can you?"

"Not without responding," I said.

"It is a difference between the genders," she said.

We were in an area where the difference between the genders was celebrated. We edged between and past the groups of men toward the entrance to Morton Street. Amelia's hand lay on my arm an ounce more heavily. Morton Street slanted down from Stockton, crowded with men. A police wagon was just turning into it, blurred in the fog, two helmeted policemen aboard, one standing with the reins, the other shouting to give way.

In the general low uproar of Morton Street female voices were raised in what sounded like lamentations, punctuated with a hysterical shriek, so that I halted with Amelia's hand clutching my arm. The pair of us was bumped by hurrying men.

In a great tangle of illumination and shadow and blowing fog were red lights and a red window shade with a ball of gaslight over it. I could make out a commotion lurching toward us, a draped figure held up on a moving dais. It was a body covered by a sheet, four men bearing it like some primitive ceremony, two policemen and two other men, one with a striped shirt. The body was carried on a door, held aloft and borne to the wagon, not thirty feet from where Amelia and I were hemmed in by silent men. The door and its burden slipped into shadow as it was stowed in the wagon bed. The helmetless policeman mounted to the driver's seat with the driver. He was Sgt. Nix, white-faced where he stood six feet above the crowd of men staring up at him.

Nix held up an arm, a hand signaling to someone; two fingers extended from his fist. A hundred feet down the street a woman shrieked again.

"We must get away from here," I said to Amelia, who was thrust against me by the press around her. "Pardon me," I said. "Pardon us, please. Pardon!"

I managed to steer her out of the crowd.

"What is it, Mr. Redmond?" she cried out.

"Another woman has been murdered," I said. "I must take you home now, Miss Brittain."

I hailed a hack on Sutter and Amelia and I rode in silence up the steep hill to Taylor Street, where I climbed a dozen steps with her and bid her good night.

At that time Bierce's prophecy that the Railroad was involved in these murders seemed preposterous to me.

"I am sorry our tour turned out so tragically," I said.

"I will never forget that scene, Mr. Redmond!" Amelia exclaimed. "The multitude of men, the smells! The fog, the reddish glow, as though there was a pink smoke rising. And those men with their swathed burden! The women's voices! The sense of terror and excitement. And the Blind Boss with those eyes like mushrooms!'' She sounded breathless, one hand clutched to her bosom. The door was opened by a liveried butler.

"Thank you and good night, Mr. Redmond!'' She disappeared inside.

I was shaken as I descended the steps, for it seemed Amelia Brittain had *seen* more of that hellish scene than I had.

I told the hackie to take me to the City Morgue in Dunbar Alley, where I would view my second corpse, the second victim of the Morton Street Slasher.

CYNIC, n.
A blackguard whose faulty vision sees things as they are, not as they ought to be.
—THE DEVIL'S DICTIONARY

n Bierce's desk was a skull, polished white as chalk, with outsize eyeholes and a grinning undershot jaw. His office was on the second floor of *The Hornet*'s premises on California Street, with a view out a window at the traffic in the street. Miss Penryn, the typewriter, rattled away on her machine in the next cubicle. Downstairs were the reporters' and Mr. Macgowan's offices. The press was in the basement. Bierce kept a neat desk, with albums of old Tattle columns on a shelf, and two of Fats Chubb's caricatures framed on the wall. One was the opera singer Adelina Patti in the shape of a plump, upright trout, mouth open singing. The other showed the Railroad as an octopus with suckers on the tentacles that were miniaturized faces of the Big Four.

Bierce and Mr. Macgowan listened to me relate what I had seen at the Morgue. Bierce stroked at the sparrow-wings of his mustache, frowning, and Mr. Macgowan leaned his big belly forward in his chair, so, with the skull, it was like having three grim faces watching me.

The stench had been terrible. The knife had opened up her bowels, the man in the leather apron had told me. "They said the two of spades was stuck in her mouth," I said.

AMBROSE BIERCE AND THE QUEEN OF SPADES

"Was she French too?" Bierce wanted to know.

"Irish. Esther Mooney."

"And the fellow was seen?" Mr. Macgowan asked. He was a beefy gent of about Bierce's age, with a walrus mustache framing a set of chins.

"One of the other girls might've seen him. Young chap with fair whiskers coming out of the room. I have this from Sgt. Nix."

"Esther Mooney and Marie Gar. Any connection?"

"Just Morton Street, as far as I can see."

"A series is certainly implied," Mr. Macgowan said. "An ace and a two. The Morton Street women must be in a fright."

I said I'd seen Captain Pusey at the Morgue.

"The photographic nonesuch," Mr. Macgowan said.

Isaiah Pusey was Chief of Detectives, Sgt. Nix's superior. He had assembled a criminal identification system of which he was very proud, albums of photographs of every criminal who had appeared in the San Francisco courts and a collection of national and international photographs as well. He bragged that he could identify any criminal whose likeness he had seen. He had made trips to London to confer on the British Crime Index, and to Paris to investigate the Bertillon system. It was considered that San Francisco criminals were sufficiently identified so long as Captain Pusey was on hand with his elephant memory and his photographic archive.

His chair creaked as Mr. Macgowan leaned forward again. "A weekly is at a disadvantage, of course," he said. "The *Chronicle* and the *Alta* can cover this day by day. Mike De Young will go the sensational route." Mike De Young was the *Chronicle*.

"Smithers can cover Central Station. That's what he's good at."

Bierce said, "I want something different than what Smithers or Gould would give us. Tom has seen the bodies. I'm going to ask him to work up supplemental material to run opposite Tattle.

"Tom and Sgt. Nix are baseball chums," he added.

Mr. Macgowan squinted at me.

"If Pusey is involved, he must have had a sniff of money," Bierce went on, with a flare of his nostrils that indicated his opinion of the Chief of Detectives. Most of the police, like the Supervisors, were on the boodle from the cribs, cowyards and parlorhouses, the gambling joints and saloons. Elmer Nix was probably relatively honest, but it was difficult to follow the straight and narrow in wide-open San Francisco. The Fire Department was proud of its rectitude.

Bierce had announced that the corruption stemmed from the State Railroad Monopoly, but it did not seem that simple to me.

"Maybe they've already got their man," I said.

"That would be the culm and crown of wonder," Bierce said.

Under the headline SECOND MORTON STREET SLASHING, the *Alta California* had printed:

> This morning the City was startled by the news that a second murder in Morton Street had been added to the terrible crime committed on Monday. The murder took place during the evening hours in an establishment presided over by Mrs. Cornford, in an upstairs room. The victim was a woman of 29 years, Esther Mooney. The same process had been followed as in Monday's case. She had been seized by the throat and her cries choked until she was strangled. Her torso was then slashed open. The murder was discovered when blood seeped beneath the door of her room.
>
> Chief of Detectives Isaiah Pusey has announced that the murderer will soon be apprehended, but no arrest has been made at this time. The tenants of Morton Street are dismayed by these crimes. Dr. Manship, who was called to view the remains of this victim, gave it as his opinion that the same man, evidently a maniac, had committed both murders. The inquest will be held at 11 o'clock Thursday morning.

There was no mention of the spades, or their progression.

Tattle, that week, made no reference to the murders, which had occurred after *The Hornet* had gone to press, but Bierce had taken shots at his usual targets:

"The worst railroads on the Pacific Coast are those operated by the Southern Pacific Company. It owes the government more millions of dollars than £eland $tanford has vanities; it will pay fewer cents than Collis B. Huntington has virtues."

He reiterated the fact that the cost of the transcontinental line had been kited to twice the maximum estimates. "Collis B. Huntington and his associates have made enormous fortunes by letting contracts to themselves—a felony under our state laws—dividing the profits and burning the books."

Of the Spring Valley Water Company he had written that it "flowed with bilk and honey," and "Included in the cost of the water is the price of nine Supervisors."

His usual theological butt was the Reverend Stottlemyer: "His latest announcements from Washington Street intimate that the praise for the propagation of the Lord's only begotten son could perhaps more fairly be shared. Certainly in the realm of plucking pigeons the proprietor of the Washington Street Church reigns supreme."

In Mrs. Cornford's establishment on Morton Street, I was taken upstairs to inspect the scene of the murder. Off a narrow corridor that bisected the second story were doors at regular intervals, tin numbers over the doors. Number 7 was a room about eight by ten feet, stinking of carbolic. It contained a bed stripped of its mattress, a straight chair, and a stand that held a white crockery bowl and pitcher. The floor had been scrubbed until the pine boards looked soft as chamois.

I interviewed Edith Pruitt in the parlor, under Mrs. Cornford's surveillance. Edith had heard some sounds in the crib next to hers and had seen the man depart. I sat in a wooden rocker with my pencil and pad, Edith on the window seat and Mrs. Cornford planted in the middle of the settee. The room was redolent of orris root, furniture polish, sweat and, faintly, an odor like rotting flowers with a medicinal tinge to it.

"He was a young man, you told Sgt. Nix."

"Maybe about as old as you, mister."

"With a beard."

"With a fair beard, yes." Edith Pruitt was a farm girl with a pleasingly plump bosom in her chaste gingham check, and a pretty piglike expression of fat cheeks and narrow eyes.

"Anything else about his appearance?"

Edith glanced at Mrs. Cornford, who smiled at her reassuringly. Edith shook her head.

"Did you see the knife?"

"She didn't see no knife," Mrs. Cornford said.

Edith showed her teeth in her nervousness. I tried to think of questions an experienced reporter like Jack Smithers would ask.

"What were the sounds like, that you heard?"

"Like somebody fell heavy on the bed. And some scraping. I didn't think what it might be. Sometimes a mister will pay extra for extra business."

"Esther would do that," Mrs. Cornford said, nodding.

"How long after the racket before you saw the man?"

"She told the copper maybe five minutes," Mrs. Cornford said.

"You kind of know how far along you are with a mister, you see," Edith Pruitt offered.

Mrs. Cornford smiled at me. She had a tapestry bag in her lap, from which she had taken a wad of blue yarn and two ivory needles.

When I returned to the subject of the man Edith had seen, Mrs. Cornford said, "The big copper had a photygraph. The higher-up one."

"Captain Pusey?"

"Older fellow with a shock of white hair. He had this photygraph."

"And was it the man?" I asked Edith.

"I told him it were him, all right," Edith said. "I told him I'd heard there was a mister, maybe it was this chap, that didn't have no dingle." She colored prettily. "Had to use a kind of leather thing strapped on. Might've been this one."

She hadn't seen this mister, only heard about him from Esther. Mrs. Cornford looked disapproving, whether of the lack of the dingle or the information proffered, I couldn't tell. No, none of the other girls had mentioned such a client.

The murder of Marie Gar had taken place at Mrs. Rose Ellen Green's place, but Mrs. Green was tired of sightseers and reporters and turned me away at the door. I inquired of other madams up and down Morton Street if there had been any reports of a mister with no dingle.

No luck.

Bierce's office was L-shaped, and I'd been promoted to a desk, a chair and a spittoon in the foot of the L.

I was writing up my notes when Miss Penryn put her head in the door to announce Miss Amelia Brittain. I jarred the desk jumping to my feet. Amelia wore a white dress with shingled lace on the bosom. Beneath a shadow of bonnet her face was stiff with anxiety. She swept the skirt of her dress past the doorjamb, her eyes fixed on me.

"Please sit down, Miss Brittain!" I dragged a chair around the corner.

She tucked her skirt under her and sat, daubing at her eyes with a handkerchief from her reticule.

"They've arrested Beau!"

I gaped at her. "For the Morton Street murders?"

"Yes! It is simply—*monstrous!*" She daubed at her lips. "They took him to *jail*. Mr. Redmond, I must again ask your assistance!"

"Anything."

"They say they have his photograph that one of the women in the premises where the murder took place has *identified*."

Captain Pusey's photograph!

"Mr. Redmond, I must believe it is a plot! Certainly Beau has enemies, any wealthy man has enemies. His mother must have enemies!"

I said it had seemed curious to me that her fiancé had not accompanied her to the Firemen's Ball and immediately wished I had not said it.

She flung herself up from the chair, her eyes blazing with indignation, then sank back.

"He had to work with Mr. Buckle on some of his mother's affairs," she said, in a controlled voice. "His mother has enormous business in the City."

"Who is Mr. Buckle?"

"He is Lady Caroline's manager here."

"Who are these enemies of Mr. McNair?"

"I don't *know!*"

Amelia's fiancé out strangling and slashing Esther Mooney while Amelia and I were waltzing at the Firemen's Ball seemed an improbable coincidence.

"I have a friend who is a police detective," I said. "I will try to find out from him what they have against Mr. McNair. Will Mr. McNair talk to me if I go to see him in jail?"

"You must tell him that I sent you!"

"Miss Brittain, I only know of Mr. McNair as the son of a very rich woman. Will you tell me something about him?"

She relaxed visibly in the chair.

"When Mr. McNair's father was still alive, they lived not far from my father's house. Beau and I attended Miss Sinclair's Seminary. He was eleven and I was ten."

A blush climbed her face, like a pink shadow sweeping upward from her throat. It was charming. "We were sweethearts. Then the elder Mr. McNair died, and Mrs. McNair—Lady Caroline—left San Francisco for England, taking Beau and Gwendolyn with her."

"Gwendolyn is Mr. McNair's younger sister?"

"Who is very beautiful," Amelia said, nodding. "A month ago Beau returned to help Mr. Buckle with his mother's affairs, and we met again. We discovered that our affection for each other is still strong. Of course our lives since we were children have been very different."

Like hers and mine, I thought. My antipathy for Beau McNair had steadily grown. I hesitated to ask Amelia if her fiancé regularly frequented the low women in the Morton Street bordellos, or the fancier ones in the parlorhouses of the Upper Tenderloin.

"He is a very eligible young man," Amelia continued. "And my mother approves of the match."

I wondered what sorts of amusements very eligible young men and women of high station engaged in. No doubt Beau McNair had a fancy turnout, and they would take trips out to Cliff House, or through the park, or down the Peninsula, where some of the instant aristocrats of the Comstock Lode, the Railroad and the banks had built their mansions. I wanted to know how much she and Beau saw of each other, and I managed to put the question so as not to seem to be prying.

"Well, of course not as much as either of us would prefer," she said. "He has been occupied with his mother's business, as he was on the night of the Firemen's Ball."

"And was Mr. McNair occupied with his mother's business the night before the Firemen's Ball?"

Her hands tightened on her handkerchief—such smooth, long-fingered, pretty hands that my heart turned over in my chest to see them.

"Mr. Redmond, you must trust me or you cannot help me!"

"I will help you any way I can," I said, in capitulation.

ARREST, *v.*
Formally to detain one accused of unusualness.
—THE DEVIL'S DICTIONARY

I took the South End–North Beach Railway out to Broadway. It was a bright day with sun gleaming on the tracks and the facades of the buildings. As we passed Kearny Street the shrill voices of the slave girls in their Chinatown cribs were audible.

I walked along Broadway to Dupont. The City Jail was a brick building with a high cornice and iron bars installed in the windows where they looked like bared teeth. A sergeant at a counter waved me down a bare-boards hallway. The third cell was the gentry cell, bigger than the others, with the same cot but with three chairs and, facing the window, a clumsy patent rocker in which Beau McNair sat with a book. I stood watching him through the bars of the door.

When I spoke his name he sprang out of the chair, setting it rocking. He came to face me through the bars. He was a handsome young fellow, no doubt about it, maybe my height but of a stringier build in his fawn-colored suit and a bow necktie. He had a fair beard, close-set blue eyes and fair hair swept over his brow. He hadn't shaved.

"Who are you?" he wanted to know.

I said I was Tom Redmond, from *The Hornet.* Miss Brittain had asked me to come to see him.

AMBROSE BIERCE AND THE QUEEN OF SPADES

"You are a friend of Miss Brittain's?" he said.

"An acquaintance."

"A newspaper fellow," he said, with a twist of his lips.

I said I was that.

"You may tell her I won't be here long. Mr. Curtis has been sent for. The governor has been appealed to. This ridiculous—" He paced across the cell, slapping the back of the rocker with his hand to set it rocking again. He returned to stand scowling at me.

"What do you make of this woman identifying your photograph?"

"She is lying, of course! For reasons I cannot imagine."

"Miss Brittain is certain it is a conspiracy against you or your mother."

"Confounded idiocy, is what it is!"

"Not a conspiracy?"

"Yes, of course a conspiracy!"

"Do you have any idea—"

"No I don't have any idea, and I am sick and tired of answering foolish questions." He glared at me with his lower lip protruding. "If you have anything of interest to say to me, will you please say it, fellow?"

I reminded myself that he was a very frightened young man. He stood with his hands jammed in his pockets, stretching the material like a Dutch boy's trousers. He filled and relaxed his cheeks as though he had a nervous problem with his breathing.

I said, "Captain Pusey has fifty albums of photographs of criminals. How would he happen to have your photograph?"

He showed his teeth like a wildcat in a trap. "I expect I have had a hundred likenesses taken," he said. "Your Captain Pusey happens to have one."

"I wonder why he would have chosen to show your photograph to the woman who saw the murderer at the scene of the murder."

He snorted.

"Do you think Captain Pusey is a part of a conspiracy?"

He seemed to regain control of himself. "See here," he said.

"There are dissatisfied people. There are demented people. There are envious people. There are people who would like to threaten any sort of eminence."

"And that is what is going on here?"

"That is no doubt what is going on here, yes."

"I'm very interested in the idea of a conspiracy," I said. "There is the matter of the playing cards—"

"It is infuriating to me," he said, "that anyone would think I would have an interest in slashing these low women from their giggle to their snatch."

I said I wondered how he knew just how they had been slashed.

"I read it in the newspapers, of course."

"It was not revealed in the newspapers."

He gave me a haughty look and turned to greet two gentlemen who had appeared.

"I advise you not to confer with journalists, Beau," a small, white-haired man said. The other was taller, graying. The fat turnkey with his hoop of keys followed them.

"What paper are you from?" the little man demanded. He had a truculent expression on a taut-skinned, shiny countenance, which looked as though his face had been scarred in a fire.

"He's from *The Hornet*," Beau said.

"I advise you especially not to confer with journalists from trash newspapers," the little man said.

"Here we are, Mr. Curtis," the turnkey said and turned a key in the lock. Beau pulled the door in toward him.

The little man was Bosworth Curtis, the bear-trap lawyer who often represented the SP, and the tall, graying man in his fine black broadcloth suit must be the Mr. Buckle, Lady Caroline's manager, of whom Amelia had spoken. I did not take offense at *The Hornet* being called a trash paper for, except for Bierce's Tattle, that opinion was a familiar one.

"Get rid of this fellow," Mr. Curtis said to the turnkey.

The turnkey shrugged at me, and I followed him along. Behind us

Beau McNair, Curtis and Buckle stood looking at each other like three actors waiting for the curtain to rise on their play.

Outside on Broadway I squinted up into the sun, and considered taking on a beer before returning to *The Hornet.*

The headline on the *Examiner* on the newsstand was NOB HILL ELITE ARREST.

In Bierce's office I was introduced to Captain Pusey, who rose from his chair for a perfunctory handshake but with a trace of pause to assure me that he was aware I was not of much account. He was in uniform, fine pressed Mission blue wool, pips on the sleeves of his long tunic to show he was a captain. His cap rested on Bierce's desk beside the skull. He was a high-nosed, false-teeth smiling fellow, maybe sixty, with pink cheeks, a Greek helmet of white hair and a belly cinched by the leather belt around his tunic waist. He smelled of hair oil and talcum, as though he'd just come out of a barber's chair.

I was informed that he had had business with Mr. Macgowan and had dropped in to see Bierce at Sgt. Nix's suggestion.

Bierce was standing intent, his arms folded on his chest as though he was learning something watching Captain Pusey greet me.

"Captain Pusey and I were discussing the great good fortune of his having a photograph of Beau McNair in his albums."

Pusey set his jaw in his perfect-teeth smile.

"I just saw Beau with Lawyer Curtis at the jail," I said.

Pusey nodded amiably. "McNair'll be out by now," he said.

"I was speculating as to how Captain Pusey happened on that particular photograph," Bierce said. "And chose to show it to Edith Pruitt."

"Showed her half a dozen photographs," Pusey said. "You don't want to confuse a witness with too many, you know. Just good luck one of them took."

"Quite remarkable luck," Bierce said. "I can't help speculating further. For instance, did you run across Beau's photograph in the

Scotland Yard archives when you were in London? Or did a friend at the Yard send it to you when Beau returned to San Francisco?"

Captain Pusey did not look pleased at Bierce's speculation.

"Guesswork," he said. "A good deal of detective work is pure guesswork, Mr. Bierce. Sometimes it proves out."

"Educated guesswork," Bierce said, nodding. "It is evident that Beau has a criminal record of some kind, or you would not possess his photograph. I believe that could be put in the form of a syllogism. Captain Pusey keeps a store of photographs of criminals. In his collection is a photograph of young McNair. Therefore young McNair has been arrested sometime in the past."

Pusey drew a fat railroad watch from his pocket to consult it, thus impressing us with the value of his time.

"Let me make an educated guess," Bierce said. "The photograph and attendant information were sent from England. They pertained to criminal activity in London. London is famous for its prostitutes. Beau McNair was involved in a criminal activity that concerned prostitutes."

Pusey bent forward to ring the spittoon.

Bierce waited.

"Well, you are just about right, Mr. Bierce," Pusey said finally. He had a hint of the stuffed-nose Australian accent that reminded you of how many ticket-of-leave convicts had settled in San Francisco in the early days.

"What did Beau McNair do?" Bierce said.

"Collegeboy scrape," Pusey said with a sigh. "Three flash young fellows with more money than is good for them. A club of them. The Diamonds, they called themselves. Had little diamond pins they wore. Some kind of initiation business."

"And what did they do?" Bierce persisted.

"Hired a couple of Whitechapel women for the night and beat them instead of the usual. Stripped them naked and drew on their bellies."

"Drew what on their bellies?"

Pusey considered for a moment. "Like a cunt all the way up to their neck. Hairs running off it. Some kind of indelible ink with acid stuff in it that burned them. Not dangerous, but painful. Now there's a stunt that would get anybody's pecker up," he said sarcastically. "Drawing cunts on whore's bellies."

It sounded like what had been done to Marie Gar, but with a knife rather than a pen. And this fellow was Amelia Brittain's fiancé!

"The entertainments of young British Futilitarians," Bierce said.

"Bit of a scandal," Pusey went on. "They thought money would buy it off, but it got out and about. Beau was the one that was forgiven a bit, being younger than the rest. And a fine-looking young fellow like he is. Probably led astray by his pals."

"Ashamed not to be shameless," Bierce said. "Embarrassing for his mother, considering her past profession."

The rumor, or more than a rumor, was that Lady Caroline had been a madam in Virginia City, on the Comstock, when she had married Nat McNair.

"What happened?" Bierce inquired.

"There was money paid out, and a judge gave them Diamonds a good talking-to. Beau's mother sent him packing back here."

"Diamonds and spades," I said.

They both gazed at me as though I was a child who had spoken his first intelligible word.

"On the evidence, it looks like you have your man, Captain Pusey," Bierce said.

Pusey produced a chuffing laugh. He pushed himself ponderously out of his chair. "Time to get back to me duties." He shook hands with Bierce, nodded to me and strode out of the office settling his cap on his head. His shiny boots resounded after he had passed from sight.

Bierce stood still gazing at the chair the Chief of Detectives had vacated. "Captain Pusey does not seem much disturbed that young McNair will have been snatched from his clutches. I would like to know just what is his game."

"Boodle," I said. "That's what he is famous for."

"Blackmail," Bierce said. "The McNair fortune. The son of the widow McNair, Lady Caroline as she now is."

I was trying to balance the young dandy I had seen in the City Jail, to whom Amelia Brittain was engaged, with the arrogant and lickerish Diamond who had drawn on whores' bodies with acid ink. And with the monster who had slashed Marie Gar to death.

I told Bierce about Beau McNair's remark of slashings from giggle to snatch. He narrowed his eyes at me and patted the skull on his desk.

"It does not immediately appear that the Southern Pacific is involved," was all he said.

"But Beau McNair is the murderer!"

Bierce shook his head. "It appears a shade too neat, and too dependent on what Captain Pusey wants us to think."

I was dismissed and returned to my desk, still appalled at what I had learned of Beaumont McNair.

"A whale of peccability has swum into our ken," Bierce remarked behind me.

In the morning papers it was noted that Beaumont McNair had been discharged from City Jail. One Rudolph Buckle had sworn that the young man had been in his company on the nights of both the playing card murders.

This week's *Hornet* featured a full-page Fats Chubb cartoon of a hairy, evil-looking assassin with a huge knife. Bierce had written: "What is one to make of our San Francisco slasher, whose affection for the soiled doves of Morton Street is so great that he must slice them open to rejoice in the beauties of their vitals? What is one to make of his deposit on his victims of the spade suit of playing cards, first an ace, next a deuce? That a trey is to follow is powerfully implied. Do the playing cards indicate a gambler, a sachem of the Faro layout suddenly overcome with recollections of female outrages? What is the message boded by those infernal black swords?"

Further along the column got on the subject of the Hawaii annexation: "The drums beat on for the damnable rape of those mid-Pacific isles whose royalty this nation has pretended to befriend, for the chief benefit of the missionaries who have invaded those paradisiacal shores, imprisoning the Kanaka on the sugarcane plantations and his women in Mother Hubbards."

I was surprised to read, in the same issue, Mr. Macgowan's editorial proclaiming the rightness of the annexation of the Hawaiian Islands before they were absorbed into the British Empire or fell prey to a German coup d'état. As though Mr. Macgowan did not read his editor and columnist, nor Bierce his publisher.

HABEAS CORPUS.
*A writ by which a man may be taken out of jail
when confined for the wrong crime.*
—THE DEVIL'S DICTIONARY

n Sunday, her fourteenth birthday, I took my friend Belinda
Barnacle for an excursion to the
park, where we strolled through
the trees, among the bicyclists, the carriages, calèches, landaus; a Clar-
ence with two ladies in the rear seat, their veils floating out from their
hats, two cigar-smoking men facing them; a four-in-hand guided by a
plump gent in a plug hat and brass-buttoned vest. The Sunday turnouts were more impressive every month, horsemen and -women
among them, mounted on expensive horseflesh.

The fog hung offshore, and the day glistened with sunlight. Belinda flourished a parasol. She wore a lacy little hat decorated with
silk rosebuds, and her shoes were polished to gleam like stars where
they slipped in and out beneath her skirts. Sometimes she held my
arm, sometimes she walked a little apart to establish her indepen-
dence.

A band of music was playing in the bandstand a quarter mile away
so that the beat reached us raggedly. Belinda smiled up at me from
the little shade of her parasol and wanted to know how many ladies
I had danced with at the Firemen's Ball.

I held up my fingers with the thumb tucked into the palm.

AMBROSE BIERCE AND THE QUEEN OF SPADES

"Were they pretty?"

"Some were pretty."

"What were their names?"

"One was Martha. I don't remember her surname. And there was Patricia Henderson, Mary Beddoes Mathews, and Amelia Brittain."

"Which one did you like the most?"

"I did like Amelia Brittain the most. She is engaged to marry a very wealthy fellow, however."

Maybe a murderer, however.

"What's his name?" Belinda asked.

"Beaumont McNair. Isn't that a high-tone name?"

"I like Tom Redmond for a name."

"Thank you," I said.

She reminded me that we were engaged to be married on her eighteenth birthday, and we stopped at a stand in the shade of an oak tree. I bought her a bottle of sarsaparilla. Belinda sipped liquid through her straw as we walked on. A trio of horsemen clopped past us, high-stepping horses with gleaming haunches. Belinda told me about the nun who was mean to her and the nun who thought she might have a vocation. I heard my name called.

In a fancy buggy gleaming with varnish were Amelia and Beau McNair, Amelia waving a handkerchief, Beau wearing a fuzzy plug hat. Halted, the chestnut horse, with blue ribbons knotted in his mane and a high curve of tail, pitched his head and pawed a hoof. I had a comprehensive sensation of low station.

Amelia beckoned. Belinda moved reluctantly at my side, and I had the further revelation of her awareness not only of station but of youth, not to speak of the sarsaparilla bottle with its straw, which she held down in the folds of her skirt.

Amelia looked splendid in a complicated white dress, a bonnet busy with ribbons and her long white gloves, which semaphored enthusiasm. "Mr. Redmond, how nice to see you! Here's my Mr. McNair certified innocent!"

Beau raised a finger from the reins in greeting.

I introduced Belinda Barnacle, whose curtsy, with her dipping parasol and concealed sarsaparilla bottle, was prettily managed.

Beau McNair's striped jacket fit him like paint.

"I've told Mr. McNair how helpful you've been, Mr. Redmond," Amelia said. "I suppose I can't thank you for the disposition of these misapprehensions, but your support was important to an anxious young woman."

I bowed and said I was always at her disposal.

Though his expression was sullen, her fiancé had such a gilded aura, with his clipped fair beard and mustache, that it was a mental effort to conceive of him as the kind of rakehell who believed his station in life gave him license for insult and injury to lesser beings, not to speak of slaughtering whores for sport.

Drawing on a whore's belly with an acid pen was so stupid and juvenile that I could hardly believe it of this sartorial paragon seated at his ease beside Amelia Brittain. He simply did not look the part.

"Mr. McNair's mother will be arriving within a fortnight," Amelia said, with a brilliant smile, leaving me to wonder whether this was for the wedding, or because her fiancé had got himself into another pickle.

I managed to summon up an amiable expression at the information.

Beau's whip tickled the back of the beautiful horse. He tipped his hat in farewell, not having spoken a word, and the varnish-shiny rig rolled away, with Amelia's gloved hand waving back at us.

"That was Miss Brittain that you liked the most," Belinda said, as we started on

"That one, yes."

Belinda looked thoughtful. "Mr. McNair doesn't like *you* much."

"Perhaps not."

"What did she mean, you'd been so helpful?"

"He was in jail, and she asked me to see if I could do anything to help."

"He's not in jail any more."

"No," I said.

It appears a shade too neat, Bierce had said.

As we walked on I found a receptacle in which Belinda could rid herself of the sarsaparilla bottle. She managed to juggle her parasol while dusting her hands together.

"She's very pretty," she said.

When I brought Belinda home, Mr. Barnacle was leaning on the fence. In the little yard behind him young Johnny Barnacle kicked a kerosene can with resounding metal thumps. Belinda slipped inside the gate and trotted into the house.

"Henry George!" Mr. Barnacle said, jutting his unshaven chin at me.

"Henry George?"

"That writing fellow was correct. The Railroad has been the ruin of us out here."

"How is that, Mr. Barnacle?"

"Just what he said would be. For awhile everybody's put to work, then the job is finished and everybody's out of work. Depression, Tom. They said San Francisco would be another Venice if we didn't connect to the east with a railroad, but we have did it and now we are up the spout."

Mr. Barnacle had not worked for some years, which his wife attributed to his weakness for whiskey. He attributed his difficulties to the Railroad, and probably Bierce would agree with him, as Henry George did.

"One rich man makes a hundred poor men," he went on, nodding sagely at the Georgian wisdom. "The fine carriages roll past the starving children!"

"Well, your children are not starving, Mr. Barnacle," I said.

"Tell me, Tom, are you still a member of the Democracy Club?"

"Yes, sir."

"Down with the SP and the Monopoly, I say! Shooting those poor farmers down at Mussel Slough!"

"Bad business!"

"Buying up legislatures like them fellows is no better than Chinee slave girls," he ranted on. "The Girtcrest Corridor Bill! Bad cess to them, I say, Tom!"

The Girtcrest Corridor Bill, which Bierce called "the Giftcrest," was being ushered through the State legislature by Senator Aaron Jennings, "the Senator from Southern Pacific," and was a giveaway of thousands of acres of San Joaquin Valley land to the Railroad. Anti-Railroad sentiment was noisiest in the Democratic Clubs in San Francisco.

"Down with the Monopoly, Mr. Barnacle!" I said, and passed through the gate and up my creaking stairs.

I had showed a piece I wrote to Bierce, and "The Monopoly" must have impressed him enough to consider me as having some promise as a journalist, also that I possessed the proper Antimonopoly fire and facts:

> For the 737 miles of line from Sacramento to Promontory, Utah, Charles Crocker, Collis B. Huntington, Leland Stanford and Mark Hopkins, the Big Four, received $38,500,000 in land grants and government bonds. They employed themselves as the Contract and Finance Corporation to build the Central Pacific line, and when the stock they turned over to this corporation was distributed, each of the partners was richer by $13,000,000.
>
> As the Central Pacific Railroad inched its way over the Sierra to join the Union Pacific and connect the two coasts of the Nation, the Big Four was already planning the Monopoly of transportation in the State of California. The first step was the acquisition of the existing local railroads, and then the construction of new interior lines. These roads were to become the Big Four's most valuable property, the Southern Pacific Railroad. Terminal facilities in Oakland and San Francisco were acquired for the same purpose.
>
> By the early '70s the SP had succeeded in controlling the movement of freight to and from California and within the

borders of the state. The roads it did not own in California numbered five, with a total of fifty-nine miles of track.

The Southern Pacific's rate-schedules are dictated by "all the traffic will bear." Rates are set to the maximum that shippers can afford, those on agricultural products based on current market prices. Rates are low where there is competing water transport, higher where there is no competition, and freight is cheaper across the country than between San Francisco and Reno.

By the time the people of California realized that they were trapped in the arms of the Octopus, the railroad had come to control the legislature, the governor, the state regulatory agencies, city and county governments, often the courts, and wields power in the National Congress.

Anti-railroad candidates are voted into office, bills empowering the State to fix railroad rates are passed into law, but they are never enforced. Always the Southern Pacific manages to frustrate legislation—by the governor's veto, by challenging the laws in the courts, and by controlling the agencies responsible for putting the measures into effect.

Railroad gangs break up Antimonopoly meetings. Railroad opponents are punished, public officials bribed, newspapermen intimidated, protesting farmers, whose claims on Railroad agricultural lands were not honored, are shot down by hired gunmen. Although Californians raise a continual wail of complaint and vituperation against the Octopus, Mark Hopkins—the only member of the Big Four of whom it was said, a man might cross the street to wish him a good day—having gone to his reward in 1878, Charles Crocker, Collis Huntington and Leland Stanford take their ease in their magnificent mansions atop Nob Hill, overlooking San Francisco beneath a cloudless sky.

Bierce did point out that he, for one, had not been intimidated by the Railroad.

OPPORTUNITY, *n.*
*A favorable occasion for grasping a
disappointment.*
—THE DEVIL'S DICTIONARY

he third Morton Street murder took place that night. The victim this time was no whore but a middle-aged well dressed woman who was strangled but not slashed, although her skirts were flung up over her head as though the murderer had been interrupted in his processes.

The body was found in a pile of rubbish in a stub of alley off the street, and the three of spades marked the victim, although it was not deposited in the open mouth this time.

I observed this third body on the slab at the Morgue in Dunbar Alley, the swollen, agonized features, gaping mouth and bruised throat. She was a woman of about fifty, stout and graying, a mole on her chin. Her skirt and jacket were black, her hands well kempt, un-calloused, neat nails. She wore a gold wedding band and a large ruby circled by tiny red stones. There was nothing to identify her, no witnesses this time.

Bierce and I met Sgt. Nix at Dinkins's. Dick Dinkins called from behind the bar, "Hear he got him another one, Mr. Bierce. This yob'll scare all the hoors back to Cincinnati!"

Bierce saluted but did not reply. Men at the bar observed us in the mirrors or peered over their shoulders in the pleasant sour stink of beer. Sgt. Nix sat with his boots spread out and his helmet in his lap.

"Our suspect was at a dinner party at some Nob Hill folks named Brittain," he said.

"His fiancée, whom you know," Bierce said to me. He sipped his beer and swabbed at his mustache with a forefinger.

I felt a queer mix of relief and disappointment.

"A different strangler?" Bierce said.

"A copycat getting an advantage out of a trey of spades. She weren't slashed, no innards spilled. It is possible."

"A ditto-maniac," Bierce said. "No idea who the victim is?"

Nix shook his head. "We're checking hotels in case she's out-of-town. The Captain thinks she is."

"Because he didn't recognize her? He is supposed to be infallible."

"What he likes to claim," Nix said. Dinkins brought him a beer.

"She was wearing black," Bierce said. "Mourning?"

A deduction! "Maybe so!" I said.

Nix looked interested. "We'll find out who she is," he said. "One thing she's *not* is some Morton Street dove. That is one spooked pack of women, over there."

We were still at the table when a policeman came in and handed Nix a folded slip of paper. He stood beside the table until Nix had perused the note and signaled for him to depart. Nix put the paper down on the table between us.

"She was staying at the Grand. Mrs. Hiram Hamon. That's Judge Hamon. He died about a month ago. She was up from Santa Cruz. Judge Hamon retired down there from the Circuit Court."

Bierce had straightened. "Mrs. Hamon had made an appointment to see me this afternoon," he announced grimly.

Nix and I stared at him.

"What about?" I asked.

"Her letter only advised me that she had information that was important and I would be interested."

"Well, now, that is something, ain't it?" Nix said.

"Allow me to extrapolate," Bierce said. His face was keen as a hawk's. "If she wanted to see me, it was probably something to do with the Railroad. My feelings about the Railroad are well known. Judge Hamon and Judge Jennings—before he got elected to the State Senate—sat on the Circuit Court. Aaron Jennings presided over the trials of the Mussel Slough farmers, if you will remember, and his every decision went against them and for the Railroad. At the time there was talk that Judge Hamon was very disturbed, and he retired soon after. And Jennings went straight into the State Senate with the Railroad blessing."

"The Railroad at last," I said, grinning at him. "The Senator from Southern Pacific."

"Girtcrest," Nix said.

"How would you like to make a trip to Santa Cruz, Tom?" Bierce said. "To see if Mrs. Hamon had a son or daughter, or a neighbor she confided in."

The train looped down to Watsonville and back up a ledge along the coast. From the car the Pacific looked deep blue with sparkles of white and gold, the bay bounded by the Monterey Peninsula to the south. A ship with stacked white sails sat motionless in the middle distance. Further out a steamer trailed black smoke. Opposite me a stout, big-hatted gent in a black suit and a face hard and pocked as granite sat gazing out my window at the maritime vistas that had opened. His eyes caught mine once, as blank as glass. In front of me a young lady in a poke bonnet perused a novel, whose title I had not managed to spy out. Two drummers had a card game going, slapping cards down on the seat between them. The tracks wound toward Santa Cruz through tan fields.

I descended at the station and took a room at the Liddell House, before strolling around the plaza to familiarize myself with the place. A soft breath of salt air came off the Bay. The post office was in the general store on the corner opposite the plaza. The gray-haired postmistress, with pencils protruding from her coif like a cannibal headdress, gave me the Hamon address, down toward the water, second right, third house on the left, a brick chimney and a covered porch with ferns in pots. Mrs. Hamon's right-hand neighbor was a Mrs. Bettis.

When I started toward the waterfront I could see smoke rising, a thin pencil of it fattening into a boa. The bell of an engine company shrilled. In minutes the engine rolled past me behind a fine team of heavy-hammed horses, three helmeted firemen hanging off the back. The smoke was flattening and spreading out. I knew it was the Hamon house before I turned the corner.

Smoke had settled into a low-lying billow in the street. Firemen were visible in the smoke, hustling around the engine. Flames climbed in bright twisting shapes. A frieze of people watched from the other side of the street, close enough to be troublesome. Always at a fire you had to deal with rubberneckers. More than once the Engine Company 13 Chief had turned a hose on them.

I joined the group on the sidewalk. Two trees behind the house were flaring like a torchlight parade. It was the Hamon house, all right. "Started in the back," a man with a bandanna tied over his head told me. "One of these fellows said you could smell the stink of kerosene all over the back of the house."

Through the smoke I saw the Chief pointing. The crystal arcs of water changed direction. They had given up on the Hamon ruin and concentrated on wetting down the neighbor houses. The engine puffed smoke into the general pall. Mrs. Bettis's bungalow sported a little porch on which a fat woman hovered, with her hands clasped together. A fireman yelled at her to move.

The second floor of the Hamon house caved in with a wrenching crash, and the mess of blazes climbed and subsided as the walls fell in.

More spectators had arrived to line the street. Among them was a man in a big hat.

The next time I looked, he was gone.

After the fire was out I sat in Mrs. Bettis's parlor in an easy chair with antimacassars on the arms and behind my head. Mrs. Bettis occupied the sofa opposite me in her flowered dress and gray felt slippers, sipping from a glass of water. She seemed stunned by the fire next door and the news that her neighbor had been murdered. I asked her if she had seen anyone in the alley behind the houses.

She had observed the top of a buggy stopped there. Outbuildings blocked her view and she hadn't seen anything but the buggy top and the smoke. She sipped her water, gazing at me with her gray lips drooping.

"Whoever it was wanted to dispose of something in the house that had to do with the murder of Mrs. Hamon. What could that be?"

She thought. "Judge Hamon's papers?"

What did she know about them?

"He was working on them when he died. Evelyn was sorting through them afterwards. There were scandals. He was very Anti-monopoly."

The Railroad.

"Do you have any idea of what the scandals were?"

She peered at me as though she had to translate my words into a more familiar language before responding. "I know Evelyn was ex-ercised."

When I pursued the thought, Mrs. Bettis said, "She was a close-mouthed woman when it came to the Judge's affairs."

Mrs. Hamon had been ten or twelve years younger than the Judge. He was a cranky old fellow who sat on his veranda with a glass of whiskey and waved his cane and shouted at the buggies and carriages that passed by too fast to suit him.

"The dust is bad when it's breezy," Mrs. Bettis explained. The Judge had retired from the Circuit Court several years ago and he and his wife moved to Santa Cruz, where he worked on the book he intended to publish.

"She was a close-mouthed woman," she said again, to forestall my asking again about the Judge's papers.

I asked about the Judge's death.

"A stroke took him like that." Mrs. Bettis snapped her fingers.

"Right there on the veranda. Evelyn went out to call him in for supper and he was gone."

The Judge had a son by his first wife back east, maybe in Philadelphia. He and Mrs. Hamon had a daughter downstate in San Diego. They had not had many acquaintances in Santa Cruz. Mrs. Bettis thought she had been Mrs. Hamon's closest friend. She sighed.

"She had made an appointment with Ambrose Bierce," I said.

Mrs. Bettis squinted at me. She seemed to have recovered herself. "That mean writing fellow?"

"He's my boss."

She squinted at the calling card I had given her, which she held cupped in her hand. "Your name's Thomas Redmond," she said.

"Yes, ma'am."

"I knew a Cletus Redmond once." Her wrinkled, soft-cheeked old face took on an unmistakable coyness. "I often wonder what happened to Cletus Redmond."

"He married my mother," I said.

"For heaven's sake! You are Cletus Redmond's son!"

"Yes, ma'am."

"And where is your dear father now?"

"He's in Sacramento working for the SP except when he's run off after the latest bonanza. Where did you know him?"

"On the Washoe."

I felt a little electric shock of connection. The Washoe was the Comstock, Virginia City, and I didn't know my father had been there, though it stood to reason. He had visited Austin, Eureka and Tonopah for varying periods of time. My father's involvements with minerals had been borrascas rather than bonanzas, but he had never given up hope of the ultimate fortune awaiting his faith and patience.

The Gent had spent his life since coming to California in '49, at the age of seventeen, chasing bonanzas and women. It seemed that Mrs. Bettis had been one who had responded to that Irish charm. On the Washoe.

Judge Hamon had been working on a memoir that would show the Railroad in general, and Senator Jennings in particular, in a bad light, revealing payoffs and corruption in the trial of the Mussel Slough farmers. Mrs. Hamon had in turn been exercised and had made an appointment with Bierce. The murderer had intercepted her before she could see him and had burned the Hamon house with Judge Hamon's papers.

The livery stable was just around the corner from the Plaza, and I inquired if anyone had hired a buggy that early afternoon. A man with a big hat, for instance?

The lame hostler spat tobacco into the dust. "Took out a rig and was back in about an hour."

"Did he give a name?"

"Name of Brown." The hostler scratched his neck, squinting into the sun. "Carried a piece. Saw it inside his coat when he climbed into my rig."

I took another turn around the plaza and dropped into Buchanan's Saloon next door to the Liddell House for a beer.

Passing through the bat-wing doors of the saloon was like coming from full day to dark of night, with a gleam of mirrors behind the bar, a moving white shirt. When my eyes were more accustomed to the dark I saw Brown hulked at the far end of the bar. He had his hat on the stool beside him, a glass of whiskey before him. There was no one else in the place but the barkeep, who approached as I selected my own stool. Brown's pale pocked face turned toward me. I could almost feel the probe of his eyes on my face.

In Sacramento our next-door neighbors had a red, cat-killing dog named Rufus. Our black and white cat loved to tease him, sitting on a fence post with her tail flicking just out of his range while Rufus gazed up at her. He was an old dog, with bloodshot eyes and an intensity of malevolence in his glare that was uncomfortable to watch. I could not see whether Brown's eyes were bloodshot or not, but I felt that same intensity in his gaze.

When he got off his stool, I retreated out the door. A boy in a vest and knickers was passing.

"Where can I find a police officer?"

"Sheriff," he said. "Next corner toward the bay."

I persuaded a deputy that a stranger named Brown had something to do with the fire at the Hamon house and the murder of Mrs. Hamon in San Francisco. But when we got back to the saloon, Brown was gone.

"Asked who you was, and I said I didn't know," the barkeep said to us, rubbing his hands together in his apron. "Used some rank language and lit out the back."

Brown hadn't been found by the time I retired to my room after supper at the hotel. I didn't think he would be found. I thought he was a professional.

I sat at the little desk, beneath the hiss and heat of the gaslamp, making notes on hotel stationery. I was aware of no sound, but for some reason I glanced at the door. The doorknob was slowly turning. It turned half a circuit, halted, then turned the half circuit back again.

There was still no sound as I rose and stood staring at the door, which I had locked. Out the window behind me I heard carriage wheels passing in the plaza. The doorknob did not turn again. I listened for the sound of retreating footsteps but heard nothing.

I did not sleep much that night and took the train back to San Francisco in the morning.

LOVE, *n.*
A temporary insanity curable by marriage or by
removal of the patient from the influences un-
der which he incurred the disorder.
—THE DEVIL'S DICTIONARY

t *The Hornet,* after I had reported
my adventures in Santa Cruz,
Bierce handed me a letter
to read:

July 14, 188–

Dear Mr. Bierce:

You have wondered in your paper about spades in connection with
the Morton Street slashings. Spades mean death. A spade is used to
dig a grave. The Queen of Spades is well known to be the lady of
death. Spades are used to dig mines as well as graves. A mine in
the Washoe was named the Jack of Spades. It belongs to the Queen
of Spades.

The Jack of Spades Mine is a part of the Consolidated-Ohio that
has been as productive a property as George Hearst's Homestake or
Will Sharon's Ophir. When it was the Jack of Spades it was pur-
chased by investors who called themselves the spades because of the
miner's implement. Two of the spades turned to hearts and bought
up a trey to fleece the pigeons. That trey was to suffer from a case of
clubs as a momento.

This is just to inform you of the various meanings of spades, although who can tell what this madman Slasher of Morton Street has in his rabid mind.

The letter was signed "A Former Spade."

Standing over me as I sat holding the missive, Bierce was beaming. "The bulk of the mail I receive, I consign to nullity after reading one sentence," he said. "But this is a lovely piece! The writer is not uneducated, except for the misspelling of 'memento.'"

"Lady Caroline," I said.

"The Queen of Spades! Is she the target of the progression of spades? Can the murderer hope to reach that unreachable lady with his strangling fingers and his questing blade? It is unthinkable! And yet once it is mentioned, not to think of it becomes unthinkable."

"Are you thinking of it?"

"I am!"

"But Beau McNair!"

"I certainly considered the idea of a young man driven to perversions and violence by the knowledge of his mother's past. But this letter seems to me a strong implication of Beau's innocence. It mentions hearts rather than diamonds, for instance! What does 'a case of clubs' refer to, please?"

"Someone was bashed?"

"Indeed!" Bierce said. He seated himself with careful tucks at the knees of his trousers. "What else can we decipher from this marvelous missive? These are all 'moling' creatures of the Comstock Lode. The two hearts would be Nat McNair and his missus, joined by a third to make a majority. Two spades were then forced out by the familiar method of pyramiding assessments. The spade who had made the majority was then disposed of by means of a club? Revenge? The remaining two bilked spades nurse their hatred. This writer must be one of them. Can there be a mad idea of murdering poor soiled doves and ultimately reaching the Queen of Spades—vengeance at last?"

It was too many for me.

"Can the fellow Brown you observed in Santa Cruz, and who may have been inclined to threaten you or worse, be the fifth spade? Was Mrs. Hamon connected to the spades? At any rate Mrs. Hamon is connected to the Railroad through her husband's association with Senator Jennings."

There he was bringing it back to the Railroad again.

As though talking to himself, nodding, he muttered, "What Mrs. Hamon had to tell me did have to do with Railroad malfeasance. Her information concerned Jennings and the Railroad."

"Well, all that is burned up," I said. "And the Queen of Spades is on her way."

"I am most anxious to meet that personage," Bierce said and sent me off to see Sgt. Nix with information from Santa Cruz.

I encountered Amelia Brittain in front of a ladies' dress shop on Montgomery Street, gazing upon a bottle-green velvet gown that gleamed in the sunlight as though it contained shifting lights in its folds. Amelia wore her usual white lace. I remarked the heartbreak slimness of her waist as it dipped into the swell of her hips. I had forgotten how tall she was.

I snatched off my hat as she turned toward me, executing a little figure with her scrolled parasol. Her eyebrows drifted up her forehead, and she smiled her bright smile.

"Mr. Redmond!"

She took my arm and we walked along together, passing gents who tipped their hats or saluted with their canes. A Chinaman in his black pajamas hawked cigars that looked like a pack of neat brown torpedoes. Brick buildings we passed had black iron shutters closed over their windows. There was heavy traffic, very noisy. I was glad I was decently dressed as Bierce's assistant and not Dutch John the printer's, in a black suit, high collar and derby hat. In Union Square and Montgomery Street, and along the north side of Market Street, the gentry dressed for each other's eyes.

"How pleasant to be strolling in this carefree manner, rather than the *fearful* circumstance of our first expedition," Amelia said. She frowned at the *Examiner*'s headline on a newsstand: POLICE PARALYZED IN SLASHINGS.

"So they have not arrested this lunatic," she said.

"No."

We strolled on. "I had some discussion with Mr. McNair about his frequenting those places I asked to see," Amelia said.

I blew out my breath at her frankness. It was as though we were old friends exchanging confidences.

"He doesn't frequent those on Morton Street, surely," I said.

"He spoke of premises on Union Square. Do you yourself visit such establishments, Mr. Redmond?"

"Not I," I lied.

"Mr. McNair has explained to me their necessity. He tells me that men of strong gender would become quite uncontrollable if they did not have recourse to these women. Is that true, Mr. Redmond?"

I said I had heard that theory. Thinking of Beau McNair frequenting whores made my skin crawl.

"He tells me that the favors of red-haired Jewesses are the most sought after. Is that true?"

I blew out my breath again. "I have heard that also."

"Why would that be, I wonder?"

"Such women are thought to be very lively," I said.

"He calls these jauntings his researches. I caught a glimpse of him once in his sweater and workingman's jacket. He thought he was invisible in his disguise."

We walked on in silence, Amelia in thought. I was very pleased to be accompanying her along Montgomery Street with her hand on my arm, even though we were headed in the wrong direction for my business with Sgt. Nix.

"So Mr. McNair's mother is en route from England," I said.

"She should arrive in ten days' time."

I hoped it was safe to say, "Does this have to do with wedding plans, Miss Brittain? If you will pardon me for asking."

She laughed lightly. "Oh, no! That is finished! I have become quite unattached." She displayed her gloved hand, as though I could make out the absence of her engagement ring through the fine leather.

We turned into the English Tearoom, where we sat with cups of tea at a marble-topped table. I watched her ungloved, unringed hand lift her cup to her lips.

I wanted to know why she had become unattached, and I said, "I suppose young English gents like that are brought up to think they are better than other people."

She frowned at me, so I assumed it was improper to criticize Beau McNair.

"He is very spirited, if that is what you mean," she said. "He does get into difficulties by it. He is afraid his mother is coming to reprimand him for the trouble he has been in through only the slightest fault of his own—which we mentioned. His sister is engaged to be married to the son of the duke of Beltravers, and Lady Caroline is anxious that no scandal disrupt that proceeding."

Interesting information for Bierce.

I said I had passed by the McNair mansion on Nob Hill. "It is very impressive."

"It is very large! Beau tells me he has never been in all the rooms. You know, there is a ghost. Isn't that European! The servants say it looks very like Beau. Of course it is old Mr. McNair when he was young, before he became such an abominable old reprobate. My father says he was terribly dishonest!

"And one evening I was there for supper when there was such a commotion! One of the maids had encountered the ghost in the solarium."

I said carefully that it seemed probable that there were similar ghosts in other Nob Hill mansions, the manifestations of other dishonest old reprobates when young.

"The simply mad thing is that sometimes the McNair ghost makes off with the cut flowers!

"And is there anything new on those horrible murders?" she asked, switching subjects.

"You must know there has been another. Not, however, one of the women of Morton Street. The widow of a respected judge. A woman from Santa Cruz, whose house was then burned no doubt to destroy some papers that would have created a scandal."

Amelia's eyebrows rose. "What fascinating work you are engaged in as a journalist, Mr. Redmond!"

I felt I had dishonestly elicited her esteem.

"Well, it is certain that Mr. McNair has been no part of any of this," she said. "And I am very grateful for anything you may have done to establish his innocence."

I had no response for that.

I accompanied her to the City of Paris, where she halted before store windows that presented laces and shimmering silks. Bedecked mannequins extended gloved hands.

"I will leave you here, Mr. Redmond. Thank you for the tea, and the interesting conversation!" With her light laugh and her parasol tapping, she strode inside.

I continued on toward Old City Hall and once jumped to kick my heels together. The fact that Amelia Brittain was no longer engaged to Beau McNair had raised my spirits.

That evening in the cellar of the Barnacles' house I took off my jacket and shirt and pummeled the buggy seat, shooting out rights and lefts, sweating in the dim cool, breathing dust from my target. I was aware that Belinda was watching me, seated on the top cellar step with her knees and feet together and her hands clasped in her lap. I banged away, flinging my fists wide open one moment, and the next pulled together defensively with my chin in my shoulder and sweat tickling on my sides.

When I stopped, panting, and draped a towel around my neck, preparatory to a visit to the baths, Belinda said, "You act like you're mad at somebody, Tom."

"Just the opposite," I told her.

FIDELITY, *n.*
A virtue peculiar to those who are about to be betrayed.
—THE DEVIL'S DICTIONARY

n Sacramento, en route by train to Virginia City, in a delay announced as not less than two hours, I walked the four blocks from the station to my parents' house, a peeling white-painted bungalow set back from the street, with a narrow porch and two dormer windows on the second story. At least three times during my youth, in the floods of the Sacramento River, the water had come up into the house and warped the boards of the hallway so there was always a reminding faint stink of river mud.

In the upstairs rooms my two brothers and my sister and I had listened to our father and mother fight downstairs, and celebrate in their bedroom their spells of concord as noisily as they fought. My brothers and sister were older than I, and they all cleared out of the house as soon as they could find the means, but I hung on to take my diploma from the Christian Brothers and then, with a twenty-dollar gold piece sewn into my pocket, rode the deck of the steamer down the river to the City.

In the dark central hallway I called my mother's name. A familiar oppression sat on my shoulders with the redolence of old mud and the waft of boiled onions and dishwater from the kitchen. My mother stood at the stove in her shoes with the sides cut out to favor her bunions. She swung toward me with her sweet, toothless smile, her blue eyes aproned with dark flesh like a raccoon's eyes.

"Tommy!"

She let herself fall into my arms with a dramatic motion. "What are you doing here, for anyway's sake?"

"Riding the cars to Virginia City."

She pursed her lips at me. "Aren't you the fine gentleman!"

I grinned back at her and said I was getting finer day by day.

"Let me get my teeth in and make some lemonade. I'll send the boy next door for the Gent."

"I've got an hour."

I sat on the porch in one of the ragged wicker chairs with my feet up on the rail gazing out on the dusty street where a ginger mutt barked at a passing Chinaman. The yelps reverberated hollowly in the heat. I remembered chasing Chinamen with the other Catholic boys. We were all dead set against pigtails, for reasons I could no longer remember.

My mother brought me the lemonade and sat down beside me. She had put in her teeth, changed her dress and combed her hair into a gray-streaked bun on top of her head.

"Have you been saying your prayers, Tommy?" she asked.

"Not as often as I should, Ma."

"The Good Lord will forgive you anything, Son. But you must ask for His forgiveness."

"Yes, Ma."

But I had come to Bierce's way of thinking, that prayer was "to ask that the laws of the universe be annulled in behalf of a single petitioner confessedly unworthy." I myself would be ashamed to pray to the Good Lord for the gift of a Nob Hill young lady, and I had too much pride to confess impure thoughts of her as well.

My mother listened to my relation of my successes in San Francisco as a fledgling reporter for *The Hornet*. I bragged a little, enlarged a bit. She appreciated good news so much it was impossible not to make some up to satisfy her appetite. I did not mention slashed whores, however, feeling I had entertained her sufficiently.

"How's the Gent?" I asked.

"He's working for the SP. Mr. Wallingford thinks he's a natural wonder. Oh, he could sweet-talk an orang-outang out of a banana." She said this with pride.

She wanted to know why I was going to Virginia City. "The Gent says the lode is all used up, people moving on. They'll be closing the mines soon. He is the world authority on anything to do with mining except how to make money by it."

I listened to secondhand reports of the successes of Michael in Denver, Brian in Chicago and Emma in Portland with her third baby.

"Do you know what he does for the SP?" I said.

She peered up and down the street and lowered her voice. "Bobby Wallingford works over at the legislature. I think he passes out money to the Representatives and Senators. The Gent probably carries his carpetbag and the account book. He'd like giving money away. He has always been good at that."

I produced the Manila cigar with its red, white and blue band someone had given Bierce and passed it on to my mother.

"Thanks, baby," she said, pocketing the cigar.

I heard the clatter of hoofs before I saw the Gent appear. He turned the corner on a handsome gray, wearing a broad-brimmed hat, holding up an arm in greeting. He tied the gray's reins to the fence and stamped up the walk to embrace me.

"Good to see you, boy!"

He was a fine-looking man, thickening through the waist but stylishly dressed, sporting black whiskers with slashes of white on either side of his big grin. My mother headed back into the house.

I told him I was bound for Virginia City on newspaper business.

"Sad place," he said, shaking his head, and settling in the chair beside me with his shiny boots up on the rail. "Thanks, hon," he said, when my mother brought him a glass of lemonade.

"You spent some time there, didn't you?" I said.

"Briefly, briefly," he said. "They got your money away from you pretty fast on the Washoe." He grinned at me, as though we both appreciated his weakness.

"Tell me about the Comstock," I said.

"Never been there, have you?"

"Never been to Nevada at all."

"The Comstock paid for the War, you know. Made San Francisco what it is today besides. Silver ore and stock games." He managed to nod and shake his head at the same time in some inner recollection and amusement. Then he assumed a serious expression.

"Well, sir, there are two canyons running off Mount Davidson, Six-mile Canyon and Gold Canyon, and there was an old bird that'd staked some claims there named Henry Comstock. Old Pancake he was called. There was some gold but an awful lot of trash blue mud with it, till somebody sent in that blue for assay and it proved out about three thousand dollars a ton silver."

My mother watched us from the far chair, gauzed in blue smoke from the cigar I had brought her. "Tell him about that mine you had an interest in," she said.

"They say there were seventeen thousand claims around Mount Davidson in the '60s, and five of them were mine," my father said. "In '63 alone there were some three thousand Comstock properties selling shares on the San Francisco Stock Exchange. Most came to naught, like mine. Or got euchered up because someone was a lot smarter than you were.

"The Ophir, the Hale and Norcross, the Yellow Jacket, the Consolidated-Virginia and the Con-Ohio had run holes down to five or six hundred feet where they begun to peter out. Shares dropped to next to nothing and the Ralston Ring and the Bank of California started buying up shares and claims, and Ralston sent Will Sharon to Virginia City to take charge of things. The Big Bonanza came in at a thousand feet and made fortunes for Ralston and Sharon, and

Nat McNair and those Irishmen that controlled the Consolidated-Virginia, and a pack of other fry. So the Bank of California and Frisco began living high on Comstock silver.

"Then there was a bewilderment of stock options and shenanigans, boomers and plungers, assessments and bankruptcies, fake bonanzas and real ones, until the whole mess of it blew up and the Bank of California went bust and Billy Ralston took his last swim. Sharon ended up with his debts and assets, paid off debts at pennies on dollars and held onto the assets and showed himself to be the sneaking rotten two-timing son of a bitch he is. I hear he has got his hands full of this Rose of Sharon lawsuit, howsomever."

I asked if he had known Highgrade Carrie. His eyes squinted just a bit before they fixed on mine.

"Heard of her, Son," he said. "Quite a woman, I believe. The Miner's Angel."

"Angel is as angel does," my mother said.

"Angel does is just why she was called the Miner's Angel," my father said.

When it was time to go my father gave me a lift on his borrowed gray, up behind his saddle, which made me feel like a boy. I looked back to wave to my mother on the porch.

Braced against my father's back, jogged with the horse's motion, I recalled the good and the bad of my childhood. The Gent had been a strong part of the good. We had fished off the riverbank by the big snag, seated side by side with our poles at the same angle, lines falling together into the brown swirl of water. He had taught me how to play ball, patiently pitching the baseball to my mitt, a hand-me-down from Michael, and patiently pitching to Brian's bat. He had brought me home new books I had known he could not afford. He had never paid attention to what he couldn't afford.

I remembered him weeping when Michael punched him in the eye and left home.

"Those were beautiful ladies in Virginia City," my father said over his shoulder. "Julia Bulette and Highgrade Carrie. Those were some times," he said.

"A Mrs. Bettis said she'd known you on the Washoe," I said.

"Don't recall anybody by that name. What's she look like?"

I didn't do very well remembering what Mrs. Bettis had looked like, much less describing her.

"Probably her married name," my father said. "Or she was using a different name. Lot of folks used different names, on the Comstock."

He left me off at the station, with promises to take me out for a fine dinner the next time he came down to the City. On the train there was a half-hour wait before the conductor called the all-aboard, and the cars lurched and jangled with the tug of the engine.

On the Truckee & Virginia headed south down the Washoe Valley, I gazed out the window at the eastern peaks of the Sierra Nevada. The snow line was so regular it looked drawn with a ruler. The snow caught the sun like some heavenly show of the purity of nature, but I could see by the sparse timbering of those lower slopes that men had been at work cutting down the forests and sawing up the logs for cordwood, and for cribbing for the stopes of the Comstock Lode.

After a halt in Carson City, the train chuffed on around the mountain, up and up, curve after curve, tunnel after tunnel lined with blackened zinc against the sparks from the smokestacks, slow enough so I could get out of the cars to stride alongside, on up toward Mount Davidson, Virginia City and the Comstock Lode. The mountain was scarred with coyote hole mines and weathered shacks. I descended from my car into the depot below the town to the thin distant crashing of stamp mills.

A few bums, a shawled woman with a sickly child by the hand and a blanket Indian with a face as dark as mud stood watching the passengers come off the train. I climbed the hill in the shadow of the mountain, with my satchel slapping against my leg, up to C Street where stores and saloons fronted on boardwalks in need of repair. Virginia City was not a bustling community.

In the International Hotel, where spittoons glinted among the potted palms on worn carpeting, the racket of the stamps was felt through the soles rather than heard. I engaged a room on the second floor. There did not seem to be any other guests. When I opened my window that looked out on C Street and down a canyon slashed with tan dumps and tailings, the stamp mills' pounding came loudly again.

A horse car with a weary gray horse and a listless driver took me and a red-shirted miner with a crippled leg north out C Street, to where I had been directed to the Consolidated-Ohio, which had absorbed the Jack of Spades. From a rutted wagon road I gazed down on a spur of track where there were flatcars stacked with cordwood and a cluster of wooden buildings with corrugated iron roofs splashed with patches of rust, all of them centered around a central two-story structure with tanks and ladders and smokeless chimneys on the roof, and a glimpse through high windows of ranks of dusty machinery. Over the tallest section of the main building were the fading letters: CONSOLIDATED-OHIO. The Con-Ohio appeared to be shut down.

As I strolled down the wagon road toward the mine, a bearded man wearing a wicker-sided conductor's cap appeared out of a shed and leaned on his crutch watching me approach; another lame man.

"We're closed up, friend," he said, when I came up.

"Just wanted to see the famous Jack of Spades," I said.

"Nothing to see. Closed down. I'm just here so nobody'll come past and see there's nobody here."

"Which part is the Jack of Spades?" I asked.

With a sweep of his arm, he said, "Jack of Spades is the near adit in there."

"I'm looking for some information," I said.

"Tell you, friend, if you want information on anything in this dead place, you just see Mr. Devers. He's editor at the *Sentinel*."

"You wouldn't give me a look-in at the Jack of Spades for a dollar?"

His tongue swiped over his lips. He had coarse whiskers that stuck straight forward out of his face like gray quills. He removed his cap and scraped his fingers through a tangle of dull hair. "Can't do that, mister. You git now."

"I'm interested in Nat McNair and his missus," I said.

"They's nothing to do with Con-Ohio any more. Anyway, he's dead, ain't he?" He peered past me. "Oh-oh!" he muttered.

A man strode toward us from a gaping door in the main building. He was black-headed, black-bearded, wearing a black suit and boots, gesturing as he came. They were not friendly gestures. I thought he was going to walk right through me, but he stopped a foot away. Staring into my face, he addressed the crippled man:

"Who's this, Phelps?"

"Says he's interested in the Jack of Spades, Major."

"Tell him we will welcome the sight of his coattails, if you please."

"Better git, friend."

I said to the younger man, "I'm interested in the McNairs—"

"Get him out of here, Phelps," he said, glaring at me. He had cheeks as red as apples. He swung around and stalked back to the open door.

Phelps pointed.

The horse car seemed to have ceased operation for the day, so I walked back to town.

I found Editor Devers, the fount of information on Virginia City, in the saloon across the street from the International Hotel. He was sitting on a stool at the far end of the bar in the stance of a jockey on a fast horse. He was clean-shaven, with an unhealthy brown complexion. His dark suit was rumpled, his collar was dirty and he looked like an editor who had seen better times and did not expect to see them again. A bottle of Old Crow spiked up on the bar before him.

"Devers," he said. He regarded me in the mirror behind the bar instead of face to face. "Josephus P. Devers, yes, sir. Wounded at Second Manassas, mustered out and came west. Seen the great days of the Comstock. Now this camp is done with. Mines closing down.

They are letting them flood to water-table level. Con-Ohio's closed down. Ophir's closed down. Nothing but assessments-due in the *Sentinel* these days. They say they've come up with new methods for working over low-grade ore in the tailings, but nothing's doing there yet." He nodded at me in the mirror.

"It'll come back, Josey," the bartender called down to him.

He shook his head. He kept shaking it for a long time.

I said I was a friend of young Beaumont McNair and held my breath.

This time he turned to glance at me directly. His teeth and eyeballs were the same tint of yellow.

"McNair," he said.

"The Comstock millionaire. His father, I mean."

"Oh, yes."

"Married a woman from here named Carrie."

There was a silence. I had a sense of having missed the ball, maybe only strike one.

"The Jack of Spades," I said.

"Oh, yes." He watched me in the mirror again.

"I understand that Beau McNair's mother no longer owns the Consolidated-Ohio," I said.

He nodded lengthily. "Sold out, closed down. Yes. Everybody with brains in their heads is clearing out. Oh, I've seen the great days, but it's all over now."

"I understand the Jack of Spades was one of the first mines," I said.

Nodding, Devers said, "Nat McNair took over in '64, I believe it was. Had some fights with the Bank Crowd—Ralston and Sharon and them. Then the Silver Kings come to bat. Flood, O'Brien, Fair and Mackay. In '75 the Bank of California went bust. Just in time for the Big Bonanzas! That's when Nat McNair made his fortune. Bought up the Peterkin and Ohio right next door to the Jack of Spades. Consolidated-Ohio! Drifted into a big orebody. But he didn't make his fortune digging silver out of the ground, he made it manipulating stocks. They all did, all the Silver

Kings." He pointed a finger at me. "There was more money made booming stocks than there was mineral taken out of the ground. Had our own stock exchange, right here! They weren't interested in mining, they were interested in the fixed poker game they had set up. And that's the tragedy of the Comstock Lode!"

"Well, Mrs. McNair is Lady Caroline Stearns now," I said.

"She is a wonder of the world, that lady," Devers said.

I said I heard something about a spades club, a Society of Spades. "Maybe it was investors who bought up Jack of Spades stock?"

He nodded for a long time. He splashed more whiskey into his glass. "Nat McNair, Highgrade Carrie—Caroline LaPlante, her name was."

"A madam."

"A damned fine woman! The Miner's Angel, some called her." Devers stuck his chin out at me as though that was a second strike. Then his forehead creased with thought. "Al Gorton. E. O. Macomber. Somebody else."

"Elza Klosters?" I said.

Devers shook his head. "No, Elza worked for Nat McNair. Enforcer. Later on he was one of the deputies at that Mussel Slough shoot-up, as I recall."

The Railroad again!

"Al Gorton's dead," he added. "Murdered down in San Francisco."

"Clubbed?" I said.

His face jerked toward me. "Why, I believe that's right!" he said. "Did you know Al?"

"I think Beau said something."

"Believe I've got a tintype of that bunch in the files," he said.

"I'd surely like to see it."

"Come by in the morning. I'm not too busy these days. We're up on B Street."

"What I'm not clear about is how McNair ended up with control of the Jack of Spades."

"What I said. You get a certain stock position and you can call for assessments until you drive out the weaker investors. Often enough that was how those Silver Kings got their control. Nat McNair was one of the worst of them. Will Sharon was the total worst. No offense to your friend meant, you understand."

"So Beau's mother got out of the Consolidated-Ohio."

"Year, eighteen months ago. Listen: between '71 and '81 the Comstock produced about $320,000,000 and paid $147,000,000 in dividends. Last year there weren't many dividends paid, and this year my pages are filled with assessment notices. There are not many stockholders paying assessments any more, I can tell you."

"Did she sell out to a man called Major?"

"Major Copley," Devers said. "He's just the super for the bunch that bought it." He poured more whiskey.

He was fading. He sat lower on his stool, and he didn't face me at all any more, gazing at the mirror with drooping eyelids. Finally the bartender said, "About time to go home, Josey?"

"Home," Devers muttered.

"Where's Jimmy Fairleigh?" the bartender said.

"Hey, Jimmy!" one of the other drinkers called, and a bunch of them began laughing and shouting, "Jimmy! Hey, Jimmy Fairleigh!"

A little man appeared, wearing a cloth cap and a tight little suit over a big bottom. He was a dwarf, with a big, ugly face that was a curious mix of old and young. He fronted up to Devers and said, "Time to go home, Mr. Devers!"

Devers slid off his stool and, leaning on the little man and stepping carefully, as though traversing treacherous ground, made his way to the street door and was gone.

"Does he do that every night?" I asked the barkeep, who was swabbing the bar where Devers had sat.

"Every night except Sundays," the barkeep replied.

"Wouldn't think he'd be much good in the morning," I said.

"He'll be right there at his desk in the morning, nose to the wind," the barkeep said.

LABOR, *n.*
One of the processes by which A acquires property for B.
—THE DEVIL'S DICTIONARY

was sitting on my bed in my nightshirt when there was a knock, and
another, very peremptory, as I
started toward the door. When I
opened it a man shoved in past me, breathing hard as though he'd
just run up the stairs. He was the gent the watchman had called "Major" from the Consolidated-Ohio Mine. Major Copley.

He swung around to face me, no one but me to talk to this time. I felt
at a disadvantage in my slippers and nightshirt. The gas jet hissed.

I asked him what he wanted.

"You are a newspaper sneak, sir!"

I had put down *The Hornet* as my employer when I had registered
at the hotel.

"Hanging around poking and prying!"

"That is my job," I said.

He folded his arms. He wore a blue flannel shirt buttoned at the
neck, beneath his black jacket. He was a big-chested, powerful man,
maybe six feet tall in his black boots.

"I know your ilk! Sniffing scandals. Sniffing and scraping for your
kind of cat's vomit tricks. Sniffing for English!"

English?

I said I was interested in the Jack of Spades Mine.

He gritted his teeth at me. "This camp was poisoned by spying and lies told and bamboozle. Spies and sneaks. I am sick of it!"

"I'm not spying on you, Major."

He snatched from his coat pocket a nickle-plated derringer and pointed it at my forehead, squinting along the little barrel. "What do you think of that, Mister Newspaper Sneak?"

It was interesting the advantage you felt when the other fellow produced a firearm.

"I don't think much of it," I said.

He held the little piece aimed at my forehead, shaking it and showing me his lower teeth.

"There are abandoned mine shafts under our feet, sir!" he said. "Dead men inhabit them, sir!" He pocketed the derringer and lurched out of the room.

He slammed the door behind him.

In the night the wind came up. Thecurtains bellied into the room like ghosts clinging to the sash. I heard cans banging together, panes rattled. I had written up my notes for Bierce. One of the Spades, Albert Gorton, had been murdered, "clubbed" as the letter to Bierce had put it; another was named Macomber, still another was so far unidentified. One of these must have written the letter to Bierce.

Lady Caroline's managers had cleared out her interests in the Consolidated-Ohio a year or eighteen months ago. Devers had spoken of her with affection, maybe more than affection—as "the Miners' Angel." That affection didn't seem to include Nat McNair.

The Major was worried that I was spying. Spying on what? What did "English" have to do with anything?

And what did any of this have to do with the murder of two Morton Street whores and a judge's widow, in San Francisco?

My waiter at breakfast was the dwarf, Jimmy Fairleigh. The wind whooped along the street in great wallops of dust that battered against the hotel windows like hail. Men came in, cursing and beating their hats against their clothing. I thought that Devers would not be early at the office so I made a leisurely breakfast. Jimmy Fairleigh cleared the table and brought me more coffee. His heavy, anxious face was out of scale to his frame, more old than young, I could see now. He identified the wind as a "Washoe Zephyr."

Before he got away, I said, "I shouldn't imagine Mr. Devers would be early at his office this morning."

"He'll be there," he said. "Comes in early rain or shine. Up on B Street."

"I'm interested in talking to anybody who knew Caroline La-Plante," I said.

He cleared the dishes and stacked them on his arm as though he hadn't heard me.

The Zeyphr scoured B Street. Sheets of newspaper flapped through the air like seabirds, and an empty fruit can rolled and clanked. A brown dog was blown along with it, trotting obliquely with the wind pushing him. I turned up my collar and kept a hand on my hat. The wind was more of an inducement to get out of Virginia City than Major Copley's threats had been.

Devers was visible through a window that had VIRGINIA SENTINEL painted on it. He wore a green eyeshade and sat at a rolltop desk with a hand supporting his cheek. He glanced up without enthusiasm as I came in, pushing the door closed against the wind.

"Does it blow like this a good deal?"

"It'll blow like this awhile," he said, nodding. "Then it will bull up and blow hard for awhile." He indicated a chair. He looked more sickly than he had last night in the dimness of the saloon.

I told him that I'd had a visit from Major Copley in the night.

"Ah!"

"Ranted about spies and sneaks."

Devers kept his eyes fixed on one of the pigeonholes of his desk. "They got pretty skittish about being spied on, there at the Con-Ohio."

"What happened?"

"There was some fuss they'd just as soon didn't get out and about."

"What's 'English' mean?"

"Well, that's the English shuffle."

"What's that?"

"Way it was worked, the stock was stuck in low figures so the news got out that a drill hole had run into an orebody. Looked like a bonanza. There was a jump in the stock, and they sold out better off. But when they drifted on in there was nothing doing. It'd been salted. Major Copley took a deal of criticism, but he was as fooled as anybody as far as I can make out."

"Why *English?*" I said. "Because of Lady Caroline?"

"No, no, no; Carrie wouldn't have anything to do with truck like that. Fellow that first devised the business was an Englishman. Maybe he was named English. The way he worked it out for McNair had one more hook to it. They leak out the news there's a strike, then nothing comes of it like it's a salting trick, but there's an orebody, all right. So then they buy up the shares on the cheap."

It was difficult to sort through the convolutions of the English shuffle.

"You said you had a tintype of the Spades I could have."

He lifted his head as though it was very heavy. "Spades?"

I reminded him.

"Oh, it wouldn't be *here,*" he said. "All the files are down in Carson, I don't have them here."

"You promised me that tintype," I said.

"Have to come back. I'll be going down there in a week or so, look for it then. You'll have to come back."

"That tintype is worth fifty dollars to me," I said, hoping I could convince Bierce and Mr. Macgowan that the tintype was worth such a sum. "You send me that tintype and I'll send you fifty dollars."

"Done!"

"In that tintype are the people I'm interested in. McNair, Caroline LaPlante, a man named Gorton and another named Macomber, and a third man. Who was the third man?"

He shook his head. A blast of wind peppered the window. "Don't exactly remember anybody named Macomber either."

"That enforcer of McNair's named Klosters. Might he have enforced Gorton in San Francisco?"

"You didn't hear that from me."

"Clubbed him why? Something to do with the Jack of Spades? Troublesome to McNair?"

"I don't know any of that," Devers said. He swung full-face toward me for the first time. "Listen, young fellow. You go around asking questions like that and you will get some answers you are not going to like."

I rose, dropped my card on his desk and said, "I want that tintype, however."

"You'll have it," Devers said. "Get out of here and blow away now."

I let myself out into a blast of wind filled with grit.

Back at the hotel I encountered Jimmy Fairleigh in the lobby. He wore a long denim apron and swabbed the tiles with a mop with a flail of soaking cloth at the end, which he slapped from side to side. He set the mop in its pail and beckoned me into the empty dining room.

"I used to work at the Miner's Rest," he said.

"I will pay for information."

He indicated the table where I'd had breakfast, and I sat down. He remained standing before me, his short arms crossed on his chest, his ugly face contorted anxiously.

"I'd work for Carrie sometimes when I was just a kit, running errands and such. She is a fine woman. I will tell you I have never thought higher of a woman than her."

He stared at me with an expression I didn't understand, maybe defiance.

I said I was a friend of her son's, inquiring into some matters that concerned him about his mother's days in Virginia City.

"After Julia Bulette got murdered there was no keeping her here. Thought it was bound to happen to her."

Who was Julia Bulette?

"Hoor. Sometimes she worked out of Carrie's place. Frenchy bastard killed her. They strung him up!"

"How was she killed?"

"Beat on, strangled, shot. Crime of passion, they called it. She was *dead.* It was a fright to Carrie. There was no holding her here then. Said she'd marry one of those fellows that was always proposing to her and get out of town and out of the business."

"Who was proposing?"

"Fancy fellows! Sharon was married, but he'd've set her up in style. Nat McNair, that she did marry. There was others, just about every Jim, George and Will in town."

I asked if he knew of the Spades. "They had to do with the Jack of Spades Mine."

"Oh, yes," he said vaguely. "Dolph Jackson and them. McNair."

"Did Carrie have a special gent?"

"She had her favorites. Dolph; he was a funny one, made her laugh, took her for rides in his buggy. She liked that. And the Englishman. Very high-tone! And there was the piano player at the Miner's Rest, I forget his name." He rubbed the back of his neck as though to revive his memory. "She was a woman any man would want to lock up in his house just for himself."

I thought he was one who had loved her, though he had said he was just a kit.

"Macomber?"

"Sure, Eddie Macomber."

"Al Gorton?"

He nodded his big head. "Bald fellow with a bunged-up eye."

"Man named Elza Klosters?"

After some thought, he shook his head. "Nothing to do with Carrie."

I took a breath and said, "Cletus Redmond?"

"Didn't know anybody by that name. Just what is it you want, Mister?"

"So Carrie was frightened when one of her whores was murdered and decided that she had to leave town and make a good marriage."

"She was in a family way!" he blurted.

"She was?"

He licked his lips. "Now you show me some money, Mister, or I don't have no more to say."

I gave him three dollars, which was all I could afford. He tucked it into a pocket inside his apron. Yes, Carrie had been in a family way. He didn't know who the father was. Could've been any of several. There was nothing more to be got out of Jimmy Fairleigh, either because he knew no more, or he had already told me more than he'd meant to, or because my three dollars had not sufficed him or because his loyalty to Caroline LaPlante prevented any more discussion of her male connections.

"If you see Carrie you tell her Jimmy Fairleigh will always remember her," he said.

In the hotel in Reno where I spent the night, I woke up with names running through my head. English. Englishman. Britain. James M. Brittain, Amelia's father, had been a mining engineer in the Comstock. Every Jim, George and Will. I didn't sleep any more, considering withholding this connection from Bierce, because of my attachment to Miss Amelia Brittain.

INTIMACY, *n.*
A relation into which fools are providentially
drawn for their mutual destruction.
—THE DEVIL'S DICTIONARY

ierce had written: "San Francisco will welcome the returning Lady Caroline Stearns, formerly High-grade Carrie of the Washoe and Mrs. Nathaniel McNair of the City."

"She is a woman of distinction, whether the bootstraps are stretched or not," he said to me." I cannot think of many such. Adah Isaacs Mencken, Ada Claire, Lillie Coit. For the most part the gender has little to recommend it except for its role in the continuation of the species, which is an arguable concept at best. I am unconcerned with her maculate past."

He often described whores as the most honest members of their sex. Sometimes he did get tiresome in his fulminations.

He had spoken with Judge McManigle, who had served with Judge Hamon on the Circuit Court, and had not been much impressed: "Who ne'er took up law, yet lays law down," he said. "Still, he knew what cock horse Judge Hamon was riding. He was denouncing Senator Jennings for subornation and barratry, never mind that it was rancor over the Railroad choosing Jennings to ordain a state senator rather than himself. He had chapter and verse on Jennings's purchase in cases that concerned the Southern Pacific in general, and the trials of the Mussel Slough farmers in particular. That was what your arsonist friend disposed of in Santa Cruz."

"Did Brown kill Mrs. Hamon then?"

"Or Jennings himself. In any case Jennings was surely the instigator." Bierce leaned back in his chair regarding me with his handsome, high-color, cold face. He wore a blue silk cravat, and his vest buttoned with the gold chain of his watch across it. The chalky skull grimaced at our conversation.

"How do these matters fit together?" I asked. "Highgrade Carrie. The Spades. The murder of Julia Bulette. The proposals. The pregnancy. The murder of Al Gorton. Beau, who is no longer engaged to Amelia Brittain. The slashed Morton Street whores. And Senator Jennings, Mrs. Hamon and the man called Brown."

I did not mention James M. Brittain.

Bierce handed me another typewritten sheet, with an item for Tattle:

"The Senator from Southern Pacific has been especially active lately, in Morton Street and Santa Cruz, as well as the Giftcrest palm-greasings."

"I will see him hanged," he said. "And the Giftcrest defeated. And the Railroad powerfully smitten."

Tattle also contained an item on a lady poet who had sent a volume of her poems to Bierce: "Miss Frye makes comment that her best inspirations come to her on an empty stomach. The quality of her verse has caused this reader's stomach to empty as well—"

And a stab at the Reverend Stottlemyer: "It has been related to me that the Reverend Stottlemyer, renowned for his ability to separate wallets from the bills within, was asked by a fellow Deacon to exercise his powers on the Deacon's congregation, for which our Stottle would receive one fourth of the monies collected. This was assented to on the proviso that Stottlemyer take up the collection himself. He did so and pocketed the funds, whereupon the Deacon raised an outcry. To this Stottle responded, 'Nothing is coming to you, Brother, for the Adversary hardened the hearts of your congregation and all they gave was a fourth.' "

"I hope to show the tintype to Captain Pusey, when it comes," I said.

"Who perhaps will have a photograph of the bravo Klosters in his archive. I wonder if we will not find that Klosters is your menacing Mr. Brown."

"Amelia Brittain told me that Beau McNair explained to her that redheaded Jewesses were the most popular of the parlorhouse women. I wonder if there is a particular one."

"I suppose the topics of conversation of the younger generation will always be shocking to the older," Bierce said. "Yes; that is grounds for investigation."

"What do you think of Beau's alibi?"

"The young man's mother's pet employee? Young McNair is not out of the forest by any means, but I don't think he is the Morton Street Slasher."

I warned myself not to become as obsessed with Beau McNair as Bierce was with the Southern Pacific Railroad.

"Would you like to come to St. Helena for the weekend?" Bierce asked. "Meet Mrs. Bierce and the children?" He looked grim again. "You will have to meet Mrs. Day as well—my Mollie's mother."

I said I would be very pleased to come to St. Helena for the weekend.

I did not know much about Bierce's family, except that they lived across the Bay to the north. Bierce himself rented an apartment on Broadway, near *The Hornet*. He kept to himself after work, although I knew he belonged to the Bohemian Club, and he often spent evenings at cards with his literary friends Ina Coolbrith and Charles Warren Stoddard, who were the editors of the *Overland Monthly*. His drinking friends were Arthur McEwen and Petey Bigelow of the *Examiner*, and there were evenings when those three cut a considerable swath at the Baldwin Theater

Bar at Kearny and Bush, and the saloon at the Crystal Palace. And I knew he consorted with women who were not Mollie Bierce, in the French restaurants such as the Terrapin Oyster House, or the Old Poodle Dog, which had elevators to the private rooms upstairs and were open all night. I had in fact met one of his women, a Mrs. Barclay, a willowy, wispy dark lady who sparkled with diamonds and fawned on Bierce as though he was in fact Almighty God.

Bierce had suggested that I try my hand on a side piece on Leland Stanford of the Big Four, who had just been nominated for the senate with more than the usual degree of political shenanigans. I showed him what I had written:

> All the surviving Big Four are big men. Collis B. Huntington weighs 240, Stanford upwards of 260, Charles Crocker downwards from 300. The Nob Hill mansions of these former Sacramento storekeepers are big. Their fortunes are big. It is estimated that when Hopkins died he was worth $19,000,000. Crocker's fortune is larger than that, Stanford's still larger, Huntington's the largest of all.
>
> Stanford, who was governor of California during the War, is pleased to be referred to as Governor Stanford. He has been likened to Alexander the Great, Julius Caesar, Lorenzo the Magnificent, Napoleon Bonaparte, John Stuart Mill and Judas Iscariot.
>
> A man of closely considered opinions, he is outspoken against the proposed government regulation of corporations. He considers such regulation contrary to America's traditional respect for property rights, and against the interests of the small man who needs the cooperation of others of his class, in the form of corporations, to protect him from the greed of the moneyed.
>
> "It is pleasant to be rich," he told a reporter. "But the advantages of wealth are greatly exaggerated. I do not clearly see that a man who can buy anything he fancies is any better off than the man who can buy what he actually wants."
>
> And he added: "If it rained twenty-dollar gold pieces until noon every day, at night there would be some men begging for their suppers."

During the governmental investigations of the profits earned by the transcontinental railroad, the partners announced that the line was "starving." This was somewhat belied by the wonders of their mansions under construction. In his California Street palace, with its fifty rooms, its seventy-feet-high glass dome and bay windows stacked like poker chips, Stanford likes to show off his orchestrion. This is a complete mechanical orchestra housed in a large cabinet. He also takes pleasure in demonstrating his aviary of mechanical birds. These are perched on the branches of artificial trees in the art gallery and operate by compressed air, opening their metal beaks to sing when the governor presses a button.

Bierce considered my piece much too long. He was not interested in the death of the boy, Leland Stanford, Jr., nor the founding of Leland Stanford Jr. University as a memorial.

He commented that I should leave irony to the ironists and satire to those who possessed a lighter touch.

"Moreover, do not employ 'moneyed' for 'wealthy.' You might thus say 'the cattled men of Texas,' or 'the lobstered men of the fish market.' "

"Yes, sir," I said.

A messenger delivered to me a scented square envelope addressed in florid feminine handwriting. I admired the look of Mr. Thomas Redmond, Esq. as penned by Amelia Brittain in bold, elaborate copperplate.

> *Dear Mr. Redmond,*
>
> *This is to inform you that since I am no longer in a situation of attachment, you are welcome to call on me at 913 Taylor Street if you are so inclined.*
>
> *Expectantly yours,*
> *Amelia Brittain*
>
> *PS I look forward to discussing with you my "shadow"! AB*

I presented myself at number 913 on a steep block of Taylor Street, a narrow, tall, bay-windowed house with the facade bisected by a porch furnished with a wicker settee, chairs and a table. Bilious stained-glass windows gazed out at me, and the late sun glinted on the cut glass of the door. A butler in a striped waistcoat answered my crank of the bell. He had pale hair combed in a pompadour, and eyes that looked straight through me to see the printer's devil instead of the journalist. He held out a silver salver, upon which I laid my calling card, and disappeared.

He returned to say that Miss Brittain was not at home and closed the door in my face. I retreated down the steps, and down Taylor Street off Nob Hill.

In the Barnacles' cellar I whaled the stuffing out of the buggy seat, panting and dusty.

When I quit the Fire Department I had kept my helmet, for I loved it dearly, with the beaked eagle on the crown and its long beavertail; the crown made of gleaming black heavy cowhide, reinforced by strips built up into gothic arches, and the inside padded with felt. I still sometimes admired myself in the mirror, capped by its magnificence. Once I had been ambitious for the white and black of a Chief's Aide's hat, and even the white of the Chief himself. I was still stirred when I heard the fire bell of the Engine Company over on Sacramento Street, and often I hastened along to see the action.

Today there was a three-alarmer on Battery Street. Pumpers and hose reels blocked the street, and arcs of shining water flashed against the sun. This was a warehouse fire, bales smoldering and flaming glimpsed through open gates. Next door was a narrow-fronted saloon with the dilapidated sign: WASHOE ANGEL.

The Chief in his white helmet was directing the fight, yelling at firefighters scampering with their hose-laying. Out of the saloon appeared a slouch-hatted young fellow in an overall, struggling with a painting that must have been four feet by six. I had only a glimpse of the naked woman delineated. She was mounted on a magnificent white horse, her long golden hair artfully arranged to advertise as much as conceal her charms, the stallion with one foreleg raised and bent. It was the typical saloon painting, but more magnificent than most. The woman's flesh, white as gardenia blossoms, seemed to illuminate that chaotic scene. Struggling with the painting, which seemed to be buffeted by winds generated by the flames and the arching sprays, the young man staggered up the street and disappeared into an alleyway. That vision of saloon female nudity moved me to start after him, but my way was blocked by the team of horses maneuvering one of the pumpers. And the Lady Godiva of the Washoe Angel disappeared from my ken.

At Mrs. Johnson's establishment in the Upper Tenderloin, I sat in the parlor waiting for Annie Dunker. Mrs. Johnson sat on the far side of the room, stout in shiny black, talking to a gray-haired man in a brown suit, to whom I had nodded politely in response to his nod, without a meeting of eyes. I lounged in an overstuffed chair looking out the window at the traffic of Stockton Street. It was early for callers, but Mrs. Johnson had always been friendly. She had a personal style of accepting dollars, folding them and with a sleight-of-hand slipping the bills inside her black cuff.

Annie tripped down the stairs in her ankle-length shift, which revealed interesting swells and swales, and had a blue ribbon at the neck. She trotted to me, pushed me back as I rose and seated herself in my lap.

"It's been so long, Tommy!"

She was a kitten-faced, dark-haired girl a couple of years older than I, who had worked in Albany and Chicago before coming to San Francisco. She squirmed in my lap for a moment before springing to her feet. We went upstairs arm in arm. In her room I sat on the bed and said I wanted to talk.

"First or second?" she said.

"Do you know who Beau McNair is?"

"*Everybody* knows of him."

"What do you mean?"

"Everybody in the better places, I mean."

"Is there a redheaded Jewess he might spend time with?"

"Rachel, at Mrs. Overton's. My cousin's there too."

"What do you know about him?"

"Just that he is—very *attentive,* Tommy. The way you used to be with me." She had a way of making a two-syllable word out of "me." She giggled, rubbing her hands down her shift.

"Can you find out about how he is with her? How he acts? What he says? Anything interesting?"

"They don't think he is that terrible—*butcher!*"

"This is just for me to know. What he's *like.*"

"I'll ask Lucille. I know Rachel is *popular.*"

"Have you ever had a client who didn't have a—" I pointed. "*You* know?"

She covered her mouth as she giggled, shaking her head. "What would be the *point,* Tommy?"

"Have you heard of anyone like that? He has to use a leather thing he strapped on. A dildo, I guess."

"Well, there are men that do that, Tommy. Old men that can't get it up any more."

"This would be a young man."

She shook her head some more, looking puzzled.

"Could you ask around about such a fellow? I'll get some money."

"I'll do it for you, Tommy. For you and me-ee."

"Anything you can find out will be helpful."

"Now?" she said, and with a swift motion stripped her shift off over her head. She stood there naked and posed like a garden statuette. I thought of her astride a white stallion and my breath caught in my throat.

"You look grand," I said. Although all I could think of was Amelia Brittain, there was no hitch at all in taking pleasure with Annie Dunker.

MARRIAGE, *n.*
The state or condition of a community consist-
ing of a master, a mistress and two slaves,
making in all, two.
—THE DEVIL'S DICTIONARY

board the ferry across the Bay, and on the train to St. Helena, Bierce and I discussed the murders.

"Senator Jennings murdered Mrs. Hamon in order to rid himself of a threat of exposure and disposed of her after the manner of the Morton Street murders," Bierce said. "I believe Captain Pusey knows it, knows more than we do in fact, but he has his own springs of action."

"His spring of action is how to get a hook into someone with money to fork over," I said.

"I believe Pusey's game has less light than shadow."

I started at the word "shadow." What did Amelia mean by her "shadow"? Surely she could have no connection with Morton Street. Her father had been on the Comstock, and the connection of his name with a conspiracy called "the English shuffle" fretted me like a pebble in my shoe. The idea of a "shadow" caused chills of anxiety to wash over me. But she wouldn't have written of it so lightly if it had been serious.

"It is the shame of the Nation that we do not have a Chief of Detectives we can trust," Bierce said in a bitter voice. "A mayor we can trust. A governor. A president! If our lives must be led in distrust and contempt of all who govern us, it would be well to accept the fact. It is my burden that I cannot. It is an affliction to me that a moth-eaten old malefactor such as Collis B. Huntington keeps a hand in my pocket, and another on my reins. It is unbearable!"

The Bierce two-story cottage faced south among pine trees that had dropped a brown carpet of needles. On a veranda were bicycles, a porch swing and a litter of baseball bats and mitts. Two boys of ten and twelve, in short pants and striped baseball shirts ran out to dance around Bierce, followed by a red-haired child in a blue jumper, who flung herself into her father's arms. She was received with the first real enthusiasm I had seen Bierce evince toward another person. There was no question from their reddish fair hair and neat counte-nances that Day and Leigh were his sons, little Helen his daughter.

Mrs. Bierce came out on the veranda, wiping her hands in a frilly apron. She was a dark-haired, smiling woman considerably younger than Bierce, with a classic straight nose, a long face and intense bars of eyebrows. She and Bierce greeted each other coolly. I liked Mollie Bierce immediately, maybe because of Bierce's cynicism about mar-riage and women. The older boy, Day, followed Bierce to the veranda with a perfect mimicry of his father's stiff-backed military gait.

Mollie Bierce's mother, Mrs. Day, was inches shorter than her daughter, with graying hair and Mollie's straight nose turned into an aggressive beak, a ram of a chin, and an upper lip wrinkled like pie crimping. She had a way of moving toward a quarry splay-footed, as though in preparation for combat, halting too close for comfort and extending chin and nose like a challenge.

If Bierce and his wife tolerated each other, Bierce and his mother-in-law did not. Mrs. Day demanded to know why Bierce had not brought Mollie down to the City for Senator Sharon's reception. She complained that Mollie had no piano on which to practice.

This conversation took place on the veranda, Mollie Bierce rolling her eyes apologetically at me. The three of them moved inside the house, where the clamor of Mrs. Day's accusations continued. I set my bag down, took off my jacket and invited the boys to a game of catch.

We spread out into a broad triangle on the pine needles and flung the ball into each other's mitts. Leigh was not as strong as his older brother, who powered the ball with a nice acceleration of his wrist. Helen watched from the veranda, seated in the swing which she pushed with her feet against the rail, her red hair a bright stain on green canvas.

At the supper table, with Bierce at the head, Mollie at the foot, her mother beside her and the children and me distributed, Mrs. Day said, "Will you say grace, Mr. Bierce?"

"A toast!" Bierce said, rising. He held out his iced-tea glass down-table toward his wife:

"They stood before the altar and supplied / the very fires in which their fat was fried!"

He was quoting himself.

His wife flushed, as though he had paid her a compliment.

"I suppose that is all the attention the Good Lord will receive at this table," Mrs. Day said. "But you will come to church with us to-morrow, will you not, Mr. Bierce?"

"No, madam, I will not."

"We will attend," Mrs. Day said, trap-mouthed. "Your wife, and Day, Leigh and Helen. But you will not accompany your family?"

"I am the sworn enemy of organized piffle, madam," Bierce said. "Including Sunday-scholiasts and Saturday pietaries." He served up meat patties and gravy, potatoes and peas, and distributed the plates.

"And you, Mr. Redmond, are you also an enemy of religion?"

"I am Roman Catholic," I said. My response was as unsatisfactory as Bierce's. Mrs. Day appeared to be girding for sectarian battle.

"Momma," Mollie Bierce said.

"Is Roman Catholic like Mikey Hennesey?" Day wanted to know.

"Yes, dear."

"It is as honest a collection-extraction system as any protestant Bible-thumping," Bierce said.

"Dr. Grove is a fine man!" Mollie Bierce said gently.

"I'm sure he is, my dear," Bierce said. "And well deserving of your tiresome panegyrics."

"Dr. Grove has a red nose!" Helen chirped.

"Helen!"

Bierce gazed at his wife with eyes in which I could discern no affection.

"And you are a journalist also, Mr. Redmond?" Mollie Bierce said. Her darkly pretty face regarded me with her gentle smile. I thought of the constant diplomacy that must be called for, with her mother and her husband. There was a brother, I knew; the third of what Bierce termed the "Holy Trinity." I thought of my father and my brother Michael and the bitterness of interfamilial contentions, more intense and thus more savage than those with no blood connection; like the ferocity of Federals and Confederates murdering each other on the Southern killing fields.

I said I was an apprentice journalist, learning what I could from *The Hornet*'s Editor-in-chief and Tattler. I was always uneasy praising Bierce, for I knew he was absolutely aware of flattery.

Mollie asked what I was writing now.

I thought it best not to mention the Morton Street murders. "I have been inquiring into the Mussel Slough Tragedy," I said. "There is some historical evidence that needs to be reconsidered."

"Those farmers were no better than Communists," Mrs. Day proclaimed, ramming her jaw out at me. "When this nation no longer respects property rights we are on the road to perdition."

Bierce regarded her calmly and held his peace, comfortable with his conviction of the Railroad's pervasive villainy. Now we knew that an enforcer from Virginia City, a connection of Nat McNair's named Klosters, had been one of the sheriff's deputies acting for the SP at

Mussel Slough, and that the trials of the settlers in Circuit Court had been decided by Judge Aaron Jennings in every instance in favor of the Railroad.

We managed to finish supper without more hostilities. I had time alone with Mollie Bierce when she was showing me to the spare bed-room, arms filled with pillows and a quilt.

"I wish Mr. Bierce could relax more when he is here," she said. "He is so busy in the City. When he comes home he brings his busy-ness with him, and by the time he can relax it is time to go back to that teeming life again. It can't be good for him, Mr. Redmond."

She bent to place the pillows and the folded quilt on the bed, and plump the pillows, bending to her work and pushing strands of dark hair back from her face.

"He is busy in many good causes, Mrs. Bierce," I said.

"I know that, Mr. Redmond."

After breakfast Day and Leigh badgered me to play ball again. This time I set up double-play practice. I lofted the ball or bowled ground-ers, to Leigh, who pegged to Day at second base, who hurled the ball to me at first, whereupon I tossed to Leigh again. The boys yelled with excitement as we pitched the ball around with increasing veloc-ity.

Bierce watched from the veranda. I thought he wished he were a father who could play ball with his growing sons, but he was not. He was a closed-in man with an affliction of hating oppression, fraud and sham, and a talent for expressing his indignation in print. He would never be a good father, nor even a decent husband, whether or not he was able to relax from the demands of the teeming City.

Little Helen came outside and leaned against his leg, and he went back into the house with her. When Mollie Bierce called to the boys to dress for church, there was a good deal of complaint.

Mollie Bierce, Mrs. Day and the children trooped off to their Sun-day duties, and Bierce and I went for a walk on the road that looped up the hillside above the town. I was in my shirtsleeves from playing ball with the boys, and Bierce left his jacket off as well, his concession to country relaxation. He carried a stick and batted at the weeds along the margins of the road, which narrowed and steepened as we mounted. It was a bright day with puffs of cloud drifting in from the coast.

"This is Larkmead," Bierce said, flourishing the stick ahead. "Lillie Coit's estate."

Every San Francisco fireman knew of Lillie Hitchcock Coit, although her years as a fire-belle were before I had come to San Francisco. She loved firemen, had proved it as Lillie Hitchcock and continued to prove it after she had married Howard Coit. The grateful fellows of Knickerbocker #5 had awarded her one of their pins.

I couldn't fault her for wanting to wear a fireman's helmet. I remembered once as a child so loving a pair of copper-toed boots my father bought me at Gus Levenson's Store in Sacramento that I took them to bed with me. Maybe it was something of the way that Lillie Coit loved the firemen of San Francisco's Engine Companies.

It occurred to me that Bierce had been looking for her when he led me up this trail into Larkmead, and there she was, in a clearing with a horse trough, standing beside a splendid bay with his muzzle in the trough. She wore a yellow-brown dress of many layers and flounces, and a broad hat heaped with feathers. She was a rather stout little woman of about Bierce's age, with a round, friendly brown face which lighted up as she swung toward us, waving her riding crop.

"Halloo Brosey!" she called to Bierce.

They embraced. I was introduced. The coldness that had hardened Bierce's features within the bosom of his family had melted in Lillie Coit's company. The two of them sat on a downed log, gossiping and laughing, while I paced the clearing gazing out over the treetops into blue distance. I was not included in their conversation, and I felt ill at ease as I patted the horse and paced some more and seated myself and looked down at my shoes.

Bierce waved me over to them.

"Listen to this," he said to me. "About Beau McNair," he said to Lillie Coit.

"He isn't Nat's son," she said. She had a lisping way of talking, with an earnest set to her round face. "I was a sweet young thing myself at the time and didn't pay much attention. I'm sure Carrie was carrying child when she married Nat. He adopted Beau."

"If he was not the father, who was?" I asked. Jimmy Fairleigh had told me this, and I did not see what it could have to do with the Morton Street slashings.

She shrugged. "Old mysteries!"

"So she bore Beau in the City?" Bierce said.

"Mammy Pleasant would know."

"Mammy Pleasant!"

"I think that woman had to do with just about every birth on Rincon Hill or South Park at that time," Lillie Coit said. "I'd bet a dollar she midwifed Carrie."

Mammy Pleasant was a quadroon woman, very light complected, who had worked for many of the "instant aristocrats" of the City, recruiting colored servants for them, who, it was rumored, then became her informants in a blackmail scheme. She had been a procuress and the proprietor of notorious houses of assignation. She was also rumored to deal with unwanted children, and to supply children to couples who were barren. Mammy Pleasant was often to be seen about the City, a tall, upright figure in black with gold hoop earrings and a big bonnet or a black straw hat tied on her head with a scarf. She was reputed to be rich.

I had the sense of the Morton Street murders swelling and expanding to involve the whole City of San Francisco.

Bierce and Lillie Coit discussed when Bierce would next visit St. Helena, and I moved out of hearing range again. Then Bierce was assisting Lillie onto her horse. She bade him farewell and walked the bay over toward me, bending down.

"Brosey says you were a firefighter."

"Up until last year," I said.

"What company?"

I told her.

"A fine outfit! I'd be pleased if you'd come visit me at Larkmead." It was an invitation. She raised her eyebrows interrogatively.

"Well, I—" I was shocked to the core. I focused on the Knicker-bocker #5 pin on her bosom.

Lillie Coit laughed, waved her riding crop at Bierce, and the bay trotted out of the glade.

Bierce and I walked back down the trail together.

"Did she invite you to Larkmead?" he asked.

I nodded.

"She takes what she likes from life," he said. "I admire that woman."

"I saw that you do."

"When falling into a woman's arms be sure not to fall into her hands," he said.

I was still shocked at the frankness of Lillie Coit's invitation.

"She is a true aristocrat from an old Southern family, not one of our instant dukes or duchesses," he went on. "Nor is she one of the female slaves who enslave their masters. She is one of the few women I know who transcends her gender."

Descending the trail to the house it was as though, stride by stride, Bierce's face returned to its usual coldness, the failings and demands of the female gender the subject. He indicated the steeple of the church, visible through the treetops, with his stick.

"The femininnies will bore themselves to insensibility every Sunday morning on the chance of getting into the 'Upper House' for eternity," he said.

"My mother likes the sociability," I said. "She sees her friends and has a chat with the priest."

"The church is the warden of the institution of marriage, in which the monogamous female seeks to imprison the polygamous male," Bierce went on, pompously.

I was afraid he was going to confide in me the unhappiness of his own marriage, but he was no more able to reveal his personal problems than he was to play catch with his sons.

"Throughout her marriage the bride continues to demand of her captive husband the same ardor he was able to summon up during the days of their courtship," he said, slashing his stick at the weeds along the path. "She will insist on the childish inanities that were the language of their betrothal. But her lover died on the wedding night."

Bierce was lecturing on the defects of marriage and the female nature at a moment when I considered Amelia Brittain the brightest star of her sex, and her gender itself the glory of creation.

The churchgoers were already at home, and dinner was presently served. Today the argument was over the *Elite Directory of San Francisco*, a social listing in which the names of Mr. and Mrs. Bierce appeared. Bierce was contemptuous of such a list, but Mrs. Day insisted that he and Mollie Bierce take advantage of their social prominence.

Bierce had more to say on the subject of gender and institutions on the train and ferry back to San Francisco.

And he said, "I know I am a bitter man, Tom. And I know I shock you. What is there to blame? The fact that I saw too much of the nature of man in a war that had no meaning, only a resolution, and men I helped to slaughter were as good and as bad as men who were slaughtered at my side? It has affected my nature, I know. I will never be a happy man. I can only hope to be an effective one."

"You know you are that," I said.

"That remains to be seen," Bierce said.

12

ROPE, *n.*
An obsolescent appliance for reminding assas-
sins that they too are mortal.
—THE DEVIL'S DICTIONARY

onday I was turned away from 913 Taylor Street again, after standing on the porch outside the closed door feeling snubbed and foolish. This time I wrote Amelia a note that I had been told twice now that she was not at home, giving the day and hour. And I said I must know about her "shadow."

By Tuesday it had been over a week without another playing card murder, whose continuation was so grimly suggested by the progression of the suit of spades. It was as though the counterfeit murder of Mrs. Hamon, like a backfire, had halted the main conflagration.

Bierce and I met with Sgt. Nix in a saloon up Kearny Street from police headquarters at Old City Hall, in a pleasant stench of beer, with the cold food layout on the bar, iron-legged chairs grating on the brick floor, and the ubiquitous sign in front advertising PRETTY WAITER GIRLS, although there were no pretty waiter girls in evidence at this time of day.

"Jennings was in Sacramento on Wednesday—that's the day the house was burned," Nix said, leaning on the table.

"But he was surely in town the night of the murder. He and his wife live on Jones Street. He belongs to the Pacific Club. A State Senator is pretty big game for the Captain to lock horns with.''

Bierce sat with his fingers knitted together looking at Nix down his nose. ''But Captain Pusey has something to go on.''

''Maybe,'' Nix said. ''He don't just show his cards around the table.''

''Specific information,'' Bierce said. ''All I have so far are implications and intimations, and a personal conviction.''

This didn't take us any further toward the identity of the Slasher. Bierce's concentration on Jennings and the Railroad galled me.

Nix said, ''There was a lawyer in Tulare who collected evidence for the Mussel Slough farmers. Jennings threw it all out of court, and something shut this lawyer up. Ran him out of the district.''

''I think the man Tom saw in Santa Cruz was Klosters,'' Bierce said.

''Might be the captain has a photograph of this Klosters,'' Nix said.

''I've wired the editor of the *Virginia Sentinel* offering him two hundred dollars for the tintype of the Spades he told Tom about,'' Bierce said. ''Tom is writing a piece recalling Mussel Slough,'' he added. ''There will be a response.''

''From the Railroad, you mean?'' Sgt. Nix said. ''If they even bother.''

''Yes,'' Bierce said sourly. ''So far they are as intact as the Prelapsarian apple.''

Bierce had written in Tattle, responding to a letter from a reader:

> To P.D.—In assuming that we have abandoned the ''fight against the railroad people'' you are in error. In the natural course of comment—verbal and graphic—upon public matters, we have often found occasion to censure the piratical methods of the Railrogues, and on similar occasions shall do so again, as you will presently observe.
>
> For instance, our Mr. Huntington has remarked that if the Railroad's profits continue to decline, he will have to resort to reducing wages. He is the largest employer in the state, and

if Mr. Huntington is not permitted to earn two millions a year on an original investment of a suspender button and a postage stamp, no mechanic shall earn more than a dollar a day if he can help it.

Mr. Huntington has announced himself opposed to politics. In the purity of his motives, as compared to Mr. £eland $tanford's, he will turn the offices at Fourth and Townsend into a Sunday School and appoint the faithful Aaron Jennings chaplain of both branches of the State Legislature. If we rightly understand him, Mr. Huntington, whose claim it is that "every man has his price," promises to renounce the sinful practice of paying money to the legislators, and substitute the saintly habit of taking up a collection, in which operation we recommend that he consult the most successful operator in that field, the Reverend Stottlemyer of the Washington Street Church.

We will have more to say of the senator from Southern Pacific presently. There is the matter of an arson in Santa Cruz that destroyed the papers of former Circuit Court Judge Hiram Hamon, which were concerned with corruption in the judiciary in general and the purchase of then Judge Jennings in particular, and with the murder in Morton Street of Judge Hamon's widow, which, as we have written, was ineptly arranged to seem to be the third of the "playing card" murders.

The column included some of his usual targets, dogs as "leakers, reekers, smilers and defilers," the Spring Valley Water Company as "the hydrants of Infamy / the springs of felony," and reflections on the politics of the Hawaiian Islands: "This bald-faced land-grab by mizzle-spouting missionaries and sugar landlords."

I was proud that Bierce had run my piece on Mussel Slough on the page opposite Tattle:

During the '70s the Railroad advertised in the East and Midwest for farmers to buy and settle Railroad-grant lands in the San Joaquin Valley. Thousands of farmers came on the Railroad's promise to sell them their land at $2.50 to $5.00 per acre.

The Railroad laid out the towns of Goshen, Tulare, Tipton and Hanford in the Tulare Basin, which came to be known as Starvation Valley from the farmers' struggle to make a living there.

In 1877, when the lands were prospering, the Railroad broke its promise. Instead of being reconveyed to the settlers at the low figures, lands that had already been settled would be sold to the highest bidders at prices ranging from $25 to $40 per acre.

The farmers sued but lost in several cases in San Francisco Circuit Court, presided over by Judge (now Senator) Aaron Jennings.

The Railroad began foreclosures on farmers who would not pay the higher price, and sent to Hanford two armed men, who had been offered free farms if they could wrest them from the settlers. These men, named Hartt and Crow, in their capacity as gunmen arrived in a buggy laden with firearms. They were met by a dozen armed farmers led by James Harris, who sought to disarm the strangers. Crow discharged his shotgun into Harris's face, and shot six other farmers. Hartt was killed in the first exchange, and Crow escaped briefly, to be shot down as he was taking aim at another farmer.

The Railroad telegraph was the only means for the news of the gun battle to be disseminated, and the Railroad shut down the line after an announcement of an "armed insurrection." The public thus knew nothing of the farmers' side of the dispute. The embattled farmers were taken into custody by Sheriff's deputies commanded by a Railroad employee named Elza Klosters, and were brought to trial in Circuit Court in San Francisco under Judge Jennings. Evidence favorable to their cause was thrown out of court. They were found guilty of resisting officers of the law in performance of their duties and sentenced to prison terms.

Information supporting the cause of the settlers has over the years become available to the public, and facts of the Mussel Slough Tragedy and the trial of the farmers may have furnished the motive for the murder last week of Judge Hamon's widow, and the arson that burned her Santa Cruz bungalow, including her husband's papers.

This time Bierce made only one comment, warning me on the selection of words, in particular Hartt and Crow's "capacity" as gunmen. "Capacity is receptive," he said. "Ability is potential. A sponge has a capacity for water; a hand, the ability to squeeze it out."

My next assignment was to gather material for a piece on Senator Jennings.

Seated in the parlor of Mrs. Johnson's house, Annie Dunker clasped her hands with the tips of her fingers beneath her chin and rocked.

"He's a very nice young man, Tommy," she said. "He takes her to the opera and sends her things. He sends her flowers! The other girls are jealous because Rachel is treated so special."

"I wondered if he beat her or hurt her, or anything like that—when he's *with* her."

"There's nothing like that my cousin knows about, Tommy."

I had the blunt feeling that this whole line of investigation had been ill-conceived.

"It just seems funny he don't—set her up in her own place!" Annie said. "The way rich men will do sometimes. Why, they will even marry some of the girls. Isn't he awful rich? It just seems like he *wants* her in the house there. That's the only thing seems funny about it. He is very nice-spoken, my cousin says."

"Nothing wrong with him—" I gestured.

"Oh, *him!* No!"

"Did anybody know of someone that had that trouble I asked you about?"

"I mentioned it to a couple of girls, but they hadn't heard anything like that."

And that was all I was to learn about Beau McNair or the mister without a dingle from Annie Dunker.

I had discovered that she was proud of being a parlorhouse girl. She had said of whoring that it was better than going blind in a sweatshop sewing, or twenty hours a day as a kitchen drudge or housemaid, with the old man and his sons laying for you in the hallways.

Except for Slashers laying for you.

Mammy Pleasant lived in the Octavia Street mansion belonging to the financier Thomas Bell, whom she had furnished with a wife from her stable of beautiful young females. Mammy Pleasant referred to herself as the "housekeeper" but her status did not seem to correspond to that title. It was rumored that she had collected so much information about Bell's youthful malefactions in Scotland, and later ones in San Francisco, that he could never rid himself of her.

A colored butler opened the door for Bierce and me and took Bierce's card back inside. He returned to usher us into a parlor so curtained and lightless that we had to feel for chairs in which to seat ourselves. Mammy Pleasant was manifested as a faceless darkness between a white lace cap and a neckpiece that glowed phosphorescently in the murk.

As my eyes became accustomed to the dark I could make out that she was seated in a straight chair with her hands folded in her lap, waiting for Bierce or me to speak.

"Madam, we are interested in some ancient history that may affect current events, and I understand that you can assist us," Bierce said with that degree of coolness that could make a person feel that he was exposed in his iniquities.

"How may I assist you?" Mammy Pleasant said. She had a rather rasping voice that made me want to clear my throat.

"When Caroline LaPlante married Nathaniel McNair, was she already pregnant with the child she named Beaumont McNair?"

"How would I know that?" Mammy Pleasant said.

"I have reason to believe you were the midwife at the birth."

"If I was professionally employed by Mrs. McNair I could not reveal such information without her consent." She had a very precise and unaccented way of speaking, with a slight puff of a pause before each word, as though she considered it carefully beforehand.

"Such information might assist the case of the young man, her son, who finds himself in some difficulties."

"Mr. Bierce, I have been employed by many different gentry in my years in San Francisco, and I owe them respect for their confidences."

This woman was by no means intimidated by Bierce. She said, "Even if I possessed the information you require, I could not supply it without the permission of Lady Caroline Stearns."

Bierce regarded her intently. "Mrs. Pleasant, you know who I am. This young man, Mr. Redmond, is a journalist with *The Hornet*. He writes occasional pieces on recent history, which are published opposite my column. Perhaps you have seen his most recent one. It is the tale of the Mussel Slough Tragedy and of certain corrupt actions and decisions on behalf of the Railroad. Mr. Redmond has asked to come along today because he also is interested in your career among the gentry in your several different capacities, and some mysteries that attend those functions.

"What particularly interests us is the charge of baby-farming that has been laid at your door. The acquisition of wanted children and the disposal of unwanted ones."

Mammy Pleasant did not move a muscle. Her gold hoop earrings caught little dipping segments of light in that dim musty room.

Bierce continued, "As to Mrs. McNair's condition when she married Mr. McNair—or shall we say her marital situation when she gave birth to Beaumont McNair—those dates are available in the Hall of Records."

After a pause, Mammy Pleasant said, "Mrs. McNair was in a family way when she married Mr. McNair."

"How far along was she?"

"About five months."

"Who was the father?" Bierce asked.

Her earrings flipped as Mammy Pleasant shook her head.

"I think you would have made it your business to know," Bierce said, leaning toward her.

"I cannot help you further," she said, rising. She swept out of the room. We heard her say to the butler, "Please show the gentlemen to the door."

I admired her dismissal of us.

As I climbed into the buggy after Bierce, I said, "You got something out of her. I didn't think you would."

"She doesn't know what information they have recorded at the Hall of Records. I do."

"What did you find out?"

"Not much," he said chuckling. "Beau was born in March 1863. Mr. and Mrs. McNair were married in December of 1862."

I couldn't think what application that information could have. "Who was the father?" I asked.

"Ah," Bierce said. "The pleasure of that discovery is still before us."

13

RECONCILIATION, *n.*
A suspension of hostilities. An armed truce for the purpose of digging up the dead.
—THE DEVIL'S DICTIONARY

t supper at the boardinghouse we were eight or nine—depending on whether or not the drummer was out of town—including The Hooter, a bank clerk, for his hoot of a laugh; and Fuzzy Bear, a horsecar conductor, both of them named by the youngest Barnacle, Johnny. After Mrs. B.'s repast of meatloaf and gravy, cabbage and mashed potatoes, with bread pudding for dessert, the Hooter, Fuzzy Bear and young Johnny Barnacle departed, leaving me with my coffee, and Jonas, Mrs. B., Belinda and her biggest brother, Colbert, a smelly twelve-year-old with a haystack of fair hair and a way of pointing his face away while his eyes regarded you, which made him resemble an apprentice cardsharp. I understood that I was part of a Barnacle family crisis.

Belinda sat with her hands in her lap and her tragic face raised like Joan of Arc contemplating the stake.

"Ain't you ashamed to have Mr. Redmond know you have done this mean thing?" Mrs. B. said.

Belinda looked unashamed. Her face was at its prettiest when she was under duress.

"What she done was," Jonas Barnacle said to me, over his coffee mug, "she stole the two bits from the jar where it was kept for the paperboy. Didn't you, Belinda?"

Belinda rolled her eyes at me. I gathered that my presence was part of the punishment.

"Then she told me Colbert had took it. What she had did, she had stuck it under the scarf on Colbert's dresser so I'd find it there. To get him whomped. Isn't that right, Missy?"

Belinda set her lips more tightly together, staring straight ahead.

"That is about as mean a trick as I can think of," Mrs. B. said. She had her hair done up in a severe bun on top of her head. She squinched her eyes at her daughter. "A mean little snip trying to get her brother in a fix."

"I just hope Father Kennedy don't hear of it," Jonas Barnacle said, leaning his elbows on the table and pushing his face toward Belinda.

"Or Sister Claire," Mrs. B. said. "That thinks little Miss Pet here might have a vocation."

The flesh around Belinda's eyes turned pink. She rose, with dignity, made her way past the empty chairs and out of the room.

"Get out of here," Jonas Barnacle said to Colbert, who left with a smug glance at me.

The parents assumed expressions of severe sadness.

"Just don't know what to do with that girl," Jonas said.

"She's going to be a fine young lady one of these days," I said.

Mrs. B. sniffed. She had a tired, angular face in which the features were set in uneasy conjunction.

"Can't even strop her like she deserves," Jonas said. "Take a strop to her and she won't cry, she won't even flinch, look you straight in the eye and make you feel like a Cossack."

"Says she's too old to be stropped," the mother said with another sniff. "Why would she do a thing like that? Sneaky!"

"Let me talk to her," I said.

"You talk to her, Tom," her father said, looking relieved.

I found Belinda seated outside on the rickety stairs to my top-floor room, with her skirt wrapped around her legs, her feet set primly side by side and her arms folded over her chest. She had been crying.

I sat down beside her and put my arm around her thin shoulders.

"They won't believe me!" she said forcefully. "They just believe *him*. I said he stole it, and he said *I* stole it and put it on his dresser. So they believe *him*."

"You shouldn't have said it."

"Oh, I know *I shouldn't have said it*," she mimicked. "But that's not the point, Tom! It's that they'd believe him and not me! Do you know *why?* Because I'm a girl and he's a boy. Boys are worth something and girls aren't worth anything. Girls are sneaky, and boys are—*stalwart!* Well, he's not stalwart, he's a mean little pig and I *hate* him."

"You don't want to hate your brother," I said.

"Yes, I do; I hate him! But I hate her worse."

"Your mother!"

"Because she hates girls. She must've been a girl once herself! She doesn't think girls are worth raising. She thinks girls are sneaky and whining. Well, that's just what *he* is!"

"She just sounds like that when she's angry with you."

"You don't *know!* Everything's for *him*. Not so much Johnny. Colbert always comes first. He gets the biggest slice of pie, and if there's only money for one of us to throw the ring-thing at the fairgrounds, Colbert gets to do it. I can throw better than he can! But I'm second, or *third,* because I'm a girl. I'm no good because I'm a *girl*. I hate her!"

"Listen, Belinda," I said. "You're a girl and that's good, and you're a very pretty girl and that's even better. One of these days—before you know it!—all the boys're going to be looking at you, and they'll be trying to talk to you, and they'll bring you presents at school and share their cookies with you. And then when you are a young woman, the men will ask to be on your dance card and want to take you for rides in their fancy turnouts. And then you will be number one, I can tell you."

"*No!*" she moaned.

"You just watch. Then, you'll see, you can have anything you want, any*body* you want! Because you are a girl, and good and beautiful. But, see, Colbert doesn't get anything like that. He has to go out in the world and make a living and try to make something of himself, and maybe he can't and then he's a failure and he'll start drinking and people will call him worthless. Because he's a boy, because he's a man, and if you're a man nobody forgives you *anything*. So then you'll have to feel sorry for Colbert."

"He's a rotten little *turd!*" Belinda sobbed.

"I know that," I said. "But you don't want to be one, too."

She leaned against me and sobbed while I patted her shoulder.

A heavy-set customer in a big hat had stopped at the Barnacles' gate to regard us with a steady gaze. It was the man who called himself Brown, with his sweat-shiny pocked face, and no doubt his revolver tucked into his belt. He drew something from his vest pocket and flipped it over the gate onto the walk twenty feet away from Belinda and me, a playing card. I had no doubt what suit it was. I felt paralyzed with fury.

Brown marched on out of sight past the next house as Belinda rose and scampered down to pick up the card.

"It's the queen of spades, Tom!"

I snatched it from her, let myself out the gate and trotted after Brown. He had disappeared. I hadn't really tried to catch up with him.

Belinda met me at the gate. She looked frightened. "What does it mean?"

I said it was just a joke.

When I brought the queen of spades to Bierce I was angered all over again because I knew that I had been counted on to deliver it to him.

"I suppose it means we should stop fretting the Railroad about Mussel Slough," I said.

"It is a clumsy attempt at intimidation," Bierce said. "The queen of spades was employed because spades have been in the newspapers in connection with murders." He slipped the card into his desk drawer. "It must be an anticipation of your Jennings piece," he said.

"I've hardly started it!"

"It is known you are researching it. Miss Penryn may have communicated the information to Smithers, or Macgowan. Someone who has a Railroad friend. There are not many secrets around a newspaper office."

The neat little man said his name was Smith. He shook hands with Bierce, and introduced himself to me. "Clete Redmond's son?" he said.

I admitted it.

He had a diamond pin in his cravat, a gold chain across his vest. Child-sized shoes gleamed beneath the cuffs of his trousers. He had silver hair and a neat triangular silver goatee. His eyes twinkled.

"We read your recent piece in *The Hornet*," he said to Bierce, when he had seated himself, crossed his legs and settled his hat in his lap. "Yours also, Mr. Redmond," he said to me.

"May I ask who 'we' is?" Bierce said amiably.

"Certain gentlemen at Fourth and Townsend, who have been regularly insulted by you, sir!" Smith chuckled.

"Why, I thought I had complimented them!" Bierce said.

"I have a message for you," Smith said.

"I am all ears."

"It is very brief," Smith said. "It is that those who investigate may also be investigated."

He rose, clapped his hat on his head, said, "Good day, sir. Good day," he said to me and was gone, his heels clicking in the corridor.

The headline in the next morning's *Chronicle* that lay on the Barnacles' breakfast table was: SPADE SLAYING #4, and UPPER TENDERLOIN SLASHING, and the smaller head: MAYOR OFFERS REWARD. I snatched it up to skim the article:

Dr. Manship, after a hasty examination of the body, said he thought the terrible deed could have been accomplished in a few moments. The victim had been attacked near the backhouse behind the establishment on Stockton Street presided over by Mrs. Mamie Overton. The victim's throat had been cut with one stroke of a sharp weapon, and, in the familiar pattern, her torso shockingly slashed. The young woman's name has not been revealed.

A reward of one thousand dollars for information that will lead to the apprehension of the knife-wielding maniac has been authorized by Mayor Washington Bartlett.

I took the horsecar to Dunbar Alley. Captain Pusey was there, with two other policemen. The Morgue stank of old blood, sweat and cigar smoke. The latest victim lay naked, paper white and pathetically thin on her slab, red-haired, a calm face unlike the contorted faces of the three who had been strangled. This one had not been strangled, but her throat was slashed to the bone. There was a gaping wound in her belly, but she had not been opened up like the others.

"Look at her fingernails," Captain Pusey said, pointing his cigar at her hand. There were deposits of flesh under her fingernails. This woman had fought her assailant.

Her name was Rachel LeVigne.

Rachel LeVigne was Beau McNair's redheaded Jewess, and Amelia Brittain was his fiancée, or had been anyway. And had a "shadow."

When I told Captain Pusey that Miss Brittain was in danger he ordered a constable to 913 Taylor Street immediately.

WORMS'-MEAT, *n.*
The finished product of which we are the raw
material. The contents of the Taj Mahal, the
Tombeau Napoleon and the Grantarium.
—THE DEVIL'S DICTIONARY

The water closets at Mrs. Overton's parlorhouse on Stockton Street had been unusable because of a sewer stoppage, and the girls and their clients were forced to use the outhouse behind the building. The area was lighted by a kerosene lamp on a bracket. A girl inside the outhouse had heard Rachel LeVigne's screams but had been afraid to come out. Two of the clients had rushed outside to find the body and had seen a man in a cloaklike garment and a slouch hat disappear through the gate leading to the adjoining property.

Earlier, Mr. Beaumont McNair had taken Miss LeVigne to supper at the Fly Trap, and to a piano recital by the Hungarian pianist Pavel Magyar but had returned her to Mrs. Overton's by ten-thirty. He was observed bidding her good night some time before she was assaulted in front of the outhouse.

Sgt. Nix had called upon Beau McNair at the McNair mansion. He told Bierce that Beau's face was unmarked by Rachel LeVigne's fingernails, and that Rudolph Buckle vouched for his return by ten-thirty the previous evening.

Now there was terror among the prostitutes of the Upper Tenderloin as well as Morton Street, and scare headlines in the newspapers. I made my third call at 913 Taylor Street.

The porch that stretched across the front of the house rose high off the ground at the west end because of the steepness of Taylor Street. A file of spindly balusters supported the railing. The facade of the house was decorated with plaster rosettes and jigsaw fretwork in a geometric tangle of light and shadow from the morning sun over Nob Hill. A constable sat in a wicker chair at a table at the end of the porch, raising a hand in greeting to me.

The butler again took my card and retired within, and this time opened the door for me to enter.

Amelia and her mother were seated in the parlor, Amelia bright-faced with her halo of curls, rising to greet me. Her mother, formidably bosomed, with a sour expression of disapproval and anxiety, remained seated as I was led to her.

"How do you do, Mr. Redmond. Do we have you to thank for this police gentleman on our porch?"

I said they did.

"Is it because my daughter has been followed?"

"That is part of it."

Mrs. Brittain left the room to call for tea, and I was alone with Amelia.

"The poor creature!" she said.

"She was the one Mr. McNair was attached to."

"Yes!"

"He was attached to you also, you see."

Her mouth opened, but she did not speak. Her eyebrows climbed her forehead.

"Was the murdered woman the reason you broke off the engagement?"

She wet her lips. "My father insisted that the engagement be ended." She was gripping her arms against her waist as though she was cold, elbows jutting.

I did not know how to pursue that. I had been assured that Beau McNair was eminently eligible. Lady Caroline's millions!

"Miss Brittain, what did you mean in your note, your shadow? Your mother said you had been followed."

"A man has followed me on several occasions."

"What does he look like?"

"I was not able to see his features. He wore a hat that concealed his face."

"A big man, older?"

"I think he is young. I would not call him big."

"I don't want to alarm you," I said. "But you must be very careful not to be alone! Maybe it is best that you are alarmed," I added.

"Be assured that I am!"

"You are aware that Mr. McNair has not been arrested?"

She nodded, her eyes fixed on my face.

Mrs. Brittain marched back in, preceding a maid with a tea tray.

"Cream and sugar, Mr. Redmond?"

Mr. Brittain joined us for tea, a lanky, limping fellow of about sixty, tailored in black broadcloth, arranging his coattails with a flair as he seated himself. Amelia favored her greyhound father more than her bulldog mother. We sipped tea and discussed the policeman on the porch. Amelia and Mrs. Brittain were nervous, but Mr. Brittain seemed not much concerned. He invited me to his study to view his collection of gold nuggets.

His limp, like the limps I had observed in Virginia City, reminded me that Mr. Brittain had been a mining engineer on the Washoe, and of the connection of Brittain to English.

The nuggets were in a glass case, gleaming twisted shapes, a couple of them quite large. I told him I had been in Virginia City last week, and he directed me to a leather chair and offered me a cigar from a humidor.

"Josey Devers!" he said, puffing smoke. "How was the rascal?"

I said Devers looked as though a lot of whiskey had been absorbed.

"It is a dying camp, certainly. It was very lively once!"

"Devers spouted figures of silver production and stock manipulations."

Mr. Brittain snorted. "I don't think there was a miner in the place who wasn't speculating. I can tell you who the winners were, Will O'Brien, Jamey Flood, John Mackay, Fair, Sharon, Nat McNair."

I asked if he recalled a group of investors called the Society of Spades.

He had a ritual of movements with his cigar, flourishing it, moistening it, drawing it beneath his nose, holding it up like a signal. This completed, he shook his head.

"They bought the Jack of Spades Mine."

"Oh, the Consolidated-Ohio, yes."

"I was told that Lady Caroline Stearns had disposed of her interest in the Consolidated-Ohio."

"I know that is true."

I hurried on: "It seemed there was some finagling over the discovery of a new orebody, so that she received a better price than may have been warranted. Devers called it an 'English shuffle.'"

He went through his tobacco ritual again, sniffing his cigar before replacing it between his teeth. He regarded me brightly. "Carrie has always landed on her feet," he said.

I couldn't press him about the English shuffle because I was in love with his daughter.

"Highgrade Carrie seems to have been highly regarded in Virginia City," I said.

Mr. Brittain frowned with reminiscence. "She was an angel in her time."

"Devers referred to her as the Miners' Angel."

"She was that, she was indeed that." Mr. Brittain nodded, his eyes hooded. "I cannot explain, I don't think, just what a place like Virginia City is like when a camp is at full flood. The frustration, the terrible, dangerous labor in the mines. The fires, the heat, the cave-ins. The hopes; the dashed hopes! The lack of any kind of loyalty or disinterested affection. Dog-eat-dog. With no respite! Carrie was able to furnish respite. Certainly she was a madam, a woman of ill-repute. Well, you had better not call her a woman of ill-repute to anyone who was in Virginia City in her time there! She was the *only* touch of grace, of human feeling, of beauty—a reminder that there were, elsewhere, civilized ways of living, civilized occupations, people who intermingled with a civilized code of conduct. She was the reminder of all that. She was the sweet-smelling bouquet flourishing in a sewer! I tell you, when Carrie walked down the boardwalks of C Street, there was not a hat that did not come off a miner's head!

"I believe she came to Virginia City to make a living selling her body and discovered that she had a higher calling. The Miners' Fund for disabled miners; it was Carrie who started it, contributed to it, shamed others into contributing. The Miners' Angel! Not just the Miners' Fund. There were a hundred other ways she helped those poor men to remember they were human beings with human emotions, fears, loves, affections, decent aspirations."

I had opened a faucet when I had brought up the subject of Lady Caroline. I asked about the woman named Julia Bulette.

"A lesser Carrie LaPlante," he said. "A prostitute, but a decent woman." But he was still full of Highgrade Carrie.

"In the end she married Nat McNair and became a millionairess," he said. "There are some to begrudge it. I am not one."

He tapped his ash into a glass tray. "I cannot be so complimentary of her son, however. Not to say that he is in any way involved in these gruesome murders. He and Amelia were great friends when they were children, but I understand she has returned his engagement ring."

At her father's insistence, according to Amelia. Maybe Mr. Brittain was aware of Beau's frequenting of women of ill-repute and of the circumstances that kept reinvolving him with the murders of prostitutes.

"I have heard a rumor that he was not McNair's son," I said. "That he was adopted after McNair married Mrs. McNair."

He scowled more deeply, as though I had insulted the Miners' Angel.

"Two who might have begrudged her good fortune would be Spades who were cheated out of their shares in the Jack of Spades by the McNairs," I said.

"Ah, well," Mr. Brittain said. "I'm afraid that was the order of business on the Washoe."

"There was a gunman—Devers called him an enforcer—who worked for McNair. Elza Klosters."

"The threat of violence was of course a valid option in a mining camp, you know. Miners' Law!"

I mentioned the murder of the man Gorton, but Mr. Brittain did not seem interested. His memories of Highgrade Carrie had been kindled.

"Someone—I can't remember who. Sharon? Yes, Sharon. A considerable sum of money was offered to the Miners' Fund if Carrie would do a Lady Godiva. Ride a white horse naked down C Street, on a Sunday. By God, she did it! She was a vision. Her pretty hair, beautiful hair! Her beautiful flesh! By God, she did it just right, not forward but shy, but proud too—of what she was doing! And the men cheering and waving their caps. Not in any way that was disrespectful, and not turning away like the townspeople in the Lady Godiva story either. By God, they watched Carrie ride that white horse down the middle of C Street and I will swear to you that not a man there ever forgot what he saw that day. And not a woman any of them ever saw thereafter in the altogether who didn't suffer by the comparison!"

He made a breathless chuckling sound, as though the vision had overwhelmed him also.

"By God that was a woman!" he said. "There's a painting of it. A German artist-fellow painted it, for a saloon there. Franz Landesknicht, something like that. Carrie posed for it." He made the snuffling chuckle again.

I had seen that painting, carried out of a saloon called the Washoe Angel! I didn't think it was information I would divulge. I said, "I wonder where the painting is now."

He reflected. He shrugged. He said, "Ah. Well, I'm afraid Mrs.

Brittain would not let *me* hang it." He laughed long. "There's no doubt in my mind about that!"

When I made an appointment with Amelia for a Sunday drive, I saw that Mrs. Brittain did not approve of that any more than she would have approved of the portrait of Caroline LaPlante as Lady Godiva hanging in the parlor at 913 Taylor Street.

I spent the rest of the morning on Battery Street, where the warehouse had burned to a smoke-stinking mess. The Washoe Angel was heavily damaged, including the sign, whose supports had collapsed so that it had fallen into the general mess. The neighborhood consisted of small businesses and shops, mainly one-story buildings, and no one seemed to know who was the owner of the saloon, or where the famous painting might have been taken. Many of them knew the Lady Godiva painting well, however, and faces lit up with pleasure to speak of its charms. When I went to the Spring Valley Water Company I found that bills for 308 Battery Street were sent to a company called Mangan Bros. on 8th Street in Sacramento.

I would see if Sgt. Nix could carry on from there, through connections with the Sacramento police.

Bierce and I took a cab to Nob Hill, slow-moving, hoof-slipping up steep California Street.

"These questions are important," he said. "Why are these murders happening *at all?* And: why are they happening *now?*"

"Something is new," I said.

"For instance?"

"Beau McNair returning to San Francisco."

He grunted, nodding. We discussed the meaning of the four of spades found on Rachel LeVigne's body. Did the four mean that the Morton Street Slasher had decided to accept the murder of Mrs. Hamon as one of his own? Then was it his purpose to run up a score in spades culminating in the queen?

The towers and domes of the Hopkins mansion came in sight. On the right was the Crocker castle, a shaggy mass of jigsawed wood with its great tower. On its far corner was the "spite-fence" surrounding the piece of property the owner would not sell to Charles Crocker. The spite-fence was such an arrogant affront you could not look at it without wishing ill to Charles Crocker of the Big Four.

"Bad cess to him," I said.

"Do a piece on it," Bierce said. "You don't have to strike an attitude. The facts will speak for themselves."

Now the McNair mansion hulked up, mansarded roofs with towers thrust through like spears, the gray of the walls relieved by splashes of green of pollarded trees and, lower, the smears of hedges and flowers; the whole surrounded by a country mile of wrought iron fence with gleaming brass knobs at ten-foot intervals.

A portly butler with slick, black center-parted hair opened the door.

"We would like to see Mr. Buckle," Bierce said. The butler retired with his card and returned to bow us inside.

The hall rose three stories past balustraded balconies to a glass ceiling. A high wall could have mounted two of the paintings of High-grade Carrie as Lady Godiva but displayed instead a pastoral scene of deer drinking at a russet pool and, in an elaborate gold frame, an old gentleman, mutton-chopped, bald and scowling, with his mouth concealed behind an aggressive mustache, who must be the late Nathaniel McNair.

Buckle strode toward us with a clatter of heels on parquet. He was the tall, graying man I had encountered at the jail, now wearing a black morning coat and striped trousers.

"Greetings, Mr. Bierce, greetings," he said, shaking hands with Bierce and giving me a puzzled smile. "And this is?"

"My associate, Mr. Redmond."

"Please come in, gentlemen." Buckle ushered us past an octagon-shaped room in which there was a gleaming grand piano, with sheet music on its rack and a tall brass lamp beside it.

I noticed a hitch in Bierce's step as he glanced at the piano. We were shown into a sitting-room with high windows dangling shade cords and crocheted rings; Bierce sat in an overstuffed chair, I on a plum-colored plush divan. Buckle seated himself facing us, long legs crossed and highly polished pumps displayed.

"You are Lady Caroline Stearns's San Francisco manager, Mr. Buckle," Bierce said.

Buckle inclined his head. He had a cropped beard, and blue eyes under black brows. "Mr. Bosworth Curtis, Mr. Childress of the Bank of California and I handle her Western interests."

"And you and young Mr. McNair are the tenants of this remarkable edifice?" Bierce said.

Buckle laughed comfortably. "Oh, there is a staff of servants. Uncounted rooms, attics filled with unused furniture and of course a ghost! All kept in readiness for Lady Caroline, should she choose to return to the City."

"And she is en route, having so chosen?" Bierce said.

Buckle raised an eyebrow. "I wonder how you know that."

"It is common knowledge," Bierce said.

"She is just now in New York."

"Is young Mr. McNair here?"

"He has gone out for the evening. He has had a terrible shock, you understand."

"I understand that he escorted this unfortunate young woman to a piano recital," Bierce said. "Then he brought her back to her boardinghouse and came directly here. It has been established that the recital was over about twenty minutes after ten. He delivered her to Stockton Street at ten-thirty and appeared here moments after that."

"I will attest to that," Buckle said gravely.

"And also to his presence the nights of the three murders in Morton Street?"

"That is correct," Buckle said. "What is your interest in these matters, may I ask, Mr. Bierce?"

"The interest of a journalist, Mr. Buckle."

"That is a beautiful piano, Mr. Buckle," I said.

He nodded, smiling as though I had flattered him personally. "It is a Bechstein. Yes, it is a beautiful instrument."

"And you play?" Bierce said.

Nods and smiles.

"Tell me," Bierce said. "Did you not play the piano in a little band of music at the Miners' Rest in Virginia City?"

Buckle's face did not change expression, but his fingers, resting on the knee of his striped trousers, contracted. The hand relaxed as he saw my eyes fixed on it.

"Why do you ask, Mr. Bierce?" he said.

"We have been told that Beaumont McNair was accepted as his son by Nathaniel McNair, although he was not actually the father," Bierce said. "We are trying to establish who is the true father. We were told that one of Lady Caroline's favorites was the piano player at the Miners' Rest."

"I am not Beau McNair's father," Buckle said. He licked his lips with a swipe of gray tongue. "Nor can I see the pertinence of this."

"Who was the father?"

"Mr. Bierce, it was twenty-odd years ago. It was another time, and it is, in fact, none of anyone's affair. I'm sorry I cannot be helpful."

"In fact, it is everyone's affair," Bierce said. "Four women have been hideously murdered by someone connected with the Society of Spades in Virginia City, which was convened in order to purchase the Jack of Spades Mine. Of the five Spades, Caroline LaPlante and Nat McNair, with the assistance of one Albert Gorton, conspired to cheat the other two out of their shares. These others were E. O. Macomber and Adolphus Jackson. Gorton was later murdered, perhaps by a hired assassin named Klosters. I am sure that you are acquainted with all these men, Mr. Buckle. Macomber, or Jackson or someone else connected with the Society of Spades is responsible for these murders or is very closely involved in them. If you will not assist us, I will have to bring what persuasions I have at my disposal to bear on you, and on Beaumont McNair."

Buckle folded his hands together. "I can give you no information without consulting with Mr. Curtis and Lady Caroline."

"Then we will continue our voyage of discovery without your counsel. I must tell you that anyone who was associated with Lady Caroline in her Virginia City past will be investigated."

Buckle looked as though he would faint.

"Where can we find E. O. Macomber, Mr. Buckle?" Bierce said, leaning toward him.

"I have no idea what has become of him."

"What has become of Adolphus Jackson?"

Buckle moistened his lips again. "Adolphus Jackson is Senator Aaron Jennings," he said.

"The initials should have so informed me," Bierce said, leaning back.

There it was, the connection he had been searching for.

Bierce rose. "Good day to you, Mr. Buckle," he said. Buckle rose also, looking exhausted. He did not accompany us to the door but summoned the butler to see us out.

On the way back down California Street, Bierce said, "We should have inquired into the flower-loving ghost of the McNair mansion."

More ghosts than one, I thought.

15

INK, *n.*
A villainous compound of tanno-gallate of iron, gum-arabic and water, chiefly used to facilitate the infection of idiocy and promote intellectual crime.

—THE DEVIL'S DICTIONARY

I was not yet allowed to think of myself as a full-fledged journalist, for I was summoned to assist Dutch John and Frank Grief printing the week's *Hornet* in the basement with the dependable-in-its-undependability Chandler & Price press, whose revolving leather belt periodically snapped off its spindles in a flailing flight around the basement, and that acid stink of ink that required much soap and hot water at the Pine Street Baths to wash away.

After supper the Barnacle children often put on a show for the assembled boarders: Fuzzy Bear, The Hooter, Jimmy McGurn and Tom Redmond. We sat with our empty cake plates and coffee cups before us and watched the young Barnacles in performance. Tonight it was charades, in which Belinda was always the principal. She appeared swathed in white, wearing a white cap, dark lines denoting age drawn on her cheeks. Colbert, in his knickers, white shirt and a necktie, stood before her. Between them was a mysterious construction of crumpled newspapers painted white, with unlighted birthday candles stuck in it. Belinda carried a kind of wand, so that at first I thought she was a fairy princess.

But she tapped Colbert on the shoulder and in a quavery voice commanded, "Play, boy!"

"*Great Expectations!*" I said. There was applause. Belinda curtseyed. The paper construction was of course the decayed wedding cake.

Later she appeared in her Sunday dress, revealing the beginnings of a bosom, hair in neat pigtails, to stand before us and declaim:

"Blow, winds, come wrack! Knit up the ravell'd sleeve of care! There is a tide in the affairs of men, which, taken at the flood, leads on to fortune. And all the clouds that lowered around our house in the deep bosom of the ocean buried. There is a willow grows aslant a brook!"

She gestured dramatically.

"Out, damned spot! Wherefore art thou Romeo? At least we'll die with harness on our back!

"The rest is silence!"

She curtseyed to thunderous applause, her parents joining in. I slapped my hands together with enthusiasm. Belinda's cheeks were pink with pleasure as she curtseyed again.

My bride-to-be enjoyed applause very much.

When at last a brown envelope arrived from Virginia City, Bierce and I examined the faces of the Spades on the tin plate. They were grouped in front of a building that might have been the Miners' Rest, with an overhanging balcony that shaded some of the faces. They were young! All smiling. Caroline LaPlante was at the center, very respectable and rather ordinary-looking in her black skirt and white shirtwaist, with a large dark saucer of a hat shading her face. On one side of her was a man not as young as the others whom I recognized as Nat McNair, on the other a large young man, clean-shaven and grinning, derby-hatted. Beside McNair was a monkey-faced little fellow and, beside him, another derby-hatted chap whose face was partially concealed by the shade of the balcony. The three young men must be Al Gorton, E. O. Macomber and Adolphus Jackson, who was

Senator Jennings. Bierce had met Jennings but could not identify him as a young man.

"Take this to Pusey," he said. "We will test his memory for faces and the vaunted Criminal Photographic Archive."

Brushing at his mustache, he said, "It will be interesting to see if Pusey identifies Jackson as Jennings. Jennings may be paying generously for not being identified."

He had obtained a magnifying glass to see if he could recognize Jennings. When he passed it to me I bent over the tintype.

The man whose face was partially in shadow was surely my father.

I was in a state when I got to Captain Pusey's office at Old City Hall with the tintype like a block of lead in my pocket, and, when I entered, it seemed that Pusey had shrunk to only three feet tall in his blue uniform tunic, standing across the room scowling at me. I thought the shock of recognizing my father's face had been too much for me, until Pusey moved sideways to put a hand on the back of a chair and I saw he was a boy dressed up in a child's-size policeman's uniform.

Pusey himself came in through a side door.

"This's my boy John Daniel," he said. "John Daniel, come and shake Mr. Redmond's hand."

The boy approached to give my hand an energetic tug and retreated again. Pusey did not proffer his own hand. "Got something for me?" he said.

I handed him the tintype, which he laid on his desk. He bent over it, resembling a heavy-bellied candle, with his shock of hair like a white flame. He poked at the images on the tintype with a blunt forefinger. "These are Bierce's Spades then. There is Nat McNair and the grand lady herself!"

John Daniel stood silently watching. The office window looked out on an area paved with stones, where a group of bummers were in conversation, passing a bottle among them. A beer wagon rolled past with a rattle of wheels.

"That's Albert Gorton," Pusey said. "Got battered on the head in February '76. Died without coming out of it."

"Who bashed him?"

"Never solved." He grinned at me with his too-perfect teeth. "Somebody that didn't like him, probably. Unless they bashed the wrong fellow."

"Could it have been Elza Klosters doing a job for Nat McNair because Gorton was trying to blackmail McNair?"

"There's other possibilities."

"The tall man must be Adolphus Jackson." And the one partially in shadow, E. O. Macomber, was Cletus Redmond. I was in a sweat that Pusey would recognize my father, although surely his face did not appear in the Criminal Photographic Archive.

They had cheated my father out of a fortune! I would have been the son of a Nob Hill millionaire.

"What's that, Poppy?" John Daniel asked.

"Tintype of some fellows in Virginia City," Pusey said. He had never taken his eyes off the images. He shook his head slightly, as though recognition did not come, or to make me think it did not.

"Jackson spent some time in jail here."

"Probably before my time," Pusey said. "I'll study on it. Who's the other one?"

"Macomber."

He shook his head.

"Do you have a photograph of Elza Klosters?"

He rose, a bulky figure in his uniform, his belly squeezed into two fat bulges by his belt. He stamped out of the office. Outside the window a policeman had dispersed the bottle bums.

I pocketed the tintype from Pusey's desk. Bierce had paid two hundred dollars for it, after all. I wished I had never heard of it.

John Daniel watched me suspiciously.

Pusey returned laden with a heavy, leather-bound album, which he opened on his desk, and slapped through the pages. There was

Brown, whom Bierce had correctly guessed to be Klosters. He was without his hat, his surly features gazing out at me. In this likeness he possessed considerably more hair. On the opposite page was a typed list that I assumed to be of offenses, but when I rose to take a look, Pusey closed the album.

"Where's the tintype?"

I patted my pocket.

"I want it."

"It belongs to Ambrose Bierce."

"It is evidence," Pusey said. He stretched his lips to show me his fine teeth. His eyes were set in his head in a disorienting irregularity. They stared at me as though to mesmerize me.

"Evidence of what?" I asked.

His face darkened. "I want that tintype. I've got to have some time with those faces."

"I'll ask Mr. Bierce," I said.

He was not content with that, but he did not pursue it further.

When I left, Pusey told John Daniel to shake hands with Mr. Redmond again, which the boy did with another abrupt motion. Outside in the areaway, when I looked back up, Captain Pusey was watching me from his window, a looming figure capped by the topknot of white hair. Beside him was his son's head, visible above the sill, peering down.

I stopped in a saloon around the corner for a beer for my dry throat. I had been in such a sweat with Pusey looking at the Gent's image in the tintype that I hadn't concentrated on Pusey, but I had the sense that he employed his cunning even when there was no need. I patted the hard shape of the tintype in my pocket uneasily. Surely Pusey could have invoked his authority to relieve me of it if it had seemed important to him.

My breath came hard when I contemplated how close my father had come to the Big Bonanza. I turned down Clay Street, striding through the pedestrians on the busy sidewalk.

I did not identify the whiff of sound as a slung shot until my head burst.

16

A man is known by the company that he organizes.

—THE DEVIL'S DICTIONARY

I came to my senses in a dark alleyway between buildings, my back against rough bricks. My head throbbed. My stocking feet were stretched out on paving stones. Where were my shoes? My hat was missing. My jacket was gone also, with it any money I'd had with me and the tintype of the Society of Spades.

No doubt Captain Pusey had got the tintype. I touched the lump on the side of my head. Probably a bum had made off with my shoes and hat.

My banging the buggy seat in the Barnacles' cellar had not helped with the defense of the realm. I had been coshed by a professional. I felt relief that the tintype was gone.

It required some scrabbling to get to my knees. I rested there. It was another long way to my feet. The little alley stank of urine. I stood looking down at my stocking feet, willing them to move.

No one paid me any attention as I limped around the corner, and around another. I stood in the paved areaway beneath Pusey's high window, waiting for him to look out. A policeman strolled up to me, tapping his nightstick against the palm of his left hand. He had a mustache that looked painted on his face. He made moving-along gestures.

I pointed to the lump on my head, but I tender-footed on away.

I found myself in Chinatown. No one noticed my stocking feet, men in blue cotton maneuvering double loads on poles through the crowds and a woman hobbling on bound feet that probably felt like mine. Brown sun-dried ducks hung on gibbets in shop windows, trays displayed unfamiliar vegetables. Slave girls called out from their up-holstered window boxes:

"Fuckee, suckee!"

My feet were on fire when I finally got home, climbed the splintery stairs, shed my worn-out stockings and flopped onto my bed. I couldn't rest the bruised side of my head against the pillow. I lay shivering with fantasies of vengeance chasing through my brain and chills of anxiety about Amelia. I couldn't let myself think about my father's connection to the Jack of Spades Mine.

Moving slowly, I dressed and headed for *The Hornet,* bareheaded because I couldn't get a hat on my head. Bierce was not in the office, so he was probably at Dinkins's. I made my way there, to find him sitting with Sgt. Nix at his usual table. Nix had spread himself over the chair seat and chair back with a long leg stretched out.

I pointed to my lump and pulled a chair up. Bierce looked as alarmed as he ever looked, which was not very. When I had told my story, not leaving out my suspicions of Captain Pusey for Sgt. Nix's benefit, Bierce said, "The tintype is gone, then."

I entertained the irritating probability that Bierce considered me at fault for losing the tintype, for which he had paid two hundred dollars. Good riddance! Nix's hatchet face was set in a scowl.

"That's a pretty good lump you've got there, Tommy."

"I'd like to find out who put it there."

"I can make a guess," Nix said but didn't.

"Captain Pusey wanted that tintype," I said, hand to my head. "He said it was evidence."

"Evidence of what?" Bierce asked me.

"He didn't say."

"Did he recognize Jackson?"

"He said he didn't."

"Let me point out," Nix said. "He is famous for collecting photographs, and he didn't have to get you bashed on the head to take that tintype away from you. If it was evidence."

"What kind of legal compulsion would that be?" Bierce inquired.

"It's a writ of I-want-what-you-have-got," Nix said, with a sour smile.

"I'm sorry about your head," Bierce said to me.

I nodded, still a little aggrieved. Nix patted his helmet on the table. I asked if there was a constable at the Brittain house.

"He's there," Nix said.

"Sgt. Nix has discovered the owner of the Washoe Angel saloon from the tax appraiser," Bierce said. "His name is Adolphus Jackson, and tax bills are sent to him at 307 Battery Street."

The painting of Highgrade Carrie was privileged information insofar as it concerned Amelia Brittain.

"Captain Pusey showed me a photograph of Klosters from his archive," I said. "He was the man in Santa Cruz, all right. The man who tossed the queen of spades at me."

Bierce squinted at the sunny doorway of the saloon, stroking a finger along his mustache. "Someone is trying to get Beau hanged," he said. "Whores on Morton Street where Beau was seen, then Beau's particular whore on Stockton Street. If it is another progression, the young woman to whom he's engaged is certainly endangered."

"The engagement is broken off," I said. "But the Slasher may not know that."

"Could she be thought of as his whore also?"

"She could not!" I said through my teeth.

"I don't know why it is impossible for young men to believe that young women have just about the same slippery morals they have," Bierce complained.

I clamped my jaw closed. I had an engagement with Amelia on Sunday!

"A lecture from the prof," Nix said.

"Cynicism is the mother of invention," I said.

"The father of wisdom," Bierce said.

"The first refuge of scoundrels," I said, at which he smiled, for it was his own twist on Samuel Johnson's aphorism.

"Let us think of it this way," he said. "All the women of San Francisco are in danger until we can discover what this madman is about, and stop him."

When Nix had gone he said to me, "How is your piece on Senator Jennings progressing?"

"I haven't got much yet. Am I to include the fact that he was a Spade named Jackson and a San Francisco jailbird?" And the owner of a Battery Street saloon called the Washoe Angel, which had displayed the portrait of Highgrade Carrie as Lady Godiva.

"Everything you can find out. We will expect a response to *that*," he said, squinting at the lump on my head.

When I got home again there was a message from my father ordering me to meet him for supper at Malvolio's Restaurant in the Montgomery Block. I sat on my bed feeling dread like an iron harness. I got a towel from the rack and set out for the baths. My bruised feet burned.

Malvolio's was on the corner of the Monkey Block, white napery and Italian waiters with handlebar mustaches and steamy smells coming out of the kitchen when the doors were opened. The Gent sat at a table across the room. His black hair was brushed straight back, and his high-color drinker's face set in a grin as he rose to shake my hand. He embraced me with one beefy arm holding me against his muscular corporation. He had a bottle and a glass of red before him, and he motioned to a waiter to pour a second glass, which the man did with the flourish of one who knows a big tip is forthcoming. The Gent had the quality of impressing lesser mortals with his greatness. What a fine millionaire he would have made!

"How is the Bonanza Trail these days?" I asked, wondering right away why I had said it. To try to get some edge on him? He had something to say to me, as I ought to have something to say to him.

But he was simply not the Slasher, even if he was E. O. Macomber. He had never known how to carry a grudge.

"It is about petered out, Tommy. Or I am, one."

"Surely not!"

"Probably not," he said, grinning. "I have a fine position, Tommy, working with the Legislature."

Carrying the boodle for the SP. "That's fine," I said.

He touched his glass to mine with an upswing that included the other diners at Malvolio's, who probably felt cheered by it.

"Course I don't see it that San Francisco's heaven-on-earth," he said in a low voice. "Sacramento's got as much interest, I'd say. Sacramento's easy, Son. Life's easy there. Good restaurants, fine people, the Governor, Senators, Representatives."

"Hot too," I said. "What is it these days, a hundred some?"

He frowned at me, the Sacramento-supporter in him challenged. "Weather's not everything, my boy. You've got that fog down here, can't even *see* sometimes. Murders too. The Morton Street Slasher! You know what causes that? People leading pissant lives, dissatisfied, hating everybody and everything. You don't get that in Sacramento."

I said I was glad to hear it. In fact, the State Capitol might be in Sacramento, but the SP Capital was at Fourth and Townsend in San Francisco.

"When did you come down?"

"Last night on the Evening Express. Lot of grand people aboard. Ollie Fenster, Rudy Buckle, a bunch from the Bank of Nevada. We played some poker. Those fellows are paying for this fine supper!" He laughed fatly.

"Got quite a lump there," he said, nodding at my head. "Some San Francisco footpad take after you?"

"I think it was a copper," I said, and we both laughed at my fine joke.

I thought of the Gent as one of the owners of the Jack of Spades Mine, and of four other properties. He had said he had been euchred in Virginia City, but he had not said it as though he carried any freight of old hatred. Money had always been a casual thing with him. He had scraped together the funds to traipse off to the latest Bonanza camp, to buy speculative stocks, liquor and fine Sacramento meals for his boomer friends and fancy women, while my mother cut pieces of cardboard and canvas into soles to stuff inside our shoes to stop the holes, and hand-me-downed our clothes.

Probably his attitude was that if Nat McNair and company had not euchred him out of a share of the Jack of Spades Mine, someone else would have.

Menus were distributed. The Gent set them aside and ordered antipasti, gnocchi, venison ravioli and clam linguine. We munched on radishes and olives.

He glanced at me keenly. "Hear you are working for that low-grade newspaper," he said. "I tell you, Son, I was proud of you when you were a firefighter. You'd've made Chief."

"Maybe," I said, nodding.

"Working for Bitter Bierce," he said.

"Yes, sir."

"What's he like, I wonder?"

If I said, "Bitter!" we would have a laugh together, but it was as though he had tossed me a floater that I could knock out of the park. If I told him how much I admired Bierce it would cut him to the bone. Or maybe he would consider that I had tossed him a floater to knock out of the park in his innings, hinting at what a disappointment to him and my mother I had been, quitting the Fire Department to run errands for Dutch John and Ambrose Bierce.

"Well, he goes after every crook, sham, cheat and humbug, crooked preacher and porkbelly politician without fear or favor."

"Lot of them in this town," the Gent said.

"Yes, sir."

The Gent refilled his glass and passed the neck of the bottle over mine, which was still brimmed.

"I'll be surprised if Aaron Jennings doesn't go after him."

"Do you think so?" I said.

"Aaron's a gentleman. Lives in the City here. Plump sweet wife and a couple of half-grown kits. Used to be a judge, you know. A fine legislator. Man to ride the river with."

"I'm writing a piece on him for *The Hornet*."

"They've got you writing pieces?" I strained to hear the emphasis on the "you."

"Yes, sir."

Serving dishes heaped with food arrived in a cloud of smells and an officious waiter shifting plates and glasses to set them down. My father beamed at the beneficence he had ordered and scowled when he remembered the subject of the conversation. He heaped our plates with a silver serving spoon. I was so tightened up inside I wondered if I could get anything down. My head throbbed as some kind of reminder.

"How do you go about 'writing pieces'?"

"There are files at *The Hornet*, and files at the *Chronicle* and the *Alta* and the *Examiner*. I go through them and put things together." And there were facts that were not in any files.

He squinted at me. "Ever occur to you that somebody might come after *you*?"

Klosters had already come after me. I said I'd only done a piece on Mussel Slough and some looking into Mammy Pleasant so far, not to mention my researches on Senator Jennings again.

"Took the side of those Sand-lappers. I couldn't believe you'd do that, Son."

"Well, it is history."

"Lot of leeway in history," my father said.

He ordered a second bottle of wine.

"I think Wally could get you a job down at Fourth and Townsend. How'd you like that? I guess they use writers down there."

"No, thanks," I said.

"What are you, Antimonopoly?"

"Yes, sir," I said, and chewed and could not swallow.

"Son," he said heavily. "Without the Railroad this City would be just a pissant Mexican mud village. This state wouldn't be a great state. This state would be nothing at all. Who is the biggest employer in this state, Son?"

I chewed and nodded. The Railroad.

"I just can't think how a son of mine can be so misguided. Almighty God Bierce. He has set you against the Railroad, has he?"

"No, sir. I joined a Democracy Club when I was a fireman."

"My, God!" the Gent said. "Son, the Railroad *runs* this State."

"Well, it shouldn't," I said.

"*Shouldn't* isn't the issue, Tommy. "*Is* is the issue. The SP *is*."

Conversation died as we forked into our food, but I could feel the electricity of my father's indignations.

The Gent detached his napkin from his collar, filled our glasses again, squared his shoulders and said, "My boy, there are two ways of looking at life. You can approve of things, go along with things, live the good life God gave you, take advantage of the pleasures, appreciate what comes your way, have good friends that would ride the river with you. So when you come to the end of the road you can look back and say, 'Thank you, Lord, for the fullness of my days.'

"Or you can be a cold, hateful, disapproving chap. I will say your Almighty God Bierce is one of those. He may hate preachers, but he is a preacher. He will find the bad spot in every apple, he will look at the foul a person has done, not the decent. I will grant you he is a powerful chap, but, Son, nobody loves a reformer. They start out sour, and they grow sourer day by day. And when they come to the end of their time they can't look back at fullness or happiness, all they can look back at is that they hated everything and they didn't change one Gol-durn thing."

"Well, but they tried, sir," I said.

"Tell me, Son, does he have any *friends?*"

"Yes, sir," I said.

"Tell me, does he love his wife?"

"I don't believe so," I said.

He looked pleased. He pointed a finger at me. "Tommy, you remember what I say. You will come to feel the chill from that damned-righteous jobationing preacher of yours. You just mark my words."

Dishes were cleared away. Spumoni was brought, and port and cigars. I turned down the cigar, but the Gent lit up and blew blue smoke.

I said, "What time does the Evening Express get in?"

"Supposed to get in at nine-thirty, I think it is. But it was powerful late. We didn't arrive until about eleven."

So much for Rudolph Buckle's alibi for Beaumont McNair! Every time Beau became a suspect again I felt the familiar check in my breath.

I said, "As Bierce says, passengers on the SP are often exposed to the hazards of senility."

"That's a good joke," the Gent said, as though he meant it. He flourished his cigar, enjoying the cigar, the flourish, the poker game that had paid for this dinner and everything but his son.

"Do you remember, Pa, when you and I used to go fishing on the River by the big snag there?"

"I do, boy; I do remember. Better days!"

"Do you remember who it was brought me the books to start me reading?"

"By George, you were a reader, weren't you?" He gave me a naked, grateful look. There were some things I could thank him for.

"Pa, there is something I am going to have to bring up, that I have found out."

"What is that, Son?"

"We were talking about Senator Jennings just now. I remember you told me a lot of people on the Washoe used false names. He was Adolphus Jackson there."

"Long time ago, Son."

"And you were E. O. Macomber."

"Why, that's right," he said, jutting his chin. The slashes of white in his whiskers gave him a theatrical, actorish air. "How do you know this, Tom?"

"That's what I went to Virginia City for. To find out about the Society of Spades. There's a picture of you all. Highgrade Carrie, McNair, Gorton, Jackson and you."

"Society of foxes and sheep," he said, with a grunt of amusement. "Sheep got fleeced, foxes got the grapes."

"Euchred," I said.

"Why would you be interested in that?"

"The Morton Street Slasher has something to do with the Society of Spades." I could feel the tickle of sweat beneath my arms.

"You are going to have to explain that, Son."

I tried to explain. Someone was murdering whores and leaving spade cards on their slashed bodies, and it had to do with the fact that Lady Caroline Stearns had been a madam in Virginia City, and because she and Nat McNair had combined with Al Gorton to swindle Adolphus Jackson and E. O. Macomber.

My father was as Railroad as Senator Jennings.

"My goodness," he said mildly. "It do look bad for Aaron and me!"

All at once I was frantic to get away from him, from here, to try to think things through. "Will you come and meet with Bierce and me tomorrow?" I said.

He gazed at me steadily for a long moment. "Son, I don't think I will. I can see through Bierce, you see. What he wants is to embarrass the Railroad. And he has got his eye on me and Aaron Jennings through this Spades business, which seems like hocus-pocus to me. I work for the Railroad, and Aaron has his Railroad connections. It won't do, you see. It is another sheep and fox game, and Bierce is a fox I would just as soon not get tangled with. So, no, Son, I am sorry, no."

"Tell me one thing," I said.

"If I can."

"Who was the father of Caroline LaPlante's child?"

"Is that what you were after in Virginia City, Son?"

I said that was what Bierce wanted to know.

"Well," my father said, laughing. "Everybody knew it wasn't Nat."

When we had parted and I was making my way back down Montgomery Street, I felt as though I had been run through a stamp mill, and I was left with trying to decide whether or not to tell Bierce my father had been E. O. Macomber.

And just then I discovered in my jacket pocket the heavy little disc of a gold eagle that the Gent had slipped there.

INDISCRETION, *n.*
The guilt of woman.
—THE DEVIL'S DICTIONARY

n Sunday I calculated that the Brittains would be attending Trinity Episcopalian Church at Post and Powell and would be back at 913 Taylor about 12:30. So at noon I rented a shiny rig with a sleek brown gelding at the Brown and Willis Livery Stables and headed up Nob Hill. Solid fog had settled into San Francisco, as though my father had put a Sacramento blight on the City weather. I shivered in my buggy, feeling depressed and inadequate, smothering in secrets.

On the porch of the Brittain house a lanky policeman sat in the wicker chair with a cup and saucer before him. I explained that I would be Amelia's guardian for the day, citing Sgt. Nix as authority. He waved a hand, looking relieved.

Amelia was waiting in the hall, wearing a tan jacket over her dress, which fitted her torso like eelskin, her bright surprised face with its fringe of curls enclosed by her bonnet. She took my arm, whispering, "Where have you *been?* I've been waiting all morning!"

"I thought you'd be at church."

"Momma and Poppa went but I didn't."

When I helped her into the buggy the sun was glaring through thinning patches of fog. It was going to be a blessed good day! Amelia shed her jacket, peering back over her shoulder as we turned out of Taylor Street.

I asked if she was looking for her shadow.

"Oh, I haven't seen him for days. I'm sure he was bored ambling along after me, and scared off by police uniforms. Where are we going?"

"Cliff House."

"Oh, Cliff House! That's lovely!"

We headed west through the greenery and sand dunes of Golden Gate Park in a traffic of buggies and carriages filled with well-dressed people. Streams of bicyclists pedaled along the margins of the road, and pedestrians saluted each other. I was feeling a member of the quality in my suit and vest, my polished boots and soft hat, and my hired rig, very proud to be seen with Amelia Brittain at my side. Sometimes she leaned against me, and always she exclaimed excitedly about the sights or called out to friends in other buggies, so that I was reminded of the class of life-livers that my father had extolled at Malvolio's.

It was two o'clock when the great square tower and the lesser towers of Cliff House reared up ahead of us down a curving slant of roadway. In the vast dining room with the fog bank hovering just off Seal Rocks and the sea lions posturing there, we dined on turtle steaks and spring duck, with Veuve Clicquot to wash it down. The other tables were occupied by fashionable gents and ladies. By its reputation, the Cliff House was patronized by bankers, rich merchants, and political bosses and their lady friends. There was a fine feeling of opulence and naughtiness in the air, with Amelia exclaiming over her duck and the champagne and the views. The waiter as attentive to me as the fellow at Malvolio's had been to my father. We became Amelia and Tom.

I knew, however, even before our bill was presented, that I was not going to be able to afford to bring Amelia in a rented rig out to the Cliff House every Sunday, without considerable help, such as my father's poker facility and goodwill.

There was a stir of attention and glances as two people entered the dining room, a woman encased in folds and gatherings of blue material with a mass of reddish hair and a doll face of small features and red lips. Her escort was a huge old man who towered over her by more than a head. He had an impressive fall of gray beard and a ponderous way of walking so that he seemed to half surround his lady friend as the head-waiter showed them to a table behind me. I realized who they were.

"Who *is* that, Tom?" Amelia asked.

"That is the notorious Miss Hill and her new lawyer, who are in court against Senator Sharon. I understand they have become romantically friendly."

Amelia gazed at them with round eyes. "She is a fallen woman!" she whispered.

"That is true."

"What a fine complexion!"

I couldn't see the pair without awkwardly turning. Amelia continued to gaze at them between sips of champagne.

"But that gentleman is old enough to be her father!" she said.

"Do you know who he is?"

"Should I know?"

"He is Judge Terry. He was once a justice of the California Supreme Court. He fought a duel with Senator Broderick back before the War."

She nodded vigorously. "He was a southerner, and they wanted California to be a Slave state!"

"Killing Senator Broderick made certain that California would be Free Soil," I said. "Terry was almost lynched. He lit out for the Comstock, where he lawyered mining claims. Now he is back in California lawyering divorce cases.

"I hope she is successful in her suit," I added, with more intensity than I had intended.

"Poppa knew Senator Sharon on the Comstock," Amelia said. "Poppa doesn't like him."

"He's a crooked, greedy, debauched old Croesus," I said.

AMBROSE BIERCE AND THE QUEEN OF SPADES

"I wonder if her hair is really that color," Amelia whispered.

When we rose from our table I had another glimpse of Sarah Althea Hill, the Rose of Sharon, past Judge Terry's broad back, her pretty face alive with motion as she talked, one hand with a finger extended making accompanying signs. No one considered her chances against Senator Sharon's millions very good, even with Judge Terry at her side.

In the late afternoon we started back along the carriage route through the Presidio. We parked in the growing darkness above the little beach at the end of Larkin Street, where the gelding bent his neck to tug at some weeds. Amelia and I watched the lights on the Marin shore past Alcatraz.

"You may kiss me if you like," she whispered, presenting her cheek.

I kissed her cheek. She smelled of flowers. Her lips were presented and I kissed them also and was suddenly short of breath.

"I have wanted you to do that," Amelia said.

I did that some more, although I could spoil the moment thinking of Amelia's degree of intimacy with Beau McNair, which Bierce had mentioned. •

Amelia rested in my arms. "You must not put your hands there," she said, twisting slightly away. "I don't want to feel funny."

I considered dying for her.

"Do you love me, Tom?"

"Yes!" I said.

"I'm very fond of you, but I don't know if I love you yet. You are very different from the other young men I know."

"How?" I said.

"Well, I don't know any other journalists. I read what you wrote about the Mussel Slough Tragedy. My father thinks the Railroad was perfectly right in evicting those men, and putting them in jail when there was shooting."

"So does my father."

"My father doesn't read novels," Amelia said, snuggling further into my arms.

"Pardon me?"

"If you read novels you sympathize with people who are different kinds of people than you are."

"Do you sympathize with Allie Hill?" I asked.

"Yes! That poor woman has only done what was forced upon her by cruel circumstance!"

"You don't believe she should have sacrificed her life rather than her honor?"

"I certainly do not!" Amelia said. "And please kiss me and stop talking about these distressful matters."

There was a good deal more kissing before I turned the rig back along Polk Street.

On Taylor Street the upstairs windows of 913 were alight, and a lamp burned in a window off the porch. Amelia started up the steps while I wrapped the reins around the iron hitching post.

Amelia screamed.

I mounted the steps in four jumps. Amelia's screams ripped the silence. In the darkness I could see two figures down the porch, and I hurled myself toward them. Amelia had got behind the table. The man swung toward me. I hit him as hard as I could drive my fist, hit him with a left and a right while he staggered away from me. He fell against the veranda railing, which smashed under his weight. He fell through the rail and was gone in the darkness below.

The Slasher!

I sprinted down the stairs and into the shadows beneath the veranda, beating my way through the undergrowth there. He was not to be found.

Down the street I heard a police whistle.

"*Tom!*" Amelia leaned over the porch railing above me. Illumination burned behind her. Her face was an oval of shadow, her bare head bright with light.

"Did he hurt you?" I called back.

"*No!*"

"Was it Beau?"

"*No!*"

I ran up the stairs into her embrace.

"Amelia!" her father shouted behind us. "What is this?"

"Tom saved my *life!*" she cried at him.

Then we were all inside in the light: Amelia, her father in a velvet jacket, her mother in a robe, hair covered by a scarf, the butler with his shirtsleeves gartered, a woman in a cook's apron holding up a kerosene lamp.

"He had some kind of bandage on his face," Amelia murmured. "His chin—"

Then they all stared at me, as though I was the Morton Street Slasher myself. Their eyes were fixed on my chest.

My vest had been severed neatly.

"He hurt *you!*" Amelia cried at me.

In my hero's pride I was not pleased to seem to have been the Slasher's victim. I denied that I was hurt but sat down while the cook and butler fussed over me, removing my coat and vest and investigating my intact shirt front. Amelia stood with her hands pressed together, elbows out, eyebrows elevated, mouth pursed into an inch-long line. She was shivering in long spasms.

Mr. Brittain had gone to find a policeman. *Where had the constable been?*

Police appeared, one, then two more, in their double-breasted tunics like John Daniel Pusey's, that somehow made them look over-burdened and disadvantaged, helmets underarm, stern faces. There were questions to answer, a constable moistening the point of his pencil with his tongue and scribbling in his notebook. Sgt. Nix came and stood with his arms folded scowling at me.

"Where was the man who was supposed to be on duty here?" I demanded.

"He was down the street." The fellow was the first policeman who had showed up, red-faced now as Nix flipped a thumb at him.

"So she was in danger," I said.

"It's not McNair. We'd pulled him in. His alibi for the last one was no good."

"I think it's terrible the way you try to blame that young man for everything!" Mrs. Brittain burst out.

"Well, he couldn't've been this one, could he?" Sgt. Nix said. "He was in the pokey."

I saw the gleam of relief on Amelia's tear-stained face, for she had also thought the Slasher was Beaumont McNair.

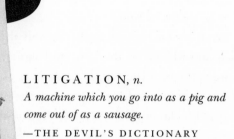

18

LITIGATION, *n.*
A machine which you go into as a pig and come out of as a sausage.
—THE DEVIL'S DICTIONARY

At this time, in Superior Court in City Hall, what was to become the sideshow of the decade was in progress; the Rose of Sharon. In *Sharon v. Sharon*, Sarah Althea Hill, claiming to be Mrs. Sharon, was suing the Senator and former King of the Comstock for divorce and a settlement, with the accusation of adultery because Sharon had admitted paternity to a child delivered of one Gertrude Dietz.

Miss Hill's supporters in the case were an Australian journalist of a shadowy past, William N. Neilson, her lawyer, George Washington Tyler and Mammy Pleasant. Judge David S. Terry was her new legal adviser.

Allie Hill had been one of Mammy Pleasant's young women.

Central to the case were several letters in which Sharon had addressed Miss Hill as "My Dear Wife," and a marriage contract written by the lady and signed by William Sharon. Allie Hill had been Sharon's mistress for some years. She lived in the Grand Hotel, across New Montgomery Street from the Palace, where Sharon kept a suite, and visited her aging lover or husband by means of the "Bridge of Sighs" passageway over the street.

"It is interesting," Bierce said, "that a gentleman can have had any number of adulterous affairs and still be considered an honest and upright man, while one lover will turn a lady disreputable in all her concerns."

"It is unfair," I said.

"What seems crucial in this case is the marriage contract, composed and written by the lady, and signed by Sharon. Oddly his signature appears at the top of the reverse of the page. Any idiot knows not to sign a blank sheet of paper at the bottom."

Miss Hill claimed that Senator Sharon had desired that their marriage be kept secret because Gertie Dietz would make trouble if he and Miss Hill were openly married. The scandal might interfere with his reelection.

A striking Fats Chubb cartoon in *The Hornet* showed the auburn-haired Sarah Althea Hill, her male supporters and a skinny black Mammy Pleasant jauntily carrying a basket filled with babies. This was a reference to Mammy Pleasant's reputation as a baby-farmer.

Mammy Pleasant had admitted to having furnished the "sinews of war" for the suit, its financing, and daily accompanied Miss Hill to City Hall in a fancy hired barouche.

"What we have here," Bierce went on, "is a confounding of the theory of oppositions. Because Senator Sharon is a bloodsucking, debauched monster does not mean that his enemy is not a perjurious harlot. The devil's horns on one side of an equation does not guarantee a halo on the opposite."

A very different Mammy Pleasant from the one we had encountered in the Bell mansion arrived at Bierce's office. She wore a handsome green cloak and a deep poke bonnet and greeted Bierce and me with a seemingly genuine smile on her dark face. Bierce proceeded in his courtly way to see her seated and settled. When she noticed the skull, she crossed herself. Bierce sat down facing her.

"I have been thinking of the matter with which you are concerned, Mr. Bierce," she said.

Bierce laid the palms of his hands together and propped his chin on the fingers.

"Mrs. McNair's marriage, the child and the child's paternity," she continued.

It was interesting that Mammy Pleasant should be speaking of babies when a color cartoon in the current issue of *The Hornet* depicted her carrying a basket full of them.

"So much talk of babies and paternity these days," Bierce said, smiling.

Mammy Pleasant nodded. "I have recalled that Senator Sharon was in Virginia City at the time of Mrs. McNair's conception."

"It seems that almost everyone in the world was in Virginia City at that time," Bierce said. "Senator Sharon, Judge Terry, Mark Twain at the *Territorial Enterprise,* and so on."

"Senator Sharon was a friend and counselor to Mr. McNair," Mammy Pleasant said. "I have heard that in Virginia City a man prospered or failed at Senator Sharon's favor. Mr. McNair prospered."

"Mrs. Pleasant, is this to suggest that Senator Sharon's favor extended so far as Mrs. McNair's womb?"

"That is for you to consider, Mr. Bierce."

"Could this visit, and this information, have anything to do with the proceedings presently taking place in Superior Court?"

She looked sour. "We would be pleased for your good opinion, Mr. Bierce. Yours is a voice that is listened to in the City."

"I see."

"When you called on me the other day, I thought: what have I to gain by assisting Mr. Bierce with the information he seeks? I could think of nothing to be gained."

"You would think it inappropriate to furnish information without some quid pro quo?"

"I do not know Latin, Mr. Bierce, but I take your meaning. Yes, that is correct. That is the way I have learned to conduct my affairs in San Francisco."

"And the information with which you hope to enlist my good

opinion is the fact that Senator Sharon was in Virginia City at the time that Mrs. McNair conceived?"

"I believe you are looking for the true father of the young Mr. McNair, and I suggest you consider Senator Sharon, who was a close friend and business associate of Mr. and Mrs. McNairs'."

"Thank you," Bierce said. "I believe you would also find it helpful to the proceedings in Superior Court if Senator Sharon was revealed as having taken part in even more adulterous affairs, with issue, than he is now renowned for."

"You leap to conclusions, Mr. Bierce."

"A rather short leap, madam."

She smiled again from Bierce to me, gathered up her large handbag and departed.

"Time cannot wither, nor custom stale, that essential malevolence," Bierce sighed, when the sound of her steps had disappeared down the hall.

"Jimmy Fairleigh mentioned Sharon," I said.

"We know that Sharon fathered Gertie Dietz's child," Bierce said. "Although fatherhood is not uncommon, as I understand it."

"No."

"What that woman carries in her very large handbag is a supply of red herrings," Bierce said.

I had attended one of the early court sessions. The courtroom was crowded because the case was a sensation, a high-ceilinged room with great windows pouring in western sunlight, and Judge Finn on the bench. Sarah Althea Hill's lawyer, Mr. Tyler, was notable for his chestful of beard, and Sharon's, a General Barnes, for mustaches which would cause him to have to pass through narrow doorways sideways. Sharon, a grizzled little man with a big head, sat grimly at one table. Miss Hill, in blue velvet faced with dark fur, and a blue hat with a veil that concealed her face, was a slim figure seated in a kind of galvanic stillness beside Mammy Pleasant.

The proceedings that day had to do with a document in the case, which Miss Hill stood before the court to draw from her bosom.

"Judge," she said in a tremulous voice. "This paper is my honor. I cannot leave it out of my hands."

"Just show it to Mr. Barnes," the Judge said.

"If your honor will take the responsibility upon yourself and compel me to, I will deliver the document."

"I cannot take any responsibility," the judge said. "Is the paper inside this envelope?"

"I desire that neither Mr. Sharon nor Mr. Barnes should handle it. I consider it my honor and have regarded it as my honor for three long years. Mr. Sharon knows all about it."

General Barnes said pompously, "I object to this lady standing there and making these statements. Mr. Sharon knows nothing about it. It is a fraud and a forgery from end to end."

"He knows every word in this paper, so help me God. He dictated it to me."

Mammy Pleasant was half-rising and subsiding in her chair, in anxiety or support.

Senator Sharon climbed to his feet. "I tell the Court this is the damndest lie that was ever uttered on this earth!"

"I do not like to offend Your Honor," Miss Hill said with dignity. "But he has got his millions against me. I have been driven from my home. He has taken my money, and I have got no money to defend myself with."

There was a good deal more wrangling before Miss Hill surrendered the paper to the Clerk who was ordered to have a copy made.

I dug through files to look over Senator Sharon's history. He had indeed been a presence in Virginia City during the '60s. William Ralston of the Bank of California was his benefactor, appointing him the bank's agent on the Washoe. Sharon made his fortune there. Mineowners had exhausted capital and credit, and the quartz mills had been so hastily constructed that many of them were unworkable. So many claims were in litigation that the courts were paralyzed. Virginia City, at the time of Sharon's arrival, was a bankrupt camp sitting on a billion-dollar ore-body. With unlimited credit from the Bank of California, Sharon began purchasing shares in the most promising mines and mills by taking over their paper from the overburdened local banks, and issuing credit at reduced rates of interest. He foreclosed like a thunderclap on nonpayment. His instincts and intuition were almost perfect. With Ralston and Darius Mills he organized the Union Mill & Mining Company to take over properties foreclosed by the Bank. He built the railroad to Carson City and Reno, controlling the traffic to Mount Davidson, and thus became one of the West's transportation magnates. He had spies to sniff out strikes that were made in competing mines, he engaged in titanic struggles for control through stock acquisitions, he boomed stocks so that their prices swooped up and down like swallows, he made secret deals between mills and mines to hide real value by spreading rumors of bonanza and borrasca. He was the most cynical manipulator of all the Comstock manipulators. At the zenith of his power and wealth he controlled the Union Mill & Mining Company and the railroad and owned seven producing silver mines, including the Ophir, which he had snatched away from Lucky Baldwin.

He was known as the "King of the Comstock," the "California Croesus," and the "Bonanza Senator." The Nevada legislature sent him to the senate in 1875.

He profited hugely on the fall of his mentor, William Ralston, who drowned in a swimming accident or committed suicide when the Bank of California closed its doors in the panic of 1875. Sharon succeeded not only to the control of the reopened Bank, but to Ralston's last great project, the Palace Hotel, and even to Ralston's country estate at Belmont. Many blamed him for Ralston's ruin. Ralston's empire had collapsed, it was said, because his closest friends, Sharon and Darius Mills, had plotted his ruin.

Sharon kept an apartment at the Palace, entertained lavishly at Belmont and indulged his taste for quoting Shakespeare and Lord

Byron. He was a pale, chilly little man with a big head, overly neat, always tight-fisted, generally disliked. His daughter Flora married a genuine British aristocrat, Sir Thomas George Fermor-Hesketh, in a splendid affair at Belmont.

His wife had died in 1874 after a marriage of trying to ignore her husband's infidelities. While he was making his millions he found time for many adulterous affairs, and he was famous for his penchant for high-class prostitutes. He was often to be seen in the company of glittering young females. He kept a number of mistresses.

The first salvo of the senator's problems with his most troublesome mistress, Sarah Althea Hill, came at his daughter Flora's wedding, when Miss Hill was physically barred from the grand event. Sarah Althea claimed she had a right to attend as a member of the family.

In September of 1883 Sharon was arrested for adultery, out of which came two current court cases, *Sharon v. Sharon* in State Superior Court, in which Sarah Althea Hill sued for divorce, a division of property and alimony, and *Sharon v. Hill* in Federal Circuit Court, which had jurisdiction because Sharon was a citizen of Nevada, in which the senator sued to have the marriage contract declared false and fraudulent and to enjoin Miss Hill from claiming to be his wife. There were to be peripheral suits for perjury, forgery, slander, libel, conspiracy and embezzlement. *Sharon v. Sharon* and *Sharon v. Hill* would be fought in California courts for almost ten years.

Bierce wrote in Tattle, "The testimony this week in the Sharon trial must be of intense interest to the readers of dime-novels. The colossal nastiness of the events divulged is the most impressive feature. The thought of a delectable young person such as Miss Hill falling into the arms of a noxious old debauchee like Senator Sharon is as revolting as is the Christian religion in the hands of Washington Street evangelists."

Pusey approached along the hallway at his stately gait and turned into Bierce's office to greet Bierce and me. He seated himself, his cap under his arm, and announced that that was a pretty scene in Superior Court. I was not summoned to join this conversation but observed it from my end of the office. I tried to set my face so as not to glower at Pusey across the office, though I didn't mind touching my head where I had been whacked certainly on his order.

"Never heard so many lies told quite so fast in all my life," Pusey said.

Bierce clicked his tongue. He wore the expression of extreme politeness that he assumed when there was a danger his feelings would show. He did not like Captain Pusey.

"Whose lies, Captain?"

"That Hill woman is one fast-talker. And temper! She's telling lies and she's got another young lady telling lies, and a young fellow, and two colored girls, all telling lies. I hear the Senator is paying a thousand dollars a day defending himself against those lies."

"No lies on his side?" Bierce said.

"Too busy brushing them off himself to tell any lies."

"Seems to me there was a young fellow that got caught in some lies saying he had had a relation with Miss Hill."

Pusey clucked and patted his white mane. "The Senator is paying out good money trying to nail down those lies that woman's suborned those people to tell about him."

"Paying money, is he?" Bierce said.

Pusey nodded. "He's got his lines out, he has. He didn't make himself twenty millions laying down and letting people walk over him."

I thought Pusey might be one of the lines Senator Sharon had out.

"He don't like people calling him names the way some have done," he said.

"As I have done?" Bierce said.

"That's right," Pusey said, displaying his splendid teeth. "Mr. Bierce, you get so many people stamping mad at you I can't be responsible for what happens."

"I understand that Miss Hill has charged him with adultery with nine women," Bierce said.

"Now, you *know* that is lies. He is a little old chap, he is sixty-four years old!"

"Five or six would be more accurate, you mean."

Pusey blew his breath out in irritation.

"Mr. Bierce, she is going to lose this case and end up in the hoose-gow for perjury. The Senator is going to win it, and he is going to remember who was a help to him and who wasn't."

"Memory like an elephant, I understand," Bierce said.

Pusey scowled at him.

"Now, Captain Pusey," Bierce said. "Don't I recollect that Senator Sharon has been one of the most active adulterers in this sinful city?"

"Where it comes to nookie, I always say all bets are off," Pusey said. He showed his teeth again. "You have done pretty well along those lines yourself, Mr. Bierce."

Bierce composed his face.

"Now what do you know about the senator in Virginia City, Captain?" he said. "Wasn't he scampering after loose women there also?"

"Not my jurisdiction, Mr. Bierce, if you know what I mean." Pusey brought his fat watch out of his pocket and scowled at it.

"I understand Mammy Pleasant has been to call," he said, switching the subject.

"That is correct," Bierce said.

"You know this is all her put in. She has laid out the money, she has furnished her lawyer to represent the young woman. George Washington Tyler, that old shyster! And Judge Terry too! Senator Sharon is not going to forget that."

"He had better be careful."

"Now why is that, Mr. Bierce?"

"I understand Mrs. Pleasant is a voodoo person. Charms, potions, sticking needles in dolls, tricks like that."

Pusey harrumphed at that, not knowing whether Bierce was serious or not.

"You have been employed by the Senator, is that so?" Bierce asked.

"I'm an employee of the City of San Francisco!" Pusey said indignantly.

When he had gone, Bierce said, "That is a pair I would not like to give aid and comfort to."

"Senator Sharon and Captain Pusey."

"We may still gain some information from Mammy Pleasant," he said. "But we can be certain we will have nothing from Pusey."

"What will we do about finding out if there is a connection between Sharon and Carrie LaPlante?"

"We will just have to ask her," Bierce said.

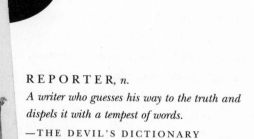

REPORTER, *n.*
A writer who guesses his way to the truth and
dispels it with a tempest of words.
—THE DEVIL'S DICTIONARY

y stock had risen at 913 Taylor Street. Amelia insisted that I had saved her life from the Morton Street Slasher, or whoever her attacker had been, and she conducted herself with me with some familiarity before her parents.

The broken railing of the veranda had been patched with pale pine boards, and the policeman on duty there was treated with more hospitality, the cook furnishing him lemonade and shortbread cookies.

I escorted Amelia to the Roller Palace. Roller-skating was a sport with which she was unfamiliar. On the gleaming hardwood floor with the racket of metal wheels on wood, under the balloon ceiling with its central boss of jewel-flashing mirrors, I held an arm around her waist while she took her first rolling steps, her left hand clutching mine, giggling, high-colored, her voice rising an octave in her nervousness. But soon she was swooping along with the best, waving long arms for balance, graceful in her lanky awkwardness with her skirts sweeping in thick folds around her legs, her tight bodice with the two lovely symmetrical mounds of her bosom, her pretty head crowned in a velvet hat with a rolled brim, laughing and laughing in her pleasure. The roller-skating seemed to help her get over her fright at the

Slasher's attentions, though still I would see her eyes fill and she would become very quiet, as if the fact that someone would want to hurt her had swept over her again.

In the steamy little tearoom over cups of Oolong she prattled about marriages of San Francisco young women to European aristocrats. Clara Huntington and Eva Mackay had married titles, Flora Sharon a baronet, Mary Ellen Donahue a baron, Mary Parrott a count, Virginia Bonynge a viscount and her sister Lord John Maxwell. The Holladay sisters had plighted troth with the Baron de Boussiere and the Comte de Pourtales.

And the widow of the multimillionaire Nathaniel McNair had married Lord Hastings Stearns.

"It is so charming!" she said. "The fathers of these women with brilliant careers were Irish saloonkeepers or hairy prospectors with their donkeys, and these European aristocrats are the descendants of crusty old warriors who chose the winning side in some war of succession. Their titles are for sale to charming females with great expectations!"

I wondered if she was regretting her own failed engagement to the son of Lady Caroline, which had been nixed by her father.

I said I didn't think any of the heiresses of the brilliant careers were as good roller-skaters as she had proved to be.

She laughed and said, "As to my own brilliant career, I'm afraid Poppa's investments are failing him just now."

I digested that.

"It is a comic spectacle, Tom," she went on. "One must learn to view it as a spectator instead of a participant."

"But you are a participant!"

"A spectator also. I insist on that!" She flattened the palms of her hands together with her chin balanced on her fingers, her eyes fixed on me.

I said I thought the whole shameless business was an affront to a democratic nation.

"It may be an affront to a Democrat, but it is fine comedy. Have you witnessed the Saturday afternoon procession on 'the line'?"

"The line" was the five blocks along Market from Powell to Kearny and up Kearny to Sutter. Saturday afternoons beautiful young women paraded along the line, for the delectation of the knots of young men watching from the open-front cigar stores on their route.

"Their toilettes are perfect," Amelia went on. "They are not 'society,' they are the daughters of shopkeepers and merchants and doctors. But they are as lovely young women as the heiress-brides of the European aristocracy. Isn't it wonderful?"

I didn't know what she was getting at.

"Tom, you must learn to appreciate *ironies!*" Amelia said. She seemed to be laughing at me. Then I saw her eyes mist again.

When I watched her lips speaking of ironies all I could think of was kissing them. I said, "I wonder if it is such a blessing to be an offspring of Nob Hill aristocrats."

"There are responsibilities, of course," Amelia said solemnly.

"So yours cannot be a free spirit."

"Yes and no."

"You are a free spirit on your roller-skates."

"Let us go pretend some more, then," she said, smiling and patting my hand.

Later she told me that I reminded her of Pierre Bezuhov in *War and Peace*.

I said, "And is Beau McNair Prince Andrew?"

"No, he is Anatole Kuragin," she said. Her nose wrinkled as she giggled.

She had read *War and Peace* in French! "It took weeks!" she said.

Women often spoke in mysterious allusions or snatches of song, so that you felt stupid when you did not catch the drift. What did her reference to *War and Peace* mean? Anatole Kuragin had failed to seduce Natasha Rostov. But Pierre Bezuhov was the man she came to love after the death of Prince Andrew. What did that tell me?

I mentioned *Vanity Fair*.

"Amelia Sedley and Captain Dobbin!"

Her face was bright with excitement to discover that we had read the same books, although I had missed *Henry Esmond,* and she had not read *The Adventures of Huckleberry Finn*. We circled the noisy floor among the other skaters with our left hands clasped again, my right arm around her waist, and compared novels.

"There isn't anybody I can talk to about books!" Amelia said, brushing her hair back from her pink face. "Beau never read *anything,* and Poppa doesn't read much any more."

I said I had enjoyed my conversation with her father.

"He is not looking forward to Lady Caroline's arrival."

"Why would that be?"

"They were friends in Virginia City but something happened so they are not friends any more," Amelia said. "Of course I know she had an ambiguous position there, and I am not allowed to speculate on what their friendship might have been." She laughed on an ascending scale.

She was the most delightful entity who had ever entered my life.

I sat with Bierce in the office. Next door we could hear the rattle of Miss Penryn's machine. Smithers shouted something further down the hall. The window was open on California Street and through it came a clamor of buggy wheels.

Bierce tapped his fingertips together. "It is someone totally committed to malevolence toward Beau McNair. To his guilt—his incrimination!—to the damage of anyone connected to him. Someone wants to drink wine out of his skull, but I can't seem to grasp the core of this anger. Is it one of the Spades?"

He peered at me through his shaggy eyebrows: "In London, as a member of the Diamonds, this young chap drew female organs on the bellies of whores with some liquid that stung but did not disfigure."

"Which Captain Pusey knew," I said. "And the Slasher must know also."

"Would it have been featured in the London newspapers? Copies of *The Times* or *The Illustrated London News* might be found in the Reading Room of the Pacific Club. But Lady Caroline would have tried to keep it out of the papers."

Bierce tugged down on the points of his vest, frowning. "The *details* of what the Diamonds did to the Whitechapel women would *not* have appeared in the papers," he said. "And *should* be known in San Francisco only to Captain Pusey. It will be remembered that Captain Pusey, by what he calls an educated guess, showed the photograph of Beau McNair to Edith Pruitt of Mrs. Cornford's establishment."

"An extremely educated guess, as you said."

"Pusey had the tintype removed from your possession because he knew that Jackson is Jennings, and he didn't want anyone else to make the connection. Why would he protect Jennings? Because Jennings is a one-time jailbird who is paying him not to reveal the fact. It is a financial arrangement he does not want disturbed."

Captain Pusey also possessed the tintype which showed the Gent to have been E. O. Macomber.

"Pusey must have his sights set on a more opulent prize," Bierce said.

"Lady Caroline. But Jennings is not the Slasher."

"Jennings is a certified peculator and murderer whom I intend to see indicted," Bierce said grimly. "The Slasher is Captain Pusey's affair. Jennings is mine."

I confessed that I had not uncovered any information on Senator Jennings that Bierce did not already know. Jennings had kept his tracks well covered.

Bierce thought that Pusey might have had a hand in the covering of tracks. I was ordered to keep digging.

When I came back from lunch, and a trot past the Brittain house to make sure a constable was on guard, Bierce was in conference. Elza

Klosters sat facing him, with his broad-brimmed hat on his lap. Hatless, with strands of graying hair combed over his pale scalp, he did not look so menacing.

"Tom, this is Mr. Klosters," Bierce said.

Klosters made no move to rise, nor I to shake his hand. I turned my own chair around to face them.

"Mr. Klosters has come to protest my attentions to the Reverend Stottlemyer," Bierce said.

"The Washington Street Church," Klosters said, nodding. He had a phlegmy rumble of a voice. "I said I would pow-wow with you." He turned his head slowly to regard me. His jaw was set in a bulldog clench.

"And what are we to pow-wow in regard to?" Bierce asked.

"I have thought of doing you some harm, Mr. Bierce."

"Is that your role at the Washington Street Church?"

"It is work I have done sometimes." Klosters ran a big hand over his balding head.

"You were chief of deputies at Mussel Slough, for the Railroad," Bierce said.

"That is neither here nor there, Mr. Bierce."

"And you have tried to intimidate Mr. Redmond here, and through him, me. That was not for the purposes of the Washington Street Church and the Reverend Stottlemyer."

Klosters shook his head patiently.

"The Reverend is as fine a man as I have ever known of," he said. "He has brought me to Jesus. He has brought the sinners in the Washington Street Church to Jesus. We have the Reverend Stottlemyer to thank for bringing us to Salvation."

Bierce's face did not reveal his opinions on organized religion.

"You have found Salvation, Mr. Klosters?" he said.

Klosters nodded his heavy head. "I was a violent man. I have become a Jesus-man in the hope of Salvation."

"You are to be congratulated."

"The Reverend is to be congratulated, not mocked as you have done. I had thought to harm you, but the Reverend has shown me that that is not the way of a Jesus-man."

"No."

"Still, you fired Judge Hamon's house in Santa Cruz," I said.

"That is one thing," Klosters said.

"And is there another 'thing,' sir?"

"The other thing is what I have told you I will not do no more. I have been offered good money to harm a person, and I have said I would not do it although that was the way of life I had led. Because I have been brought to Jesus."

"And who was the person you were to be paid to harm?" Bierce asked.

"That is neither here nor there."

Metal wheels screeched noisily past outside. A high-sided wagon rolled by, a colored man in an overall perched in the rear corner.

"Tell me," Bierce said to Klosters. "Is the person who offered you good money for this particular harm the same one who hired you to harm Albert Gorton?"

It was as though these questions required a great deal of thought on Klosters's part.

"I did not come here for this kind of palaver, Mr. Bierce. The Reverend has shown me the way and the light. I have come as a Jesus-man to tell you that the Reverend forgives you your trespasses against him, but there is others in that congregation that might not."

"Oh, this is a threat after all."

"The Reverend would not want you to think of it in that way," Klosters said.

His bloodshot eyes regarded me with a kind of total inspection and turned away as though I did not interest him.

"We are concerned with events in Virginia City in 1863," Bierce said.

"Highgrade Carrie," I said.

Klosters raised a hand, palm toward me. "Tell you something, young fellow. You too, Mr. Bierce. Just stay out of Carrie's business. You will be better off for it."

"She is a friend of yours?"

"That lady is more than friend to anybody that knew her back then," Klosters said.

"That lady will presently be in a circumstance of propinquity," Bierce said.

Klosters gaped at him.

"San Francisco," Bierce said.

"Is that a fact now?" Klosters said. He rose with a ponderous motion of shoving his chair back and heaving himself out of it. He clapped on his hat. Immediately he looked more dangerous.

"You came by my boardinghouse to deliver the queen of spades card," I said. "Did Senator Jennings hire you for that?"

Sucking on a tooth, Klosters squinted at me. "Tell you, young fellow, there is someone that is interested in you changing your ways."

"With harm in mind?" Bierce said.

Klosters shrugged. "You, too, Mr. Bierce," he added.

Bierce said, "Mr. Klosters, what would it take for you to give evidence that Senator Jennings tried to hire you to murder Mrs. Hamon?"

Klosters did not reply. He adjusted his hat and departed.

I touched the still-sore spot on my head where I had been harmed by a slung shot.

"So," Bierce said, seating himself again. "Jennings tried to hire him to murder Mrs. Hamon, but Klosters has taken the pledge, so to speak."

"Not against arson," I said.

"Nor intimidation. Although the only real threat he uttered was to stay out of Lady Caroline's business."

That consideration opened new doors.

"Both you and I have been threatened," Bierce went on. "Miss Brittain was actually assaulted, surely by the Slasher. I can only believe these were different protagonists. There is a madman out there, no doubt of *that*. There is also Jennings, who is not a madman, although he may be a frightened man by now."

"And there is Jesus-man," I said.

"Whose loyalty to Lady Caroline is evident."

"Everyone seems to be loyal to Lady Caroline."

He nodded grimly and drew his watch from his vest pocket to consult it.

"Time for Dinkins's?" he said.

I told him I had to attend a True Blue club meeting and help defend the Democracy from the Monopoly.

VALOR, *n.*
A soldierly compound of vanity, duty and the gambler's hope.
—THE DEVIL'S DICTIONARY

The meeting was in the basement of the Stoller building on Mission Street, about thirty of the True Blues on a collection of rickety wooden chairs, and Boss Chris Buckley at the podium with his toadies around him. He gazed out over us with his blind eyeballs and managed to appear amiable and impatient at the same time, as though he still had to talk to half a dozen Democracy or Antimonopoly Clubs tonight.

He waved his hands for silence.

"When the Lord created the Universe," he began, "He looked around and said it was good enough for ordinary folks, but there must be a better piece of handiwork for the Democracy, so He created California. And then He said that the special folks that lived in California ought to do something to earn this special piece of His Handiwork, so He let the Enemy create the Monopoly so that California would have to do some labors to get rid of it."

That started things off with a laugh and applause, and the Blind Boss went on from there. I sat with Emmett Moon and August Leary in the third row.

There were other matters than Regulation of the Railroad to discuss, and after Buckley and his bunch had gone on, Sam Rainey took over the meeting, and we listened to opinions on the United Street Railways of San Francisco who wanted to install overhead trolley lines, and the latest scandals from the water works.

So we were a long way off the evils of the Railroad when a dozen bullies crowded in and began breaking up the furnishings. A good many of the True Blues evaporated out the door into Mission Street, but those of us who had sworn off being pushed around went into action. I engaged a fellow with a black cap on and hit him a couple of good wallops before he took up a chair to swing at me. Emmett and August and Fred Till were in action also, but, though we outnumbered the toughs, they were more certain what they were after. I heard my name.

Three of them came for me, Small, Medium and Large, Large with a puffy clean-shaven face, an undershot jaw and a chest like a barrel in a faded blue shirt. "Redmond!" he shouted at me. He had fists balled up like melons.

I hit him left and right and backed up and hit him again, but he kept coming with his cronies blocking the flanks so I was pushed into the corner, panting like a locomotive and wondering where my own pals were. Large hit me so hard in the belly that I spewed any air I had left in me along with my dinner. When I was crawling on the floor he kicked me in the chest so I thought my ribs were broken. After that he stood back with his meathooks on his hips and watched Small and Medium kick me around.

"Back off!" Large said. "Hear?"

I lay there aching all over and half fainting, and I nodded.

"*Back off!*" the chief tough said again, and the pack of them banged off, kicking chairs over and stamping on them, and trooped out and were gone.

August and Fred Till helped me home, and up my stairs where they washclothed the blood and vomit off my face and rolled me into bed. It felt good to groan.

I waked up to see a figure in a tweed suit standing with the light from the window turning him black with bright edges. Bierce was looking through the books in my bookcase. Morning sun gleamed in his frosted hair. He swung around to stand over me, looking down.

"It wasn't Pusey this time," he said.

"No," I croaked. I ought to be asking him to take a chair, but it was too much trouble. I ached from my face on down. I moved a leg carefully.

"Back off," I said.

"Pardon me?"

"The message was to back off."

He paced over to be haloed at the window again. "Tom, I am sorry. You have taken punishment that should more rightly be mine. I cannot ask you to be the recipient of any more of it. Should we abandon the piece on Jennings? For that is what this seems to be about."

"Be damned to them."

He turned, his cold face twitching into a slight smile. "Very well. Be damned to them shall be our motto."

It was easier to nod than to speak.

"I have brought you something." He took a Colt's revolver from his jacket pocket and placed it carefully on the taboret beside my bed.

When he had gone I sat up, groaning, and stashed the revolver in the drawer of the taboret.

Mrs. B. brought me breakfast and left it even though I told her I couldn't eat anything. I slept the morning away. I was wakened by a rap on the door. "Lady to call," Mrs. B. said, disapproving. An exception to the no-women-in-the-rooms rule had been made in my case.

I was trying to sit up and brush a hand over my hair when Amelia swept inside.

She seemed to provide sunlight in the dim room as she circled around, exclaiming at everything she saw. She stood over the bed with her gloved hands clapped together, gazing down at me from under her considerable bonnet with an expression of dismay.

"My hero has been brought home on his shield!"

"You are not to leave your house without a guardian!" I raised myself to say.

She flapped a hand toward the open door. I could see a helmeted policeman leaning on the stair rail.

"Constable Button is my sentry today!" She seated herself on the end of the bed with a graceful swing of her hips. She held her hands clasped together before her as though to immobilize them.

"Mr. Bierce said it was a Railroad gang who did this."

"It was a message for me to back off."

"What does that mean, please?"

"I've been writing a piece on Senator Jennings that they don't want published."

She sat looking down at her hands with her pretty mouth pursed. I admired the sweet symmetry of her bosom. "And will you back off?" she asked.

"No."

"Poppa knows Mr. Crocker and Mr. Stanford."

I laughed, which hurt in my chest and belly. She laughed with me. I thought it must be the irony that amused her.

"What can I bring you, Tom?" she said.

"You've already brought me the best thing you could bring me."

I was astonished to see her blush. It swept up her throat and over her chin into her cheeks like a pink shadow. She clasped a hand to her throat as though to stop it.

"My mother makes a bruise remedy from cucumber cream and arnica," she said. "I will send you a bottle."

I asked if she would accompany me to Marin on Sunday, up Mount Tamalpais.

"I would love that!"

She rose swiftly. "I must be going. I don't know what Constable

Button will think!'' She swooped toward me. The brim of her hat scraped my forehead, her lips brushed mine, and she was gone.

Late in the afternoon Belinda arrived for a visit. She sat in the chair just inside the door with her feet tucked close together and her hands in her lap. She had on her Sunday dress and a bonnet that made her face look like a china doll's.

"Miss Brittain came to call on you," she said.

"Yes."

"Mother doesn't think she should have been alone in your room with you."

"She stayed two entire minutes."

"Ladies aren't allowed in the boarders' rooms."

"You are here," I said.

"I'm not a lady yet," she said, looking down at her hands in her lap. "Mother thinks she is very pretty," she said.

"Well, so are you, Belinda."

She didn't look up. "Tom."

"Yes?"

"That man followed me home from school yesterday."

"What man?" I knew what man.

"The playing-card man."

I was breathing hard suddenly. "What did he do?"

"Well, he just followed me home. Then he stood at the gate for awhile after I'd come inside. I watched through the window. Then he went away."

"Don't you worry about him," I said. "I'll walk you home on Monday."

When she had gone I lay with my eyes closed and my teeth gritted. My head felt filled with some overheated substance that ached behind my eyes. I had had no idea how vulnerable I was. But now I had an idea how the Railroad pursued its ends. I thought of the revolver in the drawer, and having come to the pass where I must carry it to walk Belinda home from school.

It seemed that when you were in possession of a firearm you began to think in terms of it.

A hackie brought me a green bottle wrapped in white tissue paper. It was Amelia's mother's bruise remedy, and I dutifully sloshed the white stuff over my bruises and rubbed it in until I stank like a cucumber stall at the Washington Street market.

Jonas Barnacle carried my supper on a tray up the stairs. "So they gave you a good pummeling, Tom."

"They did," I said.

"Those Railroad folks can get away with about anything, I guess."

"We'll see about that," I said.

2 1

FAITH, *n.*
Belief without evidence in what is told by one who speaks without knowledge, of things without parallel.
—THE DEVIL'S DICTIONARY

I was still aching and shaky on foggy Sunday morning when I presented myself at the early service at the Washington Street Church. I slid into a seat in a pew at the back of the church, which was a hollow box of bricks, with a lectern instead of an altar, a crucifix on the wall, and some numbers chalked on a blackboard, that must be hymns. These Protestants did not go in for decoration.

There were about thirty people present, and I could see Klosters's bald head in the second row. The preacher, the Reverend Stottle-myer, who had brought Klosters to Jesus, paced behind the lectern. He wore a black suit, a high collar and a four-in-hand tie. He must have been six and a half feet tall and skinny as a post.

I had brought some rage and nervousness to this brick church, together with Bierce's revolver in my pocket that seemed to weigh ten pounds.

Stottlemyer paced and halted to gaze out at the congregation with saucer eyes in his gaunt face. The eyes seemed to be fixed on me as he spoke.

" 'And the fear of you shall be upon every beast of the earth, and upon every fowl of the air; with all wherewith the ground teemeth, for into your hand are they delivered.'

"The words of the Lord! For these beasts, these fowls, represent our lower natures, my friends. And this lower nature must be subdued and disciplined by the regenerate Jesus-man.

"The Jesus-man must govern his lower nature, my friends. The ox is strong to labor, but that strength may no longer be expended without direction. Those fierce thoughts, which are as the lions and bears, must be stilled. After man has passed the flood and is regenerate, those very lions may be loosed upon him, the lower nature be slain, the Jesus-man in his higher nature left standing beside his own carcass.

"For as the beasts of the field and the fowls of the air are within our lower natures, so are the twelve apostles in our higher. They correspond to the twelve degrees of the Jesus-man, my friends, brought into perfect harmony and at-one-ment. For in the central place in these harmonies is Adonai himself, Jesus spreading his welcoming arms to the Jesus-man."

He paced, swung, and paced the other way, big-nosed and narrow-headed, with his eyes that flared like candles as he preached. He did not work himself up into any ferment, as though saving himself for the second service of the day, so it was difficult to understand what had caused Klosters to change his ways, but when he gazed out over his flock it continued to seem as though he stared straight at me. I leaned forward to cross myself and whisper a prayer, for it was like Satan himself in that jackstraw preacher knowing he had a shaky Catholic in his sights.

But after awhile he shifted into the offertory: "Our offering, my friends, is the table of Jesus. It is the food of God. The fire of heaven, which is the holiness of Jesus, consumes this offering, and all in seconds it ascends as sweet incense to Him!"

It seemed my salvation to skin out the door into the blowing fog of Washington Street when Stottlemyer wasn't looking. I took up a post in the mouth of an alley a hundred feet down the street, wondering what to do if Klosters chose the other direction. But he came my way, looming out of the fog, big-hatted and alone.

I let him pass, then stepped out and jammed the muzzle of the revolver into his kidney. "Just step this way," I heard my shrill voice say.

He stepped into the alley before he had figured out who I was. When he faced me I prodded the muzzle into his stomach. His hands were raised shoulder high. His pockmarked granite face was close to mine, his bloodshot eyes regarded me, his mouth turned down at the corners.

"What do you think you are doing?" he grated.

"You followed my landlord's girl home from school on Friday."

The corners of his mouth turned up. "These girls do like me. Can't think why."

"Don't do it again," I said.

His eyes closed in weariness, as though this was all too many for him. "You are a foolish young fellow," he said. "You know you are not going to shoot me, and I know you are not going to shoot me." But he did not lower his hands.

"I will shoot you if you offer that girl any harm," I said, and suddently I felt as futile as Major Copley.

When he lowered his right hand it came down like a hatchet on my wrist, knocking the revolver clattering to the pavement. Before I could move he slammed his boot down on it.

Panting a little from his effort, he said, "You are writing something about Senator Jennings that don't want to be published. If you leave off publishing it I will leave that girl be."

I rubbed my wrist, trying not to grimace at the pain. In fact I had not written much of the piece on Jennings, and I could rationalize that Bierce didn't actually want to publish it anyway, he only wanted Jennings to know it was being written. It was entirely probable that he had made sure that Jennings learned of that fact, which had got me the beating I still ached from, despite the cucumber arnica; and this botch as well.

"All right," I said.

He stooped to pick up the revolver and handed it to me butt first. He smiled bleakly. "Here's your piece," he said. "Don't forget the Concealed Weapon Ordinance." He opened his coat so I could see that he himself was not armed; then he lumbered off into the fog.

I was not in a good mood when Amelia and I took the ferry to Marin. I had been Futilitarian with a Concealed Weapon. In fact I had not been much of a hero since I had gone into action on the Brittain's porch, having come out on the short end of all my scrapes since.

Amelia and I stood on the deck with fog blowing past us. I put an arm around her, to which she seemed to respond. "What's the matter, Tom?"

"Things going wrong," I said.

"Can I know?"

"Not today," I said. "I wish the fog would let up, though."

"It's just what I chose for today!"

I gave her a squeeze.

The hoots of foghorns resounded down the Bay. Alcatraz loomed up like a ship bearing down on us, and faded away behind. We ascended Mount Tamalpais still in dense fog blowing over us in the open carriage with other sightseers crouched together in the seats before us, and Amelia huddled against me so that I could look down on the plane of her cheek, and the fringe of eyelashes beneath her bonnet. Suddenly we were out of the fog in brilliant sunshine.

Amelia cried out, "*Oh!*" as we sailed above the ocean of clouds that extended as far as could be seen in every direction, gleaming white, smooth as cream here and tumbled there, with Mount Diablo knifing the far billows to the east across the Bay like a fin.

As we strolled the summit she clung to my arm in the uneven

footing, matching her steps to mine. "What a lovely show you have given me!" she said.

"It is only displayed this way for beautiful young ladies," I said.

She laughed her warm breath against my cheek.

She pressed against me as we strolled like lovers among the other couples and two family groups with pinafored and sailor-bloused children running and calling to each other. We admired the prospects and walked on random paths. It was impossible to retire from the view of the others without descending two hundred feet into the clouds. It seemed to me that Amelia's discomfort matched my own.

I held my arm around her waist and she pressed against me, looked into my face with a misty expression and laughed. I laughed with her. We were very far away from the dangers of Taylor Street, and her guardian constable; and my defeats.

"This evening is the *Overland Monthly* salon," I said.

"I have heard of it," Amelia said.

"I am invited, if you wish to attend with me."

"I don't know why I should be so lucky twice in one day!"

"What do you mean?"

"I would admire very much to meet the famous poets of San Francisco!" she exclaimed, leaning her weight against me.

22

WOMAN, *n.*
An animal usually living in the vicinity of
Man, and having a rudimentary susceptibility
to domestication.

—THE DEVIL'S DICTIONARY

A s the editors of San Francisco's leading magazine, Charles Warren Stoddard and Ina Coolbrith were powerful in the literary world. Bierce had published occasional pieces in the *Overland Monthly,* which he referred to as the *Warmedoverland,* and he had invited me to accompany him to last month's salon, where I had been introduced to Stoddard, a plump, effeminate man somewhat older than Bierce. Miss Coolbrith was tall and gracious, with a frieze of fair spit curls across her forehead. Although I had no literary aspirations I had been invited to return, which I understood to be because the young lady poets outnumbered the young men who were to provide them company.

The windows of Stoddard's house on the slopes above North Beach were alight. Inside, the entryway was crowded with guests ridding themselves of coats and hats. Just past them Stoddard stood a host's post, raising his hands palms flippered back at the wrists to greet each new arrival. He wore a white gardenia in his lapel, and his active eyebrows and moues of pleasure kept his face in constant motion.

Ina Coolbrith met us inside the crowded main room. "It is Mr. Redmond, the journalist! And this is?"

"Miss Brittain," I said. "And this is Miss Coolbrith, Amelia."

"I am an admirer of your verse, Miss Coolbrith," Amelia said with an ease I admired. "And we have spent the day at Mount Tamalpais, which is the scene of many of your poems."

Smiling at her, Ina Coolbrith said, "It was there that Mr. Miller and I gathered laurels for him to take to Lord Byron's grave in England."

Joaquin Miller was holding forth to a cluster of female poets across the room, a big blowhard fraud in my estimation, in his blue flannel miner's shirt and shiny boots, which he moved forward and back so that the lady poets in their flowered frocks kept in motion evading his advances and compensating for his retreats. He was recently returned from England, where he was reported to have had a grand success. The British welcomed Westerners whom Easterners found ridiculous. Amelia gazed at the Poet of the Sierra with interest.

On the wall was an oil painting of Stoddard in a monk's cowl, contemplating a skull. I thought the painting silly, and it cast a pall of pretension on Bierce's desk skull.

Entering from a balcony were two handsome young ladies, one in black with a bouquet of violets pinned to her shoulder, the other in shimmering peach silk. Masses of golden hair were piled on her head. The two were such spectacular personages that the attention of the room was directed towards them, and I noticed one of Joaquin Miller's acolytes slip away to join the crowd assembling around these two. In other parts of the room were several portly gentlemen who looked literarily important, one with a bald head sporting sprouts of colorless hair, another in a kind of military tunic, with elaborate longhorn mustachios. Standing beside a dark wood chest inlaid with mother-of-pearl was a pair of young male poets who wore the elaborate bow ties popularized by Oscar Wilde on his recent visit to San Francisco.

Amelia looked around her with such interest that I was pleased I had thought of bringing her to the *Overland Monthly* salon.

"Tom, please inform me who these individuals *are!*" she whispered, for Ina Coolbrith had turned to greet newcomers.

I didn't know who many of them were. "That's Joaquin Miller," I said.

"Oh, there's Mr. Bierce," Amelia said. Bierce, whom I had not seen before, stood near the windows attended by his own band of females.

When I caught his eye we exchanged restrained salutes. I had to explain to him my bargain with Klosters. His glance rested appraisingly on Amelia. For someone who advertised his dislike of the female gender, Bierce did have a weakness for pretty women.

The poetess Emma McLachlan came up to be introduced to Amelia. "Please tell me who is the brilliant young lady with the violets!" Amelia said to her, when greetings and introductory comments had been run through. Miss McLachlan had mousy hair and a prim mouth. I did not find her attractive.

"That is Sibyl Sanderson," she said. "She is a talented soprano, who wishes to pursue a career as an opera singer. But her father, Judge Sanderson, will have none of it. She is very daring! She has recently returned from Paris and she dresses always in black and wears violets. When asked if that is what the fashionable ladies are wearing in Paris, she said, 'It is what the demimondaines wear!' "

Amelia looked properly shocked.

"And her companion with the magnificent hair?"

"She is Mrs. Atherton. She has recently serialized a very daring novel in *The Argonaut*. Those two are often seen together."

"*The Randolphs of Redwoods!*" Amelia said. "There was a pseudonym, as I recall."

"Yes, 'Asmodeus.' "

They were talking about matters I knew nothing about, and I was feeling sulky until Amelia touched my hand reassuringly.

"It is her first novel, I believe."

"She claims she has written another which is even better," Miss McLachlan said. "She is married to a ne'er-do-well, they say. George Atherton. She was a Miss Horn."

"What distinguished company!" Amelia said. She told me that she wished to pay her respects to Mr. Miller and departed to join the bevy around the blue flannel shirt.

I was left with Miss McLachlan, who gave me her tight-lipped smile like a wink.

"Asmodeus was some kind of devil," I said.

"The destroyer of domestic happiness," she said. "He destroyed each of Sara's seven husbands in succession."

"Think of that," I said.

"Have you read the novel, Mr. Redmond?"

I admitted that I had not and resolved not to. Amelia was now engaged in conversation with Joaquin Miller. I saw that she stood her ground when he lurched toward her.

When I had detached myself from Miss McLachlan I collected a glass of punch from a Chinese boy in a white shirt and black tie and made my way through conversational twos and threes toward Bierce's orbit. I was sweating in the heat of the crush of bodies and the gas-lights.

Bierce introduced me as his associate, which caused some interest. Amelia had abandoned Joaquin Miller and drifted over to join the group around the two daring young ladies.

Ina Coolbrith stood beside me. She seemed to be holding herself very stiffly, hands grasping her forearms. She smelled of rosewater.

In a lull in the conversation she said in a challenging tone, "I see that you have devastated another young poet in Tattle this week, Ambrose."

Bierce bowed his head to her but did not respond.

"I wonder if she will ever write another verse."

"If she does, it is probable that she will not send it to me for review," Bierce said.

There was tittering among the young ladies around him, which I saw that Miss Coolbrith did not like.

"My niece, whom you also cruelly turned into a joke, has sworn she will never write again."

Bierce said, "I wish that I were able to consider that a tragedy, Ina."

"I do," Miss Coolbrith said. "For I consider poetry unwritten to be elevated thought unexpressed, and elevated thought may help to make the world a better place. But of course elevated thought is not your metier, Ambrose."

"That is of course true, madam," Bierce said, and I saw from the whitening of his nostrils, that he had restrained himself from saying more.

"I told my niece that yours is not the voice of the muse," Miss Coolbrith continued. "But only of a cruel and disappointed man."

"Disappointed, madam?"

"Disappointed," Miss Coolbrith said, and I thought she meant it as cruelly as the cruelty of which she had accused Bierce. It seemed to me that one of them now, dramatically, must storm from the room. But Bierce only turned to address himself to one of his young ladies, and Miss Coolbrith, brushing at a wisp of hair on her forehead and affixing a smile to her face, turned to greet a young man in black broadcloth who looked like a preacher. I eased myself toward where Amelia stood listening to a speech Mrs. Atherton was making, with florid gestures.

When I looked back again Bierce had disappeared.

Amelia congratulated me on my friends as she and I walked over Nob Hill in the blessed cool air toward her home.

I said I could hardly claim they were my friends. I was no literary person.

"Surely there is a place for a journalist in such an accomplished group. Your Mr. Bierce was on a pedestal. And Miss McLachlan is quite interested in you."

"It is not a mutual interest."

She held my arm. We walked slowly so as not to arrive at 913 Taylor Street before we had to. She had a way of stretching her gait to match mine. Often our hips brushed.

The mansions of the magnates began to loom around us, facades lit by moonlight.

"What was the trouble between Mr. Bierce and Miss Coolbrith?" Amelia inquired.

"He gave her niece's poems a savage review."

"Her niece should not have sent her poetry to him. He is infamous for his savage treatment of poets."

"A word of praise from him would be important. You remarked how those young ladies flocked around him."

"Are they all poets?"

"I'm sure a number of them are. Miss McLachlan is a poet." And I told her that she herself had been the most beautiful woman in that place.

She laughed and squeezed my hand. "You just think that because you *like* me, Tom. I am so happy that you would think that! But there were two very handsome and very accomplished women there. I am not accomplished at all!"

I said I wasn't sure she should want to be as accomplished as Gertrude Atherton.

Amelia was silent for a long time, as though considering that. "She is very pleased with herself," she announced finally. "She is a wife and mother who is contemptuous of women who are wives and mothers." And she added, "She said a curious thing."

"What is that?"

"She said California girls are as flavorless as the pistachio. Doesn't that seem an odd thing to say?"

"Is the pistachio so flavorless?"

"That is not what I mean. She must have known that most of her auditors were California girls. What is the point in telling us we are flavorless?"

"You said she was pleased with herself."

"Who is herself a California girl. But I am sure she considers herself an uncommon one."

We walked on.

"I think I would not be that way," Amelia said.

I did not inquire her meaning. In the moonlit dark, scuds of fog drifted seemingly close enough overhead to reach up and touch. Down a block I could see the hulk of the McNair mansion, a line of first-floor windows alight. Beau must be there, unless he was abroad on his "researches," the idea of which angered me as much as Joaquin Miller's pretensions.

To the left the moon gleamed on the high smooth planking of Charles Crocker's spite-fence, another Railroad outrage, and a project Bierce had assigned me that I hadn't begun to work on yet. I berated myself that I would think to recoup being scared off of Senator Jennings by scarifying Charles Crocker.

Amelia said, "I would have neither the presumption nor the courage to send verses I have written to Mr. Bierce."

I said carefully that I would be pleased if she would give me her poems to read. Again she was silent for a time.

"I do not think I will do that, thank you," she said finally, and it seemed best not to disagree with her. "Tom," she said, "I think you must be very careful not to become like Mr. Bierce."

"Yes," I said, and she gripped my hand in her strong hand. The street steepened beneath our feet. Below and on the right ahead of us were the high gables and the lighted windows of the Brittain house. Amelia halted.

"If you wish to kiss me you must kiss me now!"

I kissed her lips. Embracing her affected my knees, kissing her my breath.

"That was very nice," she whispered, as we continued our descent to 913 Taylor. When we climbed the stairs a figure rose from a chair on the porch, the constable on duty, raising his helmet in salute to Amelia.

"All safe and quiet on the premises, Miss Brittain," he said.

He retreated down the porch while I bid Amelia good night. "It was such a lovely day for me, Tom," she whispered. When she turned away I saw by the light through the window that her face gleamed with tears.

23

PILLORY, *n.*
*A mechanical device for inflicting personal dis-
tinction—prototype of the modern newspaper
conducted by persons of austere virtues and
blameless lives.*
—THE DEVIL'S DICTIONARY

n Monday morning Bierce was
not in his office. The chalky skull
gaped at me as I seated myself at
my desk. I heard the approach-
ing hard rap of footsteps. It was not Miss Penryn, but a woman in a
tweedy, country jacket and skirts, and a tight-fitting cap sporting a
pheasant feather curved over her forehead like a sickle. It was Lillie
Coit.

"Good morning, Mrs. Coit!" I said, jumping to my feet.

She squinted at me out of her brown, freckled face, frowning, then
producing a smile. "Oh, it is Mr. Redmond. Bierce's not here?"

"He hasn't arrived yet, Mrs. Coit."

She moved inside the office to seat herself in the spare chair beside
Bierce's desk. She did not sit with her ankles crossed, but with her
feet planted eight inches apart in sturdy brown shoes.

"Are you a friend of Bierce's, Mr. Redmond?"

She was gazing at me with her mouth pursed and her eyes intent.
It was a serious question.

"I think so," I said.

"I am his friend also. And what a talent he has for quarreling with his
friends! What a talent he has for former friends. If I tell him what I have

come to tell him, I am afraid that I will become a former friend."

I had seen Bierce quarreling with a former friend last evening.

"Yesterday I saw Mollie Bierce and the children in the village," Mrs. Coit said with a sigh. "That is a very unfortunate situation." She leaned forward toward me.

"Mr. Redmond, Bierce likes to boast that no one, man or woman, has seen him in the buff. Are you aware of this curious source of pride? I know he was wounded in the War. Can you tell me if his wound is such a disfiguring one that he would not want even his wife to see him—*bare?*" I thought she had colored slightly, but her face was so sun-browned it was difficult to tell.

"He was wounded in the temple, at Kennesaw Mountain." It was all I knew.

She tossed her head with a commotion of the pheasant feather. "Might a head wound then explain his difficulties with friends?"

I said, "He takes certain matters very seriously, Mrs. Coit, and is apt to give his opinion seriously. I know he has recently lost a friend by an overly honest review of the poetry of a relation."

"Ina Coolbrith," Lillie Coit said, nodding. "How he loves poet-baiting. Let me tell you this, Mr. Redmond. His philanderings are too well known."

I didn't say anything to that.

"If one is unfaithful to a spouse," she went on. "One does everything possible not to advertise the fact so as not to cause unnecessary pain. That is simply decent manners."

I nodded in agreement.

"I do not take Mollie Bierce's part, you understand. But if he is so contemptuous of her and her family, why did he marry her? He is causing her unnecessary pain."

"I know that he has a number of women friends," I said.

"Young man, those are not friends, those are mistresses. They are a very different thing."

I felt my own face burn.

"He will lose her," Lillie Coit said. "Perhaps that is his intention.

There are certain men who like to boast that they are not the marrying kind, as though this makes them a more admirable member of their gender. But he will lose more besides. He will lose his children. I know he loves that girl child, and the older boy—Day. Mr. Redmond, I see Bierce, if he does not change his ways, losing his friends, losing his wife, losing his children. I shudder to think of his declining years. What can be this inclination he has to destroy every association he has of love or friendship?"

"Mrs. Coit," I said. "In the quarrel that I spoke of, his former friend spoke of him as a disappointed man."

She narrowed her eyes at me. "Do you not understand that, Mr. Redmond? He is a terribly disappointed man. He should be a great personage. He should be a writer of international fame. Instead he is merely a local poet-baiter and Railroad scold. He is mired in satire. This City, the West! has caught satire like a disease! He sees that Mark Twain has broken free of it. Mark Twain has found his heart, but Bierce cannot find his. He is a bitterly disappointed man."

I said I was sorry to hear her say this.

"I can say it because I consider him my friend, but I wonder how long it will be before there is a quarrel, or a pretext resulting in one.

"This is what I have come to tell him," she went on. "And I cannot describe how relieved I am that he is not here. I wonder if you would be able to convey my fears to him, Mr. Redmond?"

"I cannot," I said. "I am only his associate. I cannot presume to advise him. He would not wish to feel he had been judged."

She batted at the end of the pheasant feather, as though it had interfered with her vision, and rose.

"I'm sure that is true," she said. "It is a shame, however." She departed in her sudden manner, with her hard quick steps on the flooring of the hallway.

When Bierce came in, walking briskly, he slapped his hands together and insisted that I accompany him to the Palace Hotel for oysters and eggs. I told him that Mrs. Coit had stopped in to see him.

"Ah," he said. "I am sorry I missed *that* lady. There was a lady last night I wish I had missed." It was all he was to say about the quarrel at the *Overland Monthly* salon.

The Palace Hotel breakfast specialty was served from a sideboard in a mahogany-paneled room illuminated by skylights. Bierce and I sat at a marble-topped table with our yellow mix of oysters and scrambled eggs that I was not sure my bruised stomach was equal to. Bierce pitched right in. I had a sense that he did consider me a friend, as though being coshed, threatened and beaten up by a Railroad gang had proved my value to him. But not a friend who could advise him on the conduct of his life.

I told him of my bargain with Klosters, and the reasons for it.

"I told you once that I had never been intimidated by the Railroad," he said coldly.

It would be easy to find a pretext to quarrel with him, as Mrs. Coit had told me.

"I think your researches into Senator Jennings's past may have served their purpose," he said, relenting.

"Maybe so."

"So Klosters understood that you would not shoot him," he said. "His advantage is that one does not know whether he would or would not shoot."

I had Bierce's revolver in my pocket, as though it had attached itself to me, and I was presently to have employment for it.

Revolvers had played their part in San Francisco hard feelings. A man named Kalloch who was running for mayor on the Workingman's Party ticket was the target of Charles De Young's invective in the *Chronicle*. In a fracas with De Young, Kalloch was wounded. Later on his son shot De Young dead. And Bierce had acquired his own weapon when the husband of an actress he devastated in Tattle threatened him with violence.

All this crossed my mind when I recognized Senator Jennings from Fats Chubb's caricatures in *The Hornet*. He marched across the room toward us, a round-faced man with a cropped reddish-graying beard and a sweat-gleaming bald head. He was preceded by a belly so large he appeared to be carrying a bass drum under his vest. Trotting anxiously behind him, in a frock coat, was a hotel functionary.

Jennings had a booming senatorial voice and he halted ten feet away from our table to shout, "You are a liar and a calumniator, Bierce!"

I rose with my napkin in my hand, but Bierce remained seated behind his plate of oysters and eggs, his napkin tucked into his collar and a nettled frown on his face.

"You are a *Goddamned* liar and calumniator!" Jennings boomed.

Bierce said calmly, "And you, sir, are a footboy of rogues, a menial of thieves, a lackey and lickspittle, a knave, a blackguard, a sneak, a coward. And a murderer!"

"Now, Senator," the hotelman said. "Now, Mr. Bierce."

"Damned liar!" the Senator shouted.

Bierce shoveled in eggs and chewed. He said to the hotelman, "This murderer's adiposity is casting a shadow on my eggs that I fear will turn them rancid. Will you remove him?"

"Oh, Mr. Bierce," the hotelman said.

Senator Jennings produced a derringer from his pocket and leveled it at Bierce.

"Oh, Senator Jennings," the hotelman said. "Please, not in here, sir."

I took Bierce's revolver from my pocket, where its presence had asserted itself.

Bierce pushed his plate aside as though it had indeed been fouled. "You have produced a firearm, Senator Jennings. Is that the argument with which you presume to assert your innocence?"

I made sure that Senator Jennings saw the revolver, pointed at his big belly. "Are you aware of the Concealed Weapon Ordinance, sir?" I said.

His hot eyes fixed on mine. "And who are you, my man?"

"My name is Redmond."

"You are Clete Redmond's son, who has written a scurrilous piece about me."

"Yes, sir." I did not see any reason to tell him that I had been intimidated by Klosters. Perhaps he already knew of it.

The hotelman interposed himself between Jennings and Bierce. He pushed Jennings's hand holding the pistol down, muttering soothing exclamations. I returned Bierce's revolver to my pocket.

"Bierce, I have the means to make your life miserable, and short," Jennings said calmly. "And I intend to use them."

He lumbered off. Bierce motioned to the waiter to remove his plate as I seated myself again.

"We will send these away as they are quite cold," Bierce said. He rose to stride to the sideboard and load another plate with eggs and oysters from the gleaming steamer there.

I had a sense of layers of menace laid over us like blankets on a bed.

"Apparently he is not yet aware of your capitulation to Klosters," Bierce said.

When we had left the Palace after our repast, he said grimly, "I would give the devil his dues if he would provide me with the evidence I need to bring that podgy homicide to the bench of justice."

24

ROMANCE, *n.*
*Fiction that owes no allegiance to the God of
Things as They Are.*
—THE DEVIL'S DICTIONARY

gt. Nix propped his helmet on the desk beside the skull, shaking his head as Bierce told him about the encounter with Jennings at the Palace Hotel.

"He's too big for the captain to go after," Nix said. "You'd have to have a squad of ministers swearing on a carload of Bibles that they saw him strangle Judge Hamon's widow."

"Any word from the daughter in San Diego?" Bierce asked.

"She and Hamon didn't get along. She doesn't know anything."

"Tom's been nosing into Mammy Pleasant's past history," Bierce said.

"Those're tolerable high-power Nobs that used to play those games out at Geneva Cottage," Nix said, shaking his head again. "Course we always knew what Mammy was. Do you know how many abortions a month it takes to keep a crib going? Cowyards and parlorhouses? They've got some kind of pessary thing soaked in quinine and some herbs that makes them barren for awhile, but it is still abortions mostly. And was back when Mammy Pleasant was in the business. There's always midwifes around, but she was the tony one for the Nobs. Abortions and baby-furnishing. No one ever went after her for any of that. This is San Francisco. There has been funny business at the Bell house too. But they say she and Allan Pinkerton was pals from the days when she had to do with the Underground Railroad. Captain Pusey is tolerable careful with her. I've noticed.

"They say she's in court every day. Right in the middle of things too. Sarah Althea and her lawyers having a confab at their table, she'll stick her black head right in the middle of it. Of course she is paying the bills. Miss Hill and her new lawyer's a couple of turtledoves, I hear. I expect some of that's for Sharon's benefit."

There was some discussion of *Sharon v. Sharon,* which seemed to be going Sarah Althea Hill's way at the moment.

Bierce asked if Beau McNair was in custody or out.

"Out," Nix said. "His mother's on hand. Got in last night."

"Now Captain Pusey will spring his trap," Bierce said.

"Let's see what you have on Mammy Pleasant," Bierce said, when Nix had gone. I brought him the typescript:

> Mary Ellen Pleasant arrived in San Francisco in 1853, a passenger on the SS *Oregon.* Also aboard was a young Scotsman named Thomas Bell, and a long-standing connection was formed. Mrs. Pleasant was a quadroon who could pass for white and did so in a San Francisco that was more interested in handsome women than in distinctions of color. It may be that she knew of some crime or aberration in Thomas Bell's past, because she has kept a rein on him as his fortunes flourished in San Francisco. She was renowned as a chef and was passed from kitchen to kitchen among the aristocracy of Rincon Hill and Nob Hill. It was said that she could command a cook's wage of $500 a month, with the stipulation that she wash no dishes.
>
> In the employ of wealthy men she found a role as an organizer of elaborate parties, with the service of beautiful females she always seemed to know how to procure. In the late '60s she operated a prosperous house of assignation where the Bonanza kings were often to be found: William Ralston, Darius Mills and William Sharon, as well as Thomas Bell, who

had become a financier of considerable means. In 1869 she opened a Pleasure Palace at the junction of the Geneva and San Jose Roads called Geneva Cottage. Parties were limited to ten, the fee was $500. Financiers, politicians, bankers and mining kings visited Geneva Cottage for stag parties. A popular amusement was a game of Nymphs and Satyrs, with Nymphs shedding garments as they fled into the darkness of Geneva Cottage's park, and aging Satyrs puffing in pursuit. There were rumors about harsh treatment of the girls, and at least one troublesome Nymph dropped from sight. Such rumors were not pursued by the police because of Mrs. Pleasant's connections.

In the '70s she purchased a new "boardinghouse" at 920 Washington Street, where the opening revels were presided over by Governor Newton Booth and his Secretary of State, Drury Malone. William Sharon, William Ralston and Nathaniel McNair were on hand for the event.

Out of her party organization and procuring facilities, Mrs. Pleasant progressed to matchmaking. A beautiful young woman of her stable became engaged to, and later married, Thomas Bell. India Howard, who had been the chief ornament at Geneva Cottage, also married well. Another of Mammy Pleasant's girls was Sarah Althea Hill, who took up residence in the Grand Hotel that was paid for by Senator Sharon. In the current trial of *Sharon v. Sharon,* Mrs. Pleasant is the chief witness for Miss Hill, or Mrs. Sharon, as the case may be.

In the early '70s Mrs. Pleasant held San Francisco real estate of considerable value and, advised by Thomas Bell, had also prospered in mining stocks. These were lost in the crash of the Bank of California in 1875. Many considered William Sharon responsible for the Bank debacle and Ralston's suicide. Mammy Pleasant may blame her financial downfall on Senator Sharon, and her active participation in Sarah Althea Hill's claim on the Sharon fortune may be motivated by revenge.

After the Bank crash Mrs. Pleasant moved into Thomas Bell's mansion on Octavia Street as his "housekeeper" presumably under the direction of his wife, Teresa Bell, once one of the Geneva Cottage attractions.

Bierce didn't seem much interested in what I had collected, staring out the window frowning. Probably he was disappointed that I had found no Railroad connection. The fact was that the Big Four seemed not to have participated in any of the Geneva Cottage revels presided over by Mammy Pleasant but remained faithful to their wives and husbanded their money.

"She knows who the Slasher is," Bierce said. "But she does not see any 'gain' to helping us. But I will get it out of her!"

And he took the occasion to deliver a lecture concerning the usage of "shall" and "will," as though he could not pass on a piece of my writing without commentary.

"In the first person a mere intention is indicated by 'shall,' " he said. "I shall go. Whereas 'will' denotes some degree of compliance or determination. I will go—as if my going had been requested or forbidden. In the second and third person, 'will' merely forecasts, but 'shall' implies something of promise, permission or compulsion by the speaker."

"We shall track the Slasher down," I said.

"That is correct," Bierce said.

I sat with Amelia Brittain in the pergola behind the Brittain house. Squares of sunlight fell through the interstices of the laths of the roof onto the table, the pitcher of iced tea, our glasses, my hat and Amelia's hand, fingers spread on the table before her. She wore light blue with tricky sewn ridges of material that made little epaulets on her shoulders. I couldn't keep my eyes off the smooth flesh of her neck. Her pink lips smiled at me. She had greeted me as her hero, but she seemed sad today.

Constable Riley, her day-guardian, sat on the stoop above us with his chair tilted back against the wall behind him, and his trousers stretched over his fat knees.

"Do you remember the clock in *Vanity Fair?*" Amelia asked.

I sipped iced tea. "Remind me."

"In the Osbornes' house there was a clock decorated with a brass grouping depicting the sacrifice of Iphigenia."

"Sacrificed so the Greek fleet could set sail against Troy," I said, to prove I knew my mythology.

"The daughter of Agamemnon," Amelia said. It was as though she was assisting me with answers to the questions of an examination. "Because the winds were blowing the wrong way, preventing the fleet from sailing.

"In the novel the clock is tolling. Mr. Osborne is wearing a kind of military suiting, brass buttons and so on. Something is wrong. The daughters ask what is wrong. And one of them says, 'The funds must be falling.' "

I didn't remember.

"The winds were unfriendly," Amelia said, watching me. "One of the daughters would have to be sacrificed."

I was irritated that she should have read more into *Vanity Fair* than I had.

"Sacrificed?" I said.

"To a marriage for economic reasons. A girl's girlhood ended before she is ready for it, because the funds are falling."

She looked disappointed because I had had to be prompted.

I could feel my heart beating. "And the funds are falling?"

She plucked up her damp-glistening tumbler and cooled her cheek with it. She nodded.

I could hardly say it. "Beau McNair?" I asked.

She shook her head. "Poppa will not have that."

"What does he have against Beau?"

"Beau reminds him of my uncle. My Father has a twin brother who is always off somewhere writing back for money. He's a rake and a drunkard and charming. He's in the Hawaiian Islands now. I don't think Beau is like him at *all*."

I didn't care what her father had against Beau, but I cared that her face had been naked with relief when she had realized it could not have been Beau who attacked her on the porch, because he was in jail. I cared that she cared for Beau.

"Did you want to marry Beau?"

She smiled at me. "I was not ready for my girlhood to be ended." She looked down at her hands spread on the tabletop, striped with sunlight.

"Who will you be required to marry, then?" I asked. I couldn't believe that I was having this conversation with my True Love.

"Someone very wealthy. I don't know yet."

My jaws ached. "It is terrible," I said. "It is *medieval*. It's like the Middle Ages. It is a terrible thing to do to a—lovely young woman."

"Oh, I think it is a comedy. Except when it happens to you it is not so comical."

"Will you run away with me?"

She shook her head, smiling still. "Thank you, Tom."

I made a business of picking up my own tumbler, and examining the contents and sipping the sweet tea. On the stoop Constable Riley sat sweating in the sun, gazing into the distance.

"Do you love me?" she whispered.

I closed my eyes. "I thought you were my True Love. I've never—" I stopped myself.

"It's not the way it should be," she said. "You saved me from the Minotaur, so the king should give you my hand. But the funds are falling."

My anger had risen to choke me. "It is—terrible!" was all I could say.

"I am quite lucky," she said, shaking her head. "If I had no social standing, no resources, no family, my fate could very well be like that of Miss Hill."

"What's the difference?" I said.

"There is all the difference in the world! As a married woman when my husband passes on I will be a woman of independent means. Miss Hill, who has no husband, has no such bulwark."

I did not wish to argue with her about the Rose of Sharon.

"I will never forget you," she said in her cool voice. "Perhaps you will never forget me. We will go our separate ways, but it will have been—something. That will be important all our lives. That will become a part of our lives and our characters, and our *being*. It is something I have already written pages in my diary about. That I will write poems about."

"This is *America!*" I said helplessly. The Democracy! I felt sick with anger. And despite myself my anger focused on Amelia, who would let herself be sold like a Negro slave because it was part of some society comedy that amused her. For her character and *being!*

My own father and mother suddenly seemed paragons, and I felt a swell of righteousness at being poor and honest, and free. My father who might have been a silver king if the foxes and sheep had been differently arrayed. Thank the Good Lord that they had not!

I stood up. The patterns of sunlit squares swam in my eyes.

"I don't want it to be like this," Amelia said.

"I guess you don't have any say in it, do you?" I hadn't wanted to say that.

"My offer remains," I said. I knew my offer was as silly as she must know it. What did I have to offer her?

"Thank you, my hero," she whispered.

Her hand stretched across the table where I could have taken it, but I turned away from her. I didn't want her to see my face.

I tramped up the back steps past Constable Riley, who made a saluting gesture as I passed, and strode through the dark hallway and out onto the veranda, where the broken railing had now been repaired, and down the steps to Taylor Street.

It was too early in the day to visit Annie Dunker.

25

BIRTH, *n.*
The first and direst of all disasters.
—THE DEVIL'S DICTIONARY

hen I had reported my
conversation with Amelia
Brittain to Bierce, keeping
my feelings to myself, he came
out of his chair, clapping his hat on his head and beckoning me along
with him. Mr. Brittain's rejection of Beau McNair had caught his interest.

We hailed a hack to take us to Taylor Street. I had sworn I would
never return there, but at least Amelia and Mrs. Brittain were not in
evidence. The butler ushered us into Mr. Brittain's study where his
roll-topped desk was strewn with documents, and the glass-topped
cases of gold nuggets gleamed in the afternoon light. I gritted my
teeth to think of him selling his daughter into slavery because of the
falling funds.

However, he wrung my hand as his daughter's savior and greeted
Bierce amiably, a tall, thin man with a Virginia City limp and financial
difficulties.

When we were settled in chairs, Bierce said, "Mr. Brittain, we are
trying to get to the bottom of these murderous slashings of prostitutes.
Apparently the same fellow attacked your daughter."

"Young Redmond was the hero in that encounter!" Mr. Brittain had not seated himself but moved among his cases with his hands clasped behind his back, his lined face solemn. He wore pince-nez spectacles that glinted in the sunlight through the window.

"There is a connection of playing cards to events in Virginia City twenty some years ago," Bierce said.

Brittain halted to stare at him.

"The Jack of Spades Mine."

"Ah!"

"Had William Sharon any connection to the Jack of Spades, or Caroline LaPlante?"

Mr. Brittain's features contracted into a startlingly ugly expression. "She detested him! She was not often treated as a low woman, but Sharon had done so. He engineered an enterprise she felt was below her, and he enjoyed her discomfiture."

I saw Bierce digesting that. Mr. Brittain must mean the Lady Godiva ride through Virginia City. Or something else?

"You were a mining engineer there, sir," Bierce said.

Brittain dipped his head in acknowledgment. There was no point of sitting in his chair hating him. These people were different from other people. Money made them different.

"You were employed by the late Nathaniel McNair?" Bierce asked.

"That is correct."

"A pile-driver of a man, I should imagine."

"A difficult man," Brittain said. He paced, hands clasped behind his back. "It was his practice to make his associates feel small. He had an ability to estrange his friends while still binding them to him by various means."

"Such as the invention of belittling nicknames," Bierce said smoothly. " 'The Englishman' in your case. And 'English.' "

Mr. Brittain looked startled. "Now how would you know that, Mr. Bierce?"

"Tom, relate to Mr. Brittain the use of that name you encountered in the Washoe."

I said, "It had to do with a scandal that took place at the Consolidated-Ohio. There was a complication of a claim being salted that was called 'the English shuffle.' Devers told me the term referred to someone of that name who devised a particular practice."

Brittain backed away to seat himself in a leather chair. He removed his glasses from his nose with a good deal of process, folded them and slipped them into his breast pocket. His cheeks had reddened in unhealthy-looking stripes.

"It was a practice I had nothing to do with. It was a joke of Nat's. A cruel joke. My reputation—" he started and stopped.

"Your good reputation is well known, sir," Bierce said.

"Nat McNair was not an honest man," Brittain said. "He was a true disciple of Will Sharon's. He put out a great deal of rumor about drifting into a high-grade orebody. Then the rumor that the assay had been salted. These were cynical maneuvers, a dishonest, conniving business, and very effective. Mining stocks were extraordinarily volatile just then. The stock bottomed out and Nat was able to buy it up very cheaply."

"There was a Bonanza after all?"

"Yes," Brittain said.

"And your part?"

"I had been able to advise him that it looked like a considerable orebody." He held his hands to his cheeks for a moment. "May I ask the purpose of these questions, Mr. Bierce?"

"Mr. Brittain, these murders seem to be the result of a vast degree of hatred and old rage. There is a plan and purpose to them we are as yet unable to discern."

I could hear Mr. Brittain's harsh breathing. "Why *my* daughter, Mr. Bierce?"

"I think it is not a connection with you, sir. But with Beau McNair and ultimately his mother."

Brittain took his glasses from his pocket and began polishing the lenses with a bit of yellow cloth. "I am not proud of my connection with Nat McNair," he said.

"What of your connection with Mrs. McNair?"

I watched Brittain's hands halt in their employment.

"What connection can you mean, Mr. Bierce?"

"You have compelled your daughter to dissolve her engagement to Beau McNair."

Brittain's eyes swung toward me. He moistened his lips. "I believe the match would not be a happy one."

Bierce's voice was gentle. "I think your objection is because your daughter and Beau McNair are half brother and sister."

Brittain closed his eyes.

"Am I correct in this assumption, sir?"

Brittain nodded tiredly. "Can this revelation go no further, gentlemen?"

"If that proves possible," Bierce said.

Brittain looked at me and I nodded, dazed, thinking of Beau engaged to Amelia.

"She was pregnant by you, but she married Nat McNair."

"She wished to be married, but I was not prepared to marry her," Brittain said. "My family is a very proud and prominent one in New Hampshire, Mr. Bierce. It would not have done. I was tortured upon a rack."

I thought of my offer to Amelia, which she had rejected knowing it was meaningless and impossible.

"She had been frightened by the murder of another woman in Virginia City," I said.

Brittain nodded. "Julia Bulette. Yes."

"But she thought you would marry her," Bierce said.

"Yes, she thought that."

"What did she do?"

Brittain replaced his glasses again. "She was determined to have the child, but it would not have done for her to appear pregnant, you see. Her position in Virginia City was such— She disappeared. I believe she went to Sacramento where there was a relative. I don't know how Nat came into the picture. No doubt he had declared himself to her. She could have had any man she wished to choose, except for the one who failed her. It must have been that in her mood she chose the man of her acquaintance who seemed most likely to make a fortune, and one could foresee that Nat would be successful. He was lucky, he was clever, he was ruthless, and he was utterly determined."

"And he took your son as his own."

"Yes."

Brittain's face convulsed as though he were weeping without tears. His expression reminded me of Amelia; her father who would sacrifice her to the falling funds, but not to her half brother. Who remembered so passionately the painting of Highgrade Carrie as Lady Godiva.

Bierce sat thinking, the filtered sunlight silvering the curls of his graying fair hair. I could follow him so far. An English shuffle meant falsification of assay samples in conjunction with spreading dishonest rumors for the purpose of devaluing mining shares. Such a shuffle had given Nathaniel McNair control of the Consolidated-Ohio. I wondered how involved Mr. Brittain had actually been in the procedure.

He and Highgrade Carrie had been good friends, Amelia had said, but were friends no longer. He was uncomfortable with her return to San Francisco. A woman who had been the mother of his child.

"Lady Caroline Stearns is in danger," Bierce said.

Brittain stared at Bierce. His face was graven with deep lines.

"And my daughter?"

"I think her danger is past. Now that she is no longer engaged to be married to young McNair, she is of no more interest to the Slasher."

"So I have unwittingly removed Amelia from danger."

"I think so," Bierce said. He questioned Brittain about the mechanics by which Jennings and Macomber—my father—had been cheated of their interest in the Jack of Spades, but Brittain became monosyllabic and off the point, as though he was genuinely forgetful, or maybe merely distressed. It was as though he could not wait for us to be gone, and so we departed.

"He was in a panic," Bierce said. "I wonder just how innocent this well regarded mining engineer was in the original shuffle, and I wonder if that could be a part of his disaffection with Carrie, that his daughter mentioned to you."

"He refused to marry her," I said. "And she made a better match."

"A more lucrative slavery," Bierce said.

Saturday evening when I came home my father was lounging in the Barnacles' parlor in discussion with Jonas Barnacle. Belinda was seated primly in a straight chair beside the door, her polished shoes set side by side and her hands folded in her lap. She watched me enter with solemn eyes. Mrs. B., aproned, a blue scarf tied over her hair, glanced in from the next room.

My father wore a dark suit, boots and a florid tie with a diamond pin. Still jawing at Jonas Barnacle, he rose and put a possessive hand on my shoulder. The hand felt heavy as a sad-iron. He marched me outside.

"Tommy," he said. "We are heading for the Bella Union Saturday night parade. I have tickets!"

We entered the Bella Union through a large barroom packed with men and were seated at a table on the lower level of the pretty little theater, below a stage with a garishly painted drop curtain. Behind and above us were curtained stalls like a receding wall of pigeonholes. We ordered Piscos and watched a madam enter leading her bevy of handsome girls in their finery, with bright mouths and bold eyes glancing right and left while the men clapped and catcalled. The madam herself was stout, with an imperial manner of directing her flock into their stall. These were not the middle-class young ladies of "the line" who had so impressed Amelia, but they were striking women with perfect toilettes also.

It was the regular Saturday night parade where the madams showed off their girls.

"I do fancy these flaunting doves," my father confessed. "There is nothing like them in Sacramento. Women will simply not show bare arms in Sacramento."

There was whistling from the barroom as a second madam led in her charges, this one tall with feathers nodding from her hat. Her girls were indeed bare-armed, and proud in their paint and vivid fabrics, their boots crackling on the wooden floor. They were accompanied by more whistling from the barroom. The second group disappeared into their stall as a third group appeared. My father clapped for the feather-boaed madam with her blazing smile for the men appreciating her girls.

I thought of Caroline LaPlante as a madam in Virginia City, whose beauty and style had captured the town, and whose own heart had been captured by a man whose station would not allow him to marry a low woman.

And Amelia's responsibility was to marry a wealthy man. Aristocrats!

More whores passed in a cloud of perfumery, giggling, rustling fabrics, noisy boots. The gaslights gleamed on the flesh of their necks and arms.

"Other places," the Gent said, "the fancy women dress like the society women. In San Francisco it's the other way round."

Including Sibyl Sanderson, who preferred to dress like a Parisian demimondaine. I could inform Amelia that I was aware of the ironies of my father's views compared to her own, if I were ever to see her again.

Another bouquet of women made its entrance.

"I believe it does a man good to watch pretty women in their little boots," my father said.

The curtain was raised to reveal a half-circle of male and female performers. The women's outfits were as skimpy as those of the whores were lush. There was laughter and applause.

I could feel the heat from the gaslamps that illuminated the stage. A fat comedian told jokes with gestures I found distasteful.

The Gent leaned toward me. His expression was one of more sorrow than anger. "I heard you had some trouble, Son," he said.

"I would be sorry to learn you sent those ruffians after me, Pa."

He leaned toward me with a hand cupped to his ear, for the band had struck up a din of music. "What were you doing at a meeting like that anyhow? True Blue Democrats! The Boss and Sam Rainey are common malefactors, my boy!"

"Well, you work for *un*common ones."

"Tommy, those fine gents make our livings along with theirs. They make the state a better place! The railroad is like a mess of arteries that brings the blood to the organs and members, to the fingers and the head and the John Thomas. Without it you have just got nothing at all!

"Look at these folks you think you like! They have got their fingers in every till. Look at this business with the school board! Your Chris Buckley, the Blind Boss! He is not so blind as not to know the color of greenback dollars. How much do those dummies pay Buckley to be on the school board and pick the public's pocket? The Water Board? The mayor!"

"How much does the Railroad pay Senator Jennings to front up the Girtcrest Corridor Bill?"

"But that is to the benefit of this great state!"

"It is to the benefit of Leland Stanford, Charles Crocker and Collis Huntington. Will you tell me Senator Jennings is trying to make the Nation great?"

"Son, son," my father said and swung around to guffaw at the latest sally from the jokester on the stage. This one wore a hat too small for him and a long necktie, the end of which hung out of his trouser cuff. There was laughter also from the stalls where the madams had arrayed their girls.

The show of prostitutes at the Bella Union was not what I wanted to be watching when my heart was broken.

When the Gent turned back, he said, "Jennings had this painting in his office at the legislature. Lady didn't just have bare arms, she was bare all over. Horseback lady. My, she was a pure vision!"

I felt the hairs at the back of my neck prickle. "Lady Godiva," I said.

"Lady Godiva was what she was outfitted as! He had so many complaints from his constituents he had to take her down."

Constituents who didn't object to Jennings in the pay of the Railroad but did object to bare female flesh in his offices.

"What did he do with the painting?"

"Got rid of it, I guess," the Gent said, frowning. "He'd bought it from the Bucket of Blood there in Virginia City that had commissioned it."

"It was Highgrade Carrie, wasn't it?"

I thought he hadn't heard me, in another burst of laughter around us. But after a moment he looked back at me solemnly. "Yes, it was, Son."

I had not yet presented the information on the painting of Highgrade Carrie as Lady Godiva to Bierce.

"Set up by Senator Sharon, as I understand it."

"It seems you have learned a good deal about Virginia City twenty years ago, Son."

"I've learned that Senator Jennings is a murderer," I said. "Bierce is going to prove it."

The Gent did not respond to that, looking troubled. The slashes of white in his whiskers caught the light. I swigged the sour Pisco Punch.

A troupe of dancers had come onstage, waving flags in a flurry of red and white stripes, and prancing with plump legs in tights to the beat and horns of the overly enthusiastic band of music. There was a great deal of whistling.

I said, looking my father straight in the face, "Maybe when you are young you are more concerned with right and wrong. Do you still think about right and wrong?"

"Maybe I have got a more comprehensive view of what it is, Son. Mr. Bierce has got it screwed up so tight it strictures him bad, it seems to me."

"Do you think it is right for Senator Jennings to murder Judge Hamon's widow?"

His face slumped. After a long moment, he said, "No, I don't."

I thought I had spoiled his evening at the Bella Union, and I was not enjoying the show either. Amelia admitting she was for sale like any one of these painted women had screwed my insides so tight as to stricture me badly.

"Pa," I said. "Why did men change their names on the Washoe?"

"Same reason they changed their name when they came West. Forty-niners changed their names too. Change their life. Change their luck. Trouble with the law. Trouble at home. Complications with women."

I couldn't bring myself to ask which had been his reason.

"Did you know Highgrade Carrie well?"

"Not so well," he said. "Admired her till she and Nat and Will got together for the euchre. But I expect that was Nat's doing. I will admit there've been some hard feelings." He chuckled unhappily. "Well, she brought some momentoes of the Washoe to that wedding."

The word snapped in my head like a cap pistol.

"Momentoes," I said shakily. "How would you spell that?"

"How would *you* spell it, Son? You are the educated fellow here."

I spelled *m-o-m-e-n-t-o*.

"That'd be it," he said. "Why?"

"No reason," I said.

We stuck it through to the flag-waving end. When we left through the barroom I saw a familiar face. It was Beau with his fair-bearded cheeks and a gray muffler around his neck. I thought he had seen me, but he made no sign of recognition. The muffler and the ill-fitting jacket must be his disguise for the "researches" Amelia had mentioned.

"Who was that fellow?" the Gent wanted to know, when we had come out onto the street.

"That is the British gentleman Beaumont McNair," I said. "The son of Lady Caroline Stearns."

I thought for a moment he was going to insist on going back to introduce himself.

26

MUSTANG, *n.*
An indocile horse of the western plains. In English society, the American wife of an English nobleman.

—THE DEVIL'S DICTIONARY

ierce returned from St. Helena on Monday. Tuesday morning he was summoned to the offices of Bosworth Curtis in the Monkey Block. He took me along. Curtis, Bakewell & Stewart was on the second floor above Malvolio's Restaurant, with fine leather furniture in a sitting room with windows looking out over Montgomery Street, and a typewriter at a little table with her black Remington machine before her. When she swiveled ninety degrees she presided over a reception desk from which she asked Bierce and me to have a seat. A neat little person in a tan skirt and shirtwaist, she rose and left the room to tell Lawyer Curtis we were on hand.

She showed us into another big room with windows that looked out on the Customs House. Curtis was seated behind a desk the size of a Faro layout, with two people before him. One was Beau McNair, back in fancy tailoring today. The other was a lady in a shiny black hat with a veil covering her face, and gray and black layers of cloaks and jackets and skirts of materials expensive-looking just in their texture, black gloves and polished black boots, one of which twitched with a rhythm of impatience. It was Lady Caroline Stearns, though I couldn't make out her face inside the black veil. I had a sense of Bierce stiffening to military attention beside me.

Beau McNair rose. Curtis was already on his feet, an ugly little terrier of a man with his pink, shiny-skinned face and white hair brushed straight back. He didn't come around his desk to shake hands with Bierce or me.

"Mr. Bierce, I believe," he said in his bark of a voice. "Lady Caroline, this is the journalist of whom we have spoken. Lady Caroline Stearns. Mister Beaumont McNair. And this young gentleman?"

"My assistant," Bierce said. "Mister Thomas Redmond."

"We have met," I said to Beau, whom I had seen at the City Jail with Curtis and Rudolph Buckle, in the park with Amelia Brittain and at the Bella Union last night.

Beau glanced toward me solemnly, nodding. I thought it just as well not to give him the wink. He was a handsome young fellow, no doubt about it. Amelia's half brother. I could see no resemblance. I wondered if I would ever be in a situation to afford a jacket like that. It looked like he spread it on instead of arming into it like lesser beings.

"How do you do, Mr. Bierce," Lady Caroline said. Her boot had stopped twitching. Her voice was low, pleasant, with a trace of British accent. The former Highgrade Carrie of Virginia City.

"How do you do, Lady Caroline."

There was a motion of her head, possibly a nod to me.

"We have a mutual acquaintance in Miss Brittain, Redmond," Beau said to me.

"That is so," I said.

"Please sit down, Mr. Bierce, Mr. Redmond," Curtis said, seating himself. Bierce settled in a leather armchair, I on the far edge of a sofa.

"I have requested this meeting, Mr. Bierce," Lady Caroline said in her pleasant voice. "It is good of you to come. My son is in difficulty with the police, and I have been led to believe you may assist us. I am informed that you have been following these terrible murders closely and may have come to some conclusions."

"I may be able to assist *you,* madam," Bierce said.

There was a clench of tension that froze the assembled in their various postures.

Curtis tented his hands together on his desk top. "May I ask what you mean, Mr. Bierce?"

"I believe that these murders and Mr. McNair's apparent involvement in them have been contrived to bring Lady Caroline to San Francisco, where she is in danger from someone whose hatred has turned to lunacy."

The silence had texture and weight, like a block of cement.

"Who would that be, Mr. Bierce?" Lady Caroline whispered. I had a sense of slimness inside her layers of clothing, of blondness under the hat within the veil. Her black gloves worked together, one sliding over the other. I was aware of a sexual emanation so subtle it seemed to be part of her scent of flowers.

"I do not know that yet, madam," Bierce said, folding his arms on his chest.

Lady Caroline glanced at Curtis, who said grimly, "Have you evidence of this, Mr. Bierce?"

"Each of the murdered women has been marked with a playing card, a spade. Lady Caroline will remember the Society of Spades in Virginia City. Each of the murders except one has been accomplished in such a way as to implicate her son."

"I don't understand," Beau started.

Bierce interrupted. "I have seen you referred to as the Queen of Spades, Lady Caroline. Each of the numerical cards has been a progression toward the face cards."

Beneath the veil I could see Lady Caroline's lips round into an O.

"There has been a conspiracy to bring you back here, madam."

"It is young Mr. McNair we wish to consult with you about," Curtis said. "We have information that the police have evidence against him that has not yet been produced."

"Probably that is so," Bierce said.

"Captain Pusey," I said.

Curtis's eyes slid toward me, hard as agates. "Yes, Captain Pusey."
Bierce flicked a finger that I was to continue.

"It is mysterious that Captain Pusey possessed a photograph of young Mr. McNair, which he showed to a woman who might have seen the murderer in the second instance."

"That identification could be successfully challenged in a court of law," Curtis said.

"That is not the point, Bos," Lady Caroline said.

"The point is that Pusey knew of an escapade Mr. McNair was involved in in London," Bierce said. "The particularities of that escapade have been copied and made lethal, to convince the police of Mr. McNair's guilt. The murderer learned of the arrest in London by channels that lead back to Pusey. Pusey had the photograph in his archive of photographs, and he did not show it to the witness by chance. You have evidently been given notice that he has more evidence, which he is withholding."

"It is simply blackmail then," Lady Caroline said. "Captain Pusey's reputation is known to me." She did not sound much concerned.

"Captain Pusey is not as clever as he thinks himself," Curtis said.

"It seems I am the target, not my mother," Beau said. He was sitting very erect. His cropped beard looked like a sheen of gold on his cheeks and chin. I thought his eyes too close together.

"Your mother through you," Bierce said.

"Mr. Bierce, may I ask what is your interest in these horrible murders?" Curtis said.

"I am a journalist, sir," Bierce said.

"May we inquire what more you know of them?"

"A murderer, who must be considered a madman, slaughtered two women in Morton Street," Bierce said. "The third murder was not committed by the same person, but by Senator Aaron Jennings. The victim was the wife of a judge who had served with Jennings on the Circuit Court and who had evidence of Jennings's corruption. This evidence was to be made public, and to that end Mrs. Hamon had an appointment with me the next day. Jennings tried to hire a murderer

to accomplish the murder, but the man had meanwhile become religious, so Jennings did the work himself. The crime was made to look
similar to the other two murders."

"This is a base canard!" Curtis exploded. "Senator Jennings—"

"Is the murderer of Mrs. Hamon and I intend to prove it," Bierce
interrupted. Lady Caroline's gloved hand made a motion at her lawyer, who subsided.

"The fourth murder was the original Slasher at work again,"
Bierce continued. "Again it was an effort to incriminate Mr. McNair,
for the victim was an attachment of his. An attempt was made on the
life of Mr. McNair's then-fiancée, Miss Brittain, which Mr. Redmond
here was in a position to foil."

"The engagement had been broken off," McNair said in what
seemed to me an insufferable tone, as though he had done the breaking off.

"Nevertheless, she could have been considered to be an attachment at the time of the attack."

I could feel Lady Caroline's gaze. There was a silence of information being digested.

"Mr. Bierce," Lady Caroline said. "I have the sense that you want
something. Will you tell me what that is?"

"I will be able to clear this matter up if I am given some assistance,"
Bierce said. "I believe that I will soon be able to identify the person
who wishes you and your son ill, madam."

"If you are given some assistance," she said gently.

"I believe you know a man named Elza Klosters."

There was another of the stiff silences.

"Who was employed by your late husband," Bierce added.

"I remember Elza Klosters," Lady Caroline said. She was slowly
stripping the glove from her left hand, her head bowed to the process.

"And Adolphus Jackson?"

"What is the pertinence of these questions, may I ask?" Curtis
demanded.

"Senator Jennings was known to Lady Caroline as Adolphus Jackson. He was one of the Society of Spades and has cause to feel abused by Lady Caroline and her then husband.''

''Abused?'' Beau said harshly.

''Swindled then.''

Curtis said, ''Are you implying that Senator Jennings is our madman? I will not believe—''

''Senator Jennings is no madman,'' Bierce said. ''He is, however, a murderer.''

''Is he a part of the conspiracy you have mentioned?'' Lady Caroline asked. For the first time she sounded breathless. I could see her hand, spread-fingered before her bosom; it was not a young hand.

''I do not know that yet, madam. You have perceived that I want something. I am bound to see Senator Jennings prosecuted for the murder of Mrs. Hamon. You can help me accomplish that.''

Bierce would give the prosecution of Jennings precedence over the Slashings because he was set like a locomotive on rails after the SP, and he considered Jennings his particular target.

''How is that, Mr. Bierce?'' Lady Caroline said.

''Lady Caroline, it is a strength of your personality to have a power of persuasion over men. That is not an empty compliment. I ask you to persuade Elza Klosters to reveal the fact that Senator Jennings tried to hire him to murder Mrs. Hamon. Then I can promise you that the identity of the Slasher will be revealed.''

Beau started to speak, but Lady Caroline halted him with a motion of her bare hand. She whispered, ''You overestimate my powers, Mr. Bierce.''

''I believe I do not.''

''I would not be able to persuade Elza Klosters to such an action,'' she said firmly.

Bierce rose. ''Very well, madam,'' he said. ''Good day, madam. Sirs. I believe we have nothing more to communicate here.''

We left. I thought he would have his way, when they had had time to confer.

''That is a remarkable woman,'' Bierce said, in the tone in

which he had spoken of Lillie Coit, Ada Claire and Adah Isaacs Mencken.

We turned onto California Street, which slanted upward to Nob Hill, some traffic of wagons and carriages, two cable cars passing halfway up the slope. There was a shout, a cracking of hoofs, a screeching of scraped metal. Bierce grasped my arm and flung me against the brick wall behind us.

A carriage careened toward us, a pair of horses with white-rimmed eyes, forelegs flashing, the muffled figure of the driver poised whip-swinging above them. I snatched Bierce's revolver from my pocket, raised the muzzle and pressed the trigger. The shot exploded in my ear as the carriage spun away past us with its rear wheels grating and sparking on the pavement. Shouts of alarm and anger erupted further along. I held the revolver shakily aimed but did not fire again. The carriage raced away up California Street and turned at the second corner and was gone, leaving plug-hatted pedestrians staring in its wake, one shaking a cane after it. A man had leaped out of his buggy to calm his frightened horse. Smoke curled from the muzzle of the revolver.

"Missed," I said.

Bierce said in a flat voice, "I read in one of the Penny Dreadfuls that Billy the Kid holds his forefinger along the barrel of his weapon and simply points the finger at his target."

I seemed to have become his bodyguard. I pocketed the revolver. The barrel was hot. "That was a response, not a threat," I said. "Senator Jennings still has not heard from Klosters."

"No, that was for me," Bierce said. "That was not intimidation, that was an attempt to shorten my life." He sounded pleased.

Mammy Pleasant came again to visit him in the office of the editor of *The Hornet.*

She wore black bombazine that rustled like a forest when she seated herself. She had a black straw hat tied on her head with a black scarf and carried a black bag that would have contained a fair-sized infant. The gold hoop earrings glinted at her ears. She pointed her fierce, dark face at Bierce.

"I'm glad to see you, Mrs. Pleasant," Bierce said. "Why does it occur to me that your visit has to do with the return to San Francisco of Lady Caroline Stearns?"

Mammy Pleasant looked down at her hands folded in her lap and said, in her manner that was both assertive and hesitating, "It is because that is your nature, Mr. Bierce."

Bierce stroked the fair sparrow-wings of his mustache.

"And what do you have to say to me, Mrs. Pleasant?"

She turned her white-rimmed eyes toward me. "I understand that information is being collected for a news article on aspects of my life in San Francisco," she said.

"That is correct," Bierce said.

"I have some information that may be of assistance to you, if you will guarantee that my history will not be made public at this time. It would be most inopportune for me, Mr. Bierce."

Bierce sat silently for a moment, studying her. "I believe you can tell me the identity of the Slasher."

A dark hand pulled her shawl more closely around her. She leaned forward with a show of teeth in her lean face, shaking her head.

"Mr. Bierce, I believe I understand your way of thinking. You will be thinking because Mr. James Brittain forbade his daughter to marry Beau McNair that you have uncovered the truth. You have not uncovered the truth. You have only looked at half a picture."

She gathered up her bag and rose and, a hunched figure, hurried out.

Bierce and I stared at each other. "What does that sibylline utterance mean, please?"

I shook my head helplessly.

"Is our solution to Beau's parentage brought to question? Brittain did admit to it."

I said I didn't know what to think.

EDUCATION, *n.*
*That which discloses to the wise and disguises
from the foolish their lack of understanding.*
—THE DEVIL'S DICTIONARY

gt. Nix arrived at *The Hornet* with the latest news from Old City Hall.

"Bos Curtis come in the station like a wagonload of wildcats," he said. "There was fur flying in the Captain's office."

"Is it a fact that Pusey has a witness to Rachel LeVigne's murder?" Bierce asked.

"Fellow named Horswill. Showed him the photograph and he said it was Beau McNair, all right. And Mr. R. Buckle had sworn false that Beau was with him."

"Pusey was waiting to broach that to Lady Caroline?"

Nix managed to shrug and nod at the same time.

Bierce said, "I imagine Curtis told Pusey what he would do to Edith Pruitt, and this Horswill, on the witness stand—as identifiers of photographs. Not to speak of why the Captain chose to show Beau McNair's photograph in the first place."

I wondered aloud if police were stationed at the McNair mansion.

"The lady don't want anybody there," Nix said. "I understand the place is forted up pretty good from back when those Sandlotters would mob up on Nob Hill and raise the dickens. Your pal Klosters has been there," he added.

"Tom and I have been invited to call upon Lady Caroline after supper tonight," Bierce said.

"Wouldn't it be better for you to go alone?" I asked, when Nix had departed.

"I want you to observe. You will be listening, to her and to me, in order to inform me later of anything I may have missed."

At nine o'clock we rolled up California Street in a hack, jolted when the horse's hoofs slipped on the paving stones, the hackie cursing and using his whip. We came out among the edifices of the Big Four, passing the Crocker mansion with its scrollwork facade and its tower, and the loom of the spite-fence beyond it. A fog bank blocked out the lights of the western part of the City.

I said, "It must have been frightening for the Nobs when the Workingmen were rallying up here."

"Denis Kearney versus Charles Crocker," Bierce said. "Property rights versus workingman's rights. Think of the rights that have been abused in struggles over rights! Wars are caused by rights. The rights of the Negro, the rights of slaveholders. The Fugitive Slave Law! How could our legislative chambers have given birth to such a monstrosity? I say down with rights!"

The hack clattered on. "What you come to," Bierce said gloomily, "is finally that nothing matters. Nothing. The passing scene is to be watched, and ridiculed, but it is not to be *felt,* for there is nothing worth feeling. We are as flies to wanton boys, et cetera."

It seemed to be the theory of social comedy that Amelia had enunciated, but with despair instead of irony. I felt a continuing smothering anger over what she had called her responsibility. I regarded that feeling as important, even though it made me miserable.

"I hold that there are emotions worth feeling," I said.

"Just what moves the sleeping lion in your heart?"

I said I had been informed by Amelia Brittain that she was required to marry a wealthy man because of her father's financial situation, and the sensations were painful but honorably felt.

"My dear fellow, what did you expect?" Bierce said kindly. "You have read too many novels. They reinforce the preposterous view of the happy ending."

"If nothing matters, why is it important to find out who murdered three whores?" I asked.

"It is not important, it is only interesting," Bierce said. "It is a puzzle to be solved."

"Why is it important to confound the Railroad?"

"It is not important, it is only gratifying," Bierce said.

"Well," I said. "Gratification is something felt."

Bierce laughed. "I am sorry about Miss Brittain. She is a charming young woman, and no femininny if she knows her fate."

"Her happy ending," I said, bitterly.

The rig rolled on among the mansions that loomed like ancient monsters frozen in an ice age. There was some traffic of buggies and other hacks with their lamps burning, an occasional spark from metal rims on paving stones. The fog bank surged up toward us, but the sensation was of the world turning slowly to deposit us in that gray, damp maw.

The McNair mansion was one of the lesser beasts, first and second floor windows alight in the fog, misty reflected gleams dancing off the fence against a dense darkness of shrubbery. The hackie turned in under the lights of the porte cochere, where we were let off.

The heavyset butler with patent-leather hair bowed us inside. He showed us up a curving flight of stairs as broad as Morton Street, which we mounted under the glowering eyes of the portrait of Nathaniel McNair, and into a room brilliant with glowing balls of light. The butler directed Bierce to a noble overstuffed chair, and me to a divan of fat pillows. Then he poured port from a cut-glass decanter. I saw that one glass had already been filled, resting on a low table beside a chaise longue across the room.

We hurried to our feet as Lady Caroline Stearns entered.

She wore a long gown embroidered in gilt and silver, high necked, long sleeved. Within the stiff fabric there was a sense of her body in motion independent of the material that covered her. She crossed to us to greet Bierce, with a welcoming motion of her hand to me. Her hair was brushed up into a burnished knot at the back of her head above a slender neck. Her complexion was pale, no doubt with powders, her mouth tinted, her eyes a calm blue surveying us. She was no longer young, but she was very beautiful.

"Please sit down, Mr. Bierce, Mr. Redmond." She swept on across the parquet to recline on the chaise longue. I felt in her presence a queer diminution of Bierce's force, almost a shyness.

There was a moment of silence, each of us with a glass of port raised as though in a toast.

"It is time to talk about Virginia City," Bierce said.

She inclined her neat chin in what must be assent.

"You were greatly loved there, madam."

"Thank you," she said.

"Yet there has been a continuing hatred. I assume that is because of the manipulations of ownership of the Jack of Spades Mine."

"There were investors who had cause to feel they had been cheated," Lady Caroline said. The elegant folds of her heavy gown made me conscious of her reclining body and reminded me of Annie Dunker in her shift.

"Adolphus Jackson, Albert Gorton, and a man named Macomber," Bierce said. "Of these, E. O. Macomber seems to have disappeared. Detective Sergeant Nix has made some efforts to find him, with no result. Albert Gorton is apparently dead. The latter, who was an accessory to the Jack of Spades 'shuffle,' may have been murdered because he became an embarrassment to your late husband."

"That is an unfounded assumption, Mr. Bierce."

"It is not even an assumption."

"Mr. Bierce, I cannot believe that any of these men are so consumed with old wrongs that they would begin the conspiracy of revenge against me of which you seem convinced."

"Will you accept the fact that there has indeed been a conspiracy?"

"I suppose I must."

"That you are in danger?"

She inclined her coiffed head silently.

"There is another matter than the Jack of Spades Mine, madam," Bierce said. "It is the paternity of your son."

She lifted a hand to a bell that hung from a braided rope. The butler appeared. "Cigars, if you please, Marvins."

The butler brought a silver-chased humidor from a sideboard and offered it to Bierce and to me. Bierce took one, I declined. Marvins returned the humidor and carried to Lady Caroline a small box of Egyptian cigarettes. She chose one, and he lighted it for her with a flourish, then came to light Bierce's cigar. The smoke from the cigarette was a paler hue than that of the cigar, coiling upward from the tan tube between her fingers.

I thought the distribution of smokes had given Lady Caroline time to prepare herself.

"Mr. Brittain is convinced that he was the father," Bierce said. "But I have had a communication to the effect that that may not be the case."

"May I ask from whom this communication was received?" Lady Caroline asked. She braced an elbow on the chaise in order to raise her hand to hold the cigarette six inches from her lips.

"That is unimportant," Bierce said. "But I hope you will be forthcoming in the matter."

I could see her gown move with her breathing. "There was a murder," she said. "A friend of mine was horribly murdered—not slashed, in case you should leap to a conclusion. It was a violent time, a violent place. All at once that violence quite overwhelmed me. I had had proposals of marriage. It seemed that a signal had been given that I had better accept one of them and end the life I had been leading before that life ended me.

"James Brittain was the first choice," she said. "Nat McNair the last."

I wondered who had been in between.

"But I believe neither of them was actually the father of your child," Bierce said.

"Mr. Bierce, will you embarrass me into revealing the fact that I am uncertain?"

"This determination may be essential to the solution of these murders, madam."

"I admit I informed James Brittain that he was the father. That was because I had decided to accept his proposal. He was a gentleman, a cultivated man. He proved to be a four-flusher, however." She laughed lightly.

I thought her ease and calm were pretense.

"Was Senator Sharon one of the possibilities of fatherhood?"

"In one regard I may be uncertain, but in the other I am very certain. No, he was not."

"Was he one of those offering proposals?"

"Only a proposition," she said. "It would have resulted in a relation very like the one in which the valiant Miss Sarah Althea Hill became dissatisfied. My inclination was for marriage.

"Mr. Bierce, allow me to say this," she continued. "It may be an excess of pride on my part, but I do not believe I am to blame for the Jack of Spades contrivances. It was Nat's doing. It was the kind of proceeding that he became famous for. No doubt he learned it from William Sharon. I believe my role must be described as passive. Can it be that you should extend your researches beyond this little circle of five people?"

"It is possible," Bierce said, without, I thought, meaning it. "Is it possible that Macomber changed his name, as Jackson changed his?"

I felt an invisible weight press on my shoulders. Lady Caroline sighed and shrugged in her gilt and silver casing.

"What was Macomber like, Lady Caroline?" I asked.

Her blue eyes shifted toward me, blinking as though she had difficulty changing their focus. "He was a pleasant young man, rather talkative. I don't remember much more about him, Mr. Redmond."

"How did the five of you, who joined together to purchase the Jack of Spades, know each other?"

She blew smoke before addressing my question. "We were friends."

Clients? Customers? "The woman who was murdered was Julia Bulette?"

She looked suddenly wary. "Yes. She was a friend also, a business friend but a good friend, a good woman, a good, good friend."

"Might she have been included among the Spades?"

"There was a blackball system. She had been blackballed."

"May I ask by whom?"

She considered, her eyes slitted against the smoke. "It would have been my husband."

"Why would it have been, madam?" Bierce said.

"Mr. Bierce, I will confess something to you. I wonder if it will even surprise you. Nat McNair was a cruel, dishonest, coldhearted, ungrateful monster who never forgave a slight or forgot to remember a favor."

"Why did you marry him, madam?"

"I thought he would become the richest man in California." She uttered a small laugh. "He did not quite achieve that goal, but his achievement was impressive. I earned my share of it."

I thought she did not mean by her part in the Jack of Spades contrivances.

"Why was Will Sharon not an investor in the Jack of Spades?"

"Why does this name *continue* to come up in our conversation? Senator Sharon was and is a detestable man. I hope Miss Hill wins her case and takes half of his millions away from him."

She leaned back in the chaise as though satisfied with her denunciation. Bierce inquired what her son might be blamed for.

"As I have learned, he was adopted by Mr. McNair some months after he was born. He lived in San Francisco in circumstances of increasing wealth until he was ten or eleven—when he and James Brittain's daughter were sweethearts."

Lady Caroline nodded, leaking smoke through her nostrils.

"Did you approve of that connection?" Bierce asked.

"Not particularly, Mr. Bierce. Not at all, in fact."

"Her father did not approve of it because he thought them brother and sister."

Lady Caroline sipped her port, her cigarette smoking between the fingers of her other hand. They seemed to me defensive devices, as her embroidered gown was a kind of cage of armor.

"I know of your son's troubles in London, by the way," Bierce said.

"He was victimized by false friends. I do not excuse him, mind you." Even when she spoke with force there was a serenity to her words that seemed to me the product of a considerable will. She addressed herself to me:

"Mr. Redmond, I would prefer that any further confidences be revealed only to Mr. Bierce."

"Certainly," I said, rising. "Lady Caroline, I bring a message from Jimmy Fairleigh in Virginia City. He asked me to tell you that he will never forget you."

The beautiful mask suddenly became an unhappy human face. Her lips parted, her eyes flared at me, lines showed in her throat.

"That sweet unfortunate boy! What is he doing, please?"

"He is a waiter at the International Hotel there."

"And the mines are closing down. The town must be dying. I must do something for him!" she whispered, and the mask reformed itself. I bade her good night.

Marvins showed me into another sitting room downstairs and busied himself lighting lamps and bringing me another glass of port. I had difficulty sitting still, and the wine seemed an overly heavy and sweet appurtenance of aristocracy. After twenty minutes I asked Marvins to tell Bierce I was taking the air and went outside into the brisk damp, to walk along the McNair brass fence toward the top of Taylor Street hill, where a single streetlamp shed a circle of pale illumination in the fog, as though its flame burned under water.

I stopped before I reached a point where I could look down on the Brittain house and retraced my steps toward the porte cochere. I turned again just in time to see a figure detach itself from the shrubbery, straddle the fence and hurry away from me. As he passed under the streetlight he glanced back and I thought I caught a glimpse of a glint of fair beard.

When Bierce joined me I told him I had seen Beau leave the house.

"I believe it could not have been Beau you saw," he said. "He was playing chess with Rudolph Buckle in the Billiard Room."

"Did you see him?" I asked.

"No," he said thoughtfully.

"But Beau was the subject of our conversation," he went on. "You said once that Miss Brittain had spoken of his researches. He is obsessed with prostitutes. Lady Caroline is disturbed by this and fears he may get himself into trouble again as he did in London. The fact is, he *is* in trouble! And how can I discuss with her the probability that his obsession stems from his knowledge of his mother's former profession? Now he is infatuated with a young Chinese woman, no doubt a prostitute."

"She is in danger from the Slasher, then," I said.

We started back down California Street toward the lights of Chinatown beneath us.

"There was a general obsession with Chinese prostitutes in the old days," Bierce went on. "It is still the case! Every yokel who comes to the City must see for himself. The burning question is not What is man? or Why are we here? but Does the Chinese female possess a different arrangement of sexual apparatus than her white sister? Imagine it! Ah Toy is reputed to have made her fortune by this quest for the essential knowledge. Her price list read 'Two bits lookee, four bits feelee, six bits doee.' And I believe the bulk of her fortune came in the satisfaction of the lookees." He laughed, striding along at his military gait. He seemed pleased with himself.

He announced that he wished to smoke a few pipes of opium, and he commanded me to accompany him. He needed my counsel.

We descended into Chinatown, where he seemed familiar with an odoriferous alley off Kearny Street. This was not one of the tourist opium dens. We descended four brick steps and passed along a mossy wall in a play of shadows as dense as black velvet. I could smell the opium before we got to the door of the parlor, that pervasive odor that reminds you of something you can't quite recall. An old Chinese bowed us inside. In an outer room six men, not all Chinese, lay on wooden bunks alcoved into the wall, jackets hanging beside their heads, which rested on leather-covered bricks. Smoke massed gray against the painted ceiling. On the wall was a price list in English and Chinese, for small pipes and large. In an inner chamber was a cot with a taboret beside it, a lamp burning on the table. The old Chinaman indicated this. Bierce, in turn, pointed me to a straight chair, which I pulled over.

"Tell me everything you know, saw, heard, thought—everything," he said. "Not just tonight. Everything. There is something I've missed. Just keep talking."

I began talking.

A younger Celestial in a pink silk shirt with decorative frogs down the front appeared and, squatting, kneaded a ball of dark brown gum over a flame until it began to bubble and then plunged it into the bowl of the pipe, which Bierce inhaled. The first pipe seemed to take only moments, and the young man went through the preparations for the second. I inhaled free smoke. Bierce had removed his coat and loosened his tie. It was the first time I had seen him with his collar button undone.

"Continue!" he commanded.

I pulled from my memory everything I knew about the murders, the trip to the Washoe, the tintype of the Spades, the interview with Pusey, my conversations with Amelia and her father. But not with my father, E. O. Macomber, who had written the Former-Spade letter to Bierce.

Bierce smoked the second pipe, and a third. "Does Amelia have brothers?" he asked.

She had a brother named Richard, whom I'd glimpsed at the Firemen's Ball and who was studying at the Sheffield School at Yale.

"And she has an uncle, who is her father's twin, and whom Beau resembles?"

"Amelia does not think he does."

I told Bierce about seeing Beau at the Bella Union, and catching sight in Battery Street of the painting of Lady Caroline as Lady Godiva—which Mr. Brittain had described and which was apparently Senator Jennings's property. Bierce demanded a description of the man carrying the painting to safety, which description I was unable to supply other than that the fellow had been young.

There were more questions, all with no apparent focus to them.

After what seemed hours of my increasingly dry-mouthed account, Bierce muttered in Chinese to the young man, who bowed and retired. Presently a female entered. I was shocked to see that she was an Oriental prostitute in a short white shift. She had a piquant face, slit-eyed, with high cheekbones. A gap between her front teeth gave her an attractive hoydenish appearance. She squatted to prepare what I counted as the fifth pipe and tossed her head at me with a smoldering eye.

I went out into the common room where I stood ill-at-ease and angry among the recumbent smokers, and their attendants moving in the dim light. I felt trapped in the wrong place and time, breathing smoke of which I disapproved even as I felt drowsy from its fumes.

I had not told Bierce everything, so I was perhaps hindering his solutions. But I did not want those solutions to involve my father.

Presently the girl reappeared and with another toss of her head directed me back inside. It occurred to me that I had become prudish since my attachment to Amelia Brittain, but I disapproved strongly of the enslavement of young Chinese girls in Chinatown.

Bierce lay with one knee raised. He sat up, holding his hands to his cheeks, and shook his head once.

"I think I have it," he said.

"That's good," I said. I wanted to get out of this place.

"I must do Captain Pusey's work for him in order to accomplish my own ends," Bierce said, standing unsteadily. I helped him with his coat.

"Are you going to tell me?" I asked.

"Not yet. In case I am wrong."

28

When I got to Pine Street and started up my creaking outside stairs in the darkness, I could see some white object on the top step, like a large bag of laundry there. It rose, extending in height, as I climbed toward it, and it was Amelia Brittain in a white dress.

"What are you doing here?" I whispered.

"I had to see you!"

"Where's your guard?"

"I took a hack. I've been waiting for *hours!*"

I unlocked the door and let us in and bent to light the lamp. Amelia sat on the bed with her hands clasped under her chin. "You smell funny!" she said.

I said I'd been in an opium den with Bierce.

"Did you smoke opium?"

"I did not."

"There are *ladies* that do that. Eleanor Bellingham told Momma it is so marvelously relaxing."

She made me feel stodgy and disapproving. "You shouldn't—" I started.

"Oh, don't say *that!* I'm going to be married!"

I couldn't get my breath. When I sat down beside her she leaned her head against my shoulder.

"He's a friend of Poppa's. He's nice. He's—"

"What's his name?"

"He is Marshall Sloat. He's a banker."

I didn't know the name.

"It is to be very soon!" She put her arms around me. "It's a wonderful marriage! Please kiss me, Tom!"

I kissed her. The kissing progressed.

"The wedding will be at Trinity, and the reception in the Palace. Everyone will be there!" She was breathing hard. "Governor Stanford will be there. Mr. Crocker will be there, and Mr. Fair. Senator Jennings will be there."

I said I didn't think Senator Jennings would be there, but she paid no attention. Somehow her blouse was off, and her undergarments slipped down to her waist. I kissed her bare bosom. She had raised her arms above her head, twining there like swans' necks while she sighed, and closed her eyes and turned her face one way and the other. I kissed her breasts and felt the perfumed down beneath her arms tickle my cheek. I kissed her belly. When I tried to go further she whispered, "No, no, no, no, no, no!" on an ascending scale. So I kissed her breasts while she sighed and sobbed and twined her arms above our heads and talked on:

"Maybe General Sherman will be there," she panted. "And the Mackays, and the Millses and Mr. and Mrs. Reid, and Miss Newlands, and the Blairs and the Martins and the Tolands. The Thomsons and the Blakes and the Walkers and Miss Osgood and Mr. Faber."

It was the *Elite Directory of San Francisco.*

Where were her ironies now?

The ache in my groin felt as though I'd been clubbed there. I kissed Amelia's breasts while she listed the names of San Francisco's elite who would attend her marriage to Mr. Sloat, the banker. Her nipples were like pink fingertips. I kissed her nipples while she moaned. She would not lie back on the bed or permit any other attentions. I kissed her until my lips ached.

When I took her home in a hack she was weeping. This time I mounted the steps at 913 Taylor Street with an arm supporting her. She let herself inside and was gone.

When I returned to my room a note had been slipped under the door:

> *Since you have ignored the rule against bringing women to your room we will require you to vacate these premises as of Monday next.*

Mrs. Adeline Barnacle

In the morning the books I had lent Belinda were stacked neatly on the fourth stair: *Ivanhoe, The Mill on the Floss* and *Great Expectations,* along with three neatly penned lines of script on a page torn from a school notebook ending our engagement.

Thursday at *The Hornet* offices I was discussing with Bierce my piece on Crocker's spite-fence, trying to pretend that my heart was not broken into halves of fury and grief.

I knew that when Charles Crocker was praised as a public-spirited man who had constructed many works of great and permanent value to the State, Bierce had responded:

"His tendency to make improvements is merely a natural instinct inherited from his public-spirited ancestor, the man who dug the post-holes on Mount Calvary."

He also showed me a newspaper clipping he had saved, a denunciation of Crocker by a lawyer with whom the Railroad magnate had quarreled:

"I will show the world how an intelligent patron of the arts and literature can be manufactured by the process of wealth out of a peddler of needles and pins. I will visit Europe until I can ornament my ungrammatical English with a fringe of mispronounced French. I will wear a diamond as big as the headlight of one of my loco-motives; and my adipose tissue shall increase with my pecuniary gains until my stomach is as large as my arrogance, and I shall strut along the corridors of the Palace Hotel a living, breathing, waddling monument of the triumph of vulgarity, viciousness and dishonesty."

"You can't hope to equal that for invective," Bierce said. "Just leave the vituperations to others," he said, and that is what I had tried to do:

> Charles Crocker of the Big Four was the superintendent of construction of the Union Pacific Railroad. He accomplished wonders with the thousands of coolies, "Crocker's Pets," who made up the bulk of his construction crews, and were released to unemployment when the Railroad was completed.
>
> Unemployed himself, he traveled abroad to purchase furnishings and art objects for his Nob Hill mansion, to serve which he financed a cable car line up California Street. The Crocker palace cost in the vicinity of a million and a half dollars to build. The architectural style is called "Early Renaissance." Its 172-ft. facade is a masterpiece of carpenters' scrollwork, and its 76-ft. tower commands a magnificent view of the City.
>
> Although he could have extended his domain to almost any corner of the country that he desired, he was unable to purchase the northeast corner of the block of Nob Hill bounded by Jones, California, Taylor and Sacramento Streets. He had acquired all the other lots that made up the block for his mansion, but a stubborn German undertaker, Nicholas Yung, would not sell his corner.
>
> Crocker consequently had constructed on three sides of the Yung property a fence 40 feet high, closing off Yung's sunlight and views except for a narrow frontage on Sacramento Street. Eventually Yung moved his house to another part of the City but would not release the property, so Crocker left the fence standing.
>
> The spite-fence has become one of the landmarks of Nob Hill and has come to signify the arrogance of the rich in general and the Railroad millionaires in particular.
>
> Denis Kearney's Workingman's Party was viewed by Nob

Hill as anarchistic. Kearney's Irishmen often gathered at the spite-fence as the focus for their rage against the Railroad moguls who had amassed fabulous wealth and who had discharged an army of Chinese after the completion of the Railroad, contributing to the post-Railroad depression and to general unemployment. It is claimed that Crocker had his tower fitted with slots for pouring boiling lead down on the heads of besieging Communists, but, although the Sandlotters' rallies began at the spite-fence, the rioters usually drifted downhill to sack Chinatown. The hot-lead slots have so far not been put to use.

"That is adequate," Bierce said. "Now go through and take out half the adverbs."

"There are only three."

"Remove two."

Miss Penryn announced Mr. Beaumont McNair. Beau strode into the office, with his gold-leaf beard, his arrogant chin, his close-set eyes, his well fitted jacket and his affected manner of walking, as though testing the floor with the stretched-out toe of his gleaming boot before trusting his weight to it.

He halted gazing at the chalk-white skull on Bierce's desk. Bierce rose. I did also.

"Good morning, Mr. McNair."

"Good morning, Mr. Bierce. Redmond," Beau said, with a dip of his head in my direction.

I produced a chair and he seated himself with some style, this young man whose pleasure it was to draw cunts on the bare bellies of whores and who was, in fact, obsessed with low women.

"There was an incident last night," Beau said, chin up, eyes fixed on Bierce. "An intruder."

Bierce glanced once at me but only nodded to Beau.

"Someone broke in," Beau said. "Marvins pursued him but lost him. There was a window open."

"The ghost," Bierce said.

Beau looked startled.

"Mr. Buckle told us there was a permanent ghost."

"Well, yes," Beau said.

"This was when I was in conference with your mother?" Bierce asked. "If so, Mr. Redmond observed the ghost leaving the house. He thought it was you."

Beau looked confused and irritated.

"Have the police been notified?"

Beau removed a linen handkerchief from his pocket and patted his forehead. "My mother thought you should be advised first."

Bierce leaned back in his chair with his fingers knitted together over his vest. "Someone hates you, Mr. McNair."

"I understand that. And I understand that you and my mother came to some meeting of the minds last night. She is prepared to meet your condition, Mr. Bierce. I am to inquire if you will come to us this evening and present your solution to these matters. She believes that you will require that others be on hand also."

"I shall present you with a list. Tom, if you would write down these names for Mr. McNair."

I did not much like taking orders in Beau's presence, but I brought out notebook and pencil. Bierce dictated. I wrote. It was not the *Elite Directory of San Francisco,* but it was not entirely different.

With his list in hand, Beau McNair remained standing, scowling. "I must speak with Redmond," he said.

"I'll just take these to the typewriter," Bierce said, flourishing a sheaf of papers. He left us there.

"I will ask your intentions towards Miss Brittain," Beau said.

I still ached from last night's frustrations. "My intentions are not intentions," I said.

"That is very glib," Beau said. "I say, I demand to know your intentions!"

"I am telling you I have no intentions. Miss Brittain is engaged to marry a man named Marshall Sloat."

"Her mother is worried that you have formed an attachment to Miss Brittain. She does not wish any complications."

His coat fit him so prettily it weighed on me. I said I didn't consider that any of his business.

"I speak for Mrs. Brittain, and I will speak frankly. Miss Brittain belongs to a station in life to which you cannot aspire."

I blew out my breath to keep calm. "I wish you would come down to the True Blue Democracy Club and explain your meaning," I said.

His face was pinched and schoolmasterish. He looked at me as though I was being purposefully stupid. How I disliked him, Amelia's half brother.

"We call folks who live on Nob Hill 'instant Aristocrats,' " I said. "Is that what you mean? For instance, your putative father went to the Washoe and found a bonanza, while mine found nothing but borrascas. Is that the difference?" Mine, in fact, had been euchred by his.

I said, and immediately wished I hadn't, "Aristocrats go to whores and draw all over their bellies. Is *that* the difference?"

His face turned a dangerous red. "*How dare you?*"

"You don't want to try tricks like that here," I said. "San Francisco whores are *tough*."

He stared at me with his mouth open. "*Damn* you!"

"No, damn *you!*" I said. "For the spoiled presumptuous twit you are." I was aware of pushing this into something from which I could not withdraw, which pleased me.

He glared at me down his nose. "I demand satisfaction!"

I laughed at him. "Manhole covers at twenty feet?"

"Damned fortune hunter!"

"Bare knuckles in the basement," I said.

I led him downstairs into the basement and through the door into the cellar next door, where there was an empty storeroom lighted by dusty clerestory windows that gave onto California Street.

Beau stripped out of the beautiful jacket. He'd had some boxing instruction. He danced around me, feinting lefts and rights while I took off my coat. I felt heavy, lumpish and poisoned.

He danced toward me. I knocked him down. It is easeful to your inner furies when you have bashed someone on the jaw, but the demands and responsibilities of the Brittain family were not Beau's fault.

He bounced up again. The second time I knocked him down he managed to pop me on the nose, and I felt the claret starting.

Sprawled on the floor he gazed up at me as I mopped at my nose with my handkerchief. He pronounced himself satisfied.

He climbed to his feet, massaging his jaw and moving his shoulders in a manner distasteful to me.

"You know what the Morton Street whore who identified your photograph said?" I said.

"What is that?"

"She said there was a client of Esther Mooney's who didn't have a dingle. He used some kind of leather dildo. He might have been the one that killed Esther. That wouldn't be you, would it?"

"*Certainly not!* The police—"

"Did they ask to see your dingle?"

"I don't know what you are getting at, Redmond!"

Glaring, he stood poised with his elbows folded back and his chin out, as though he was going to assault me again or take flight. Suddenly he ripped at his placket and exhibited himself for my inspection.

"What about balls?" I said.

He cursed me in an unaristocratic manner.

"Listen," I said, holding my handkerchief to my nose. "I apologize for my childish behavior. Don't you know we are trying to save your bacon?"

"Yes, I do know that, Redmond."

In the end we shook hands.

"Here's another communication from our Comstock correspondent," Bierce said, passing me a handwritten note when I returned to the office with my nosebleed stanched.

Dear Mr. Bierce,

If you are worried about who fathered Highgrade Carrie's get, worry no more. Everybody knew Dolph Jackson was her beau.

A Former Spade

"He has no occasion for a 'momento' in this missive," I said.

"It is the connection between the murderers!" Bierce said. "The 'Former Spade' is my benefactor!"

Who was the Gent.

TRUTH, *n.*
An ingenious compound of desirability and appearance.
—THE DEVIL'S DICTIONARY

ierce and I arrived at the McNair mansion fifteen minutes later than the six o'clock appointed hour. Marvins let us in, and we followed his stately guidance down an expanse of gleaming parquet past the piano octagon to a large room with windows looking south over the City. Chairs had been set facing a presiding table, as for a ceremony. Lady Caroline was seated at the table, flanked by Beau and Lawyer Curtis. In the chairs, craning their necks as Bierce and I entered, were Senator Jennings and a balding man with Yankee chin whiskers who had a lawyer look to him; Rudolph Buckle; Captain Pusey; and Mammy Pleasant in her black bonnet. I had been halfway afraid the Gent would be on hand, summoned behind my back; or Senator Sharon.

Sgt. Nix stood straddle-legged, hands clasped behind him, against the walnut paneling. Elza Klosters sat with his broad-brimmed hat in his lap in a chair beside the door. His pale scalp gleamed with sweat.

Marvins closed the double doors behind us with a slap of sound.

I slipped into an empty chair while Bierce remained standing, his cold face glancing around at the company that had been summoned at his request.

Senator Jennings heaved himself to his feet. "What the devil is all this, Bierce?"

"Sit down, sir," Bierce said. He moved at his stiff gait over to the broad window, where he could face the three at the table and the rest of us as well. His expression was that of having the Railroad where he wanted it. Jennings remained standing, big-bellied.

"I have asked Mr. Bierce to conduct these proceedings," Lady Caroline said in her soft, British-accented voice, smiling a kind of general smile out of her porcelain mask. The fingers of her white gloves were tented together as she spoke. She wore a dress of black velvet trimmed with lace, with a high neck. Her pale hair flowed in waves to a high French knot stabbed with a diamond-headed pin. Diamond dewdrops glistened from her earlobes. She turned her smile to Bierce.

Jennings sat down. His cheeks were the color of raw beef. He leaned his head sideways to something his lawyer whispered.

Bierce said, "We are concerned with two murderers here. We will dispose of the obvious one first. I have already warned Senator Jennings that I will prove he murdered the widow of Judge Hamon."

"One moment, if you please," Jennings's lawyer said, rising, a hand and a finger raised as though to a point of order.

"I do not please," Bierce said. "Mr. Klosters, did Senator Jennings offer you money to murder Mrs. Hamon?"

There was a moment of silence, the lawyer still standing. Lady Caroline turned her fixed smile on Klosters. Jennings rose again, to hulk beside his lawyer, glaring at the enforcer.

"Offered me three hundred dollars," Klosters said in his heavy voice. He remained seated, his hands holding his hat on his lap. "Told him I wouldn't do it, so he offered me five hundred. Told him I was not in that game any more."

"The Society of Spades," Bierce said. "Was formed to purchase control of the Jack of Spades Mine in Virginia City. There were five members. Two of them married, Caroline LaPlante and Nathaniel McNair. They enlisted a third, Albert Gorton, to form a majority to cheat the other two out of their shares of what was to become an incalculable profit. One of these others was an E. O. Macomber, who has disappeared or changed his name, the fifth person was Adolphus Jackson, who became Aaron Jennings and was elected a State Senator.

He let that settle, pacing, before he continued: "Jackson and probably Macomber were rightfully infuriated at the swindle that had been perpetrated upon them. Gorton was brained out of revenge, or because he had become a liability to McNair. That murder does not concern us, although Mr. Klosters may be able to clear it up."

"It is not necessary that you respond to that, Elza," Lady Caroline said. Her voice was drowned by Senator Jennings's bellow:

"I do not intend to listen to this twaddle!"

"Then why are you here, sir?" Bierce said. "Captain Pusey, will you arrest Senator Jennings for murder?"

"I do not take my orders from journalists, Mr. Bierce," Pusey said calmly. He was sitting with his arms folded on his uniformed chest, his legs crossed; he looked as though he had been trussed.

"Very well," Bierce said. "I will have more to say of Senator Jennings as we proceed."

He strutted before the window, a little showily I thought. He held up a finger before his chin.

"Some things have been clear from the outset. Captain Pusey knew from his connections with the London police that young Mr. McNair had been involved in a scrape in which he and some companions abused low women in ways that were to be transformed into butchery in the murders of the Morton Street prostitutes. It is clear that Captain Pusey knew of this from the fact that he showed Mr. McNair's photograph, from his archive, to a prostitute who had had a glimpse of the murderer.

"Captain Pusey had also told another person of Beau McNair's arrest in London."

Bierce paused to pace some more.

"And the identity of that person, Mr. Bierce?" Curtis asked, peering past Lady Caroline. Beau was studying his hands.

"In good time, Mr. Curtis. There was great hatred here. As we have seen, Senator Jennings had been wronged, but there is another who was much more terribly wronged, and whose hatred turned to murderous insanity."

This time when Bierce paused, no one spoke. Lady Caroline had her chin raised regally.

"Nathaniel McNair was not the father of Beaumont McNair," Bierce continued. "Two other men had been told they had fathered Caroline LaPlante's son. In one of those men's family there is an occurrence of twins."

Suddenly Rudolph Buckle was on his feet, his lips working as though trying to form words that would not come. Lady Caroline made an imperious motion with her hand. She had removed one of her gloves.

"Mrs. Pleasant pointed out to me that I was only looking at half the picture," Bierce said. "Twins," he repeated. "One of the twins was given to Mammy Pleasant. The disposer of unwanted babies disposed of the unwanted twin."

Heads turned to Mammy Pleasant. Her gold hoop earring caught the light in a shivering round as she drew herself up.

"You may address this matter, Mrs. Pleasant," Lady Caroline said.

In her soft staccato, Mammy Pleasant said, "The child was given to a Mr. and Mrs. Payne to rear. He was a stonemason. They had lost a child of their own."

"Was there money involved, Mrs. Pleasant?"

"They were given two thousand dollars," Mammy Pleasant said.

Lady Caroline had removed both gloves and was smoothing a cream-colored liquid from a small silver bottle onto her hands.

It was as though Bierce was a schoolmaster calling on her. He did not look at her directly but raised a finger inclined toward her.

"McNair would allow me to keep one baby but not two," she said. "It was a punishment."

"You chose to keep the better-looking or the stronger of the twins?" Bierce said. "Or was there some defect?"

"I do not intend to discuss that, Mr. Bierce."

"I will point out that the hatred would be intensified if there was a defect. Hatred against his perfect brother as well as his mother."

Lady Caroline wrung the liquid into her hands.

"I believe there was some flaw, a deformation," Bierce said. "I believe the deformation was genital."

He paused to glance at Lady Caroline. Color had mounted in her cheeks, but she did not respond.

Bierce continued, speaking very carefully: "As Beaumont McNair's scrape with London prostitutes seems to show a discomfort with his mother's history, so does the other twin's particular viciousness.

"The twin's object was to see his brother punished for these murders, but it was primarily to punish his mother. The incrimination of Beau was to serve the purpose of bringing his mother to San Francisco. There he would punish her as he had punished the other prostitutes. Certainly it was a mad scheme. It was a madman's scheme."

Lady Caroline now sat motionless with her beautiful head erect, watching Bierce with the smile that was no longer a smile.

"What is this young man's name, Senator?" Bierce asked suddenly.

His name must be Payne.

Heads turned toward Jennings, who glared back at Bierce with his lips pressed together like a scar.

Mammy Pleasant enunciated the name softly: "George Payne."

Bierce pointed a finger at Senator Jennings. "You believed you were the father of Caroline LaPlante's offspring, the father of George Payne. The pregnant mother told you that you were, as she had also told another. She had decided that she wanted to be married, and you were her second choice, but you were a four-flusher as well. Nat McNair was her third choice. Perhaps you were, in fact, the father. The mother claims to be uncertain."

Jennings snarled at him.

I wondered suddenly who else had been informed of his paternity. Was *this* the connection with Sharon that everyone denied?

"I don't pretend to know how you came to know George Payne or his identity," Bierce went on. "But encounter him you did. He worked as a barkeep in your saloon on Battery Street. Adolphus Jackson's saloon, actually. It was George Payne who carried away from the fire the painting of Caroline LaPlante as Lady Godiva—it once hung in a saloon in Virginia City, and then in your office in Sacramento. And later still in the Washoe Angel saloon. It was the twin who carried off the famous painting of his mother, wasn't it, Tom?"

Heads turned toward me. "Yes," I said.

"The young man's hatred was fed," Bierce said, turning toward Lady Caroline. "Captain Pusey had conveyed the information about Beaumont McNair's London transgression and arrest to Senator Jennings. They were well acquainted. Pusey knew Jennings was a convicted arsonist named Adolphus Jackson and had been blackmailing him for years. Jennings passed along Pusey's information to his employee. There had to be a starting time for these vicious murders. The starting time was Beaumont McNair's return to San Francisco.

"George Payne's hatred was fed by Senator Jennings," Bierce said.

"One moment!" Jennings's lawyer said, rising, hand and finger rising also.

"You have no proof of any of this!" Jennings shouted. He shoved his chair noisily back as he lurched to his feet. "You damned calumniator! I am getting out of this shithole, Ted!"

Shoulders hunched and head forward as though ducking beneath rifle fire, he plunged toward the double doors Marvins had closed behind Bierce and me. He flung them open and disappeared with a hurrying crack of footfalls on the parquet. Neither Pusey nor Sgt. Nix made any move after him. His lawyer, grimacing at Lady Caroline, followed more sedately, closing the doors behind him.

"May we call this murderer an extrapolation, or merely hypothetical?" Curtis said in a stifled voice.

"Bos," Lady Caroline said.

"Are you saying that Senator Jennings was the intellectual author of these murders?" Buckle said.

"At least the impulse to them."

"Can the police find this twin?"

"We will find him," Pusey said calmly.

"You will find a man who has been mistaken for Beaumont McNair many times," Bierce said. He paced before the window. Lady Caroline's eyes never left him.

"The hatred these two shared was very powerful," Bierce said. "They complemented each other. The twin might not have turned murderous without Jennings. Jennings might have forgotten his old grudge without George Payne, whom he considered his wronged son."

He had broken through to the Railroad at last. He had connected the SP with the Slasher.

"So Lady Caroline is in danger," Pusey said, still with his arms and legs entwined.

"George Payne has been gaining access to this mansion for years," Bierce said. "He believed it should have been his house. The servants knew of him as the ghost. It may be that Mr. Buckle has actually encountered him."

Heads turned to Buckle, who was still standing. His lips moved, but he did not speak. He was breathing heavily.

"Is this true, Rudy?" Beau demanded.

"I believe this meeting can be concluded," Lady Caroline said, before Buckle could respond. She rose to her feet. "Thank you, Mr. Bierce. I am very impressed by your conclusions. We have certainly been forewarned."

Curtis rose. Others shifted in their chairs, rising, Mammy Pleasant elbowed and switched herself around. Her posture, and her first steps as she turned toward the door, were those of an old woman.

I heard the clatter of heels on the parquet of the hallway outside. The door burst open. Beau McNair, in a slouch hat and a gray muffler, panting, pale-faced, took two steps inside, his face aimed at Lady Caroline like a weapon. But it was not Beau.

It was the young man I had seen in the barroom at the Bella Union, and whom I had seen appear out of the shrubbery here, night before last.

A shot convulsed the room. The hat on Elza Klosters's lap exploded into the air, where it flopped and fell like a shot duck. George Payne toppled straight forward, arms extended, dropped with a crash and did not move again. Klosters rose, his smoking pistol in his hand. There was an acrid whiff of gunsmoke. I snatched Bierce's revolver from my pocket.

I slammed it down on Klosters's hand. He yelped and dropped his own weapon. He yelped again as I jammed the muzzle into his ribs.

"Tom!" Bierce called, as though I was a puppy who had misbehaved. "*Tom!*" Klosters stared at me with his catkiller eyes and his mouth open in a circle of pain, his right hand gripped in the other. I kicked his smoking gun under the chairs.

Lady Caroline had risen to stand looking down at her dead son. Beau moved to embrace her. She raised her chin, pointed her face to the ceiling, white as Bierce's skull but so very beautiful. Marvins, holding a Navy .44, filled the doorway. Mammy Pleasant backed away from the body, crossing herself.

I could see the cheek of the Morton Street Slasher, furred with a short fair beard like Beau's. The muffler had fallen open to reveal the two parallel scabs from Rachel LeVigne's fingernails. His blue eye was open, staring into infinity; the unchosen boy, the abandoned child crazed by it; the son of James Brittain or Aaron Jennings or someone else, and of Caroline LaPlante. A tongue of dark blood seeped from beneath his side.

No one else seemed to understand that we had witnessed an ambush and an execution, or maybe they all did.

COGITO COGITO ERGO
COGITO SUM —
*"I think that I think, therefore I think that I
am"; as close an approach to certainty as any
philosopher has yet made.*
—THE DEVIL'S DICTIONARY

The headline in the *Chronicle* the morning I cleared out of my room at the Barnacles' was SENATOR JENNINGS INDICTED. In the text he was referred to as the "Senator from Southern Pacific." Bierce had struck his blow at the Railroad.

Jennings was indicted for the death of Mrs. Hamon.

The Slasher murders remained unsolved.

Jonas Barnacle helped me tote bags, boxes, books and a bottle of cucumber arnica down the rickety stairs. I glimpsed Belinda through a window and detached a hand from my load to wave to her, but she did not wave in return.

In my last mail on Pine Street was an announcement of the wedding, in the Trinity Episcopalian Church at Post and Powell, of Miss Amelia Brittain to Mr. Marshall Sloat. The reception would be held at the Palace Hotel.

Sloat was a childless widower, more than twice the age of his bride-to-be. I remembered Amelia commenting on Judge Terry's age compared to Sarah Althea Hill's. A fallen woman, she had called Miss Hill.

I left my buggy seat nailed to the wall in the Barnacle cellar.

In the editor's office at *The Hornet* Bierce sat with Bosworth Curtis. He beckoned me to a chair, although I saw that Curtis disapproved.

"Lady Caroline is anxious that George Payne not be identified as her son," Bierce said. "She has made an arrangement with Captain Pusey."

"So Pusey got what he was after," I said. I was having difficulty controlling my feelings, which Bierce thought not worth having. The chalky skull gaped at Curtis.

"Her daughter is engaged to a member of the British aristocracy," Curtis said. "She is anxious to avoid scandal."

I wondered if Curtis disliked favors done for the aristocracy as much as I did. I considered Bierce a sitting duck for a grand female like Lady Caroline Stearns.

Curtis unfolded a sheet of creamy paper.

"Lady Caroline thought it appropriate to show you this," he said.

He handed the paper to Bierce, who studied it before passing it on to me. It was a list of Lady Caroline's philanthropies.

Nathaniel McNair had conspired, cheated, swindled, strong-armed and bribed to control his mining properties and fleece the fools who gambled in mining shares to make his pile. Now his widow redistributed it with interest to the needy.

The item caught my eye: Washoe Miners' Fund, $10,000. A miners' fund in Wales was listed as well. There were funds for neglected children and for wayward girls. The Frances Castleman Home for Indigent Women in San Francisco had received $7,000. There were some twenty items, ranging from $20,000 to $500. About half were in England, half in San Francisco and Nevada, two in New York. The $20,000 was for the Sanctuary for Homeless Young Women in Cleveland. The total was a magnificent sum of money.

"Her secret is safe with us," Bierce said.

"She will be grateful," Curtis said, standing and refolding the paper. The shiny skin of his face gleamed pinkly.

"Her man Klosters may think he and I have uncompleted business," I said. "Perhaps she would curb him."

"It shall be done," Curtis said. He clicked his heels and pitched his head at Bierce, with a little bow. He made a lesser bob at me and departed.

"So you let her off," I said.

"You saw the list."

"Fancy paper," I said.

"She is well known for her generosity," Bierce said.

It was true. "That was a murder," I said stubbornly. "A door was left open, or the same window he got in before. It was a trap. He wasn't even armed. How was it that he arrived there at just that moment? It was planned."

"Tom, we have been over this too many times." His forehead was creased with irritation as he gazed at me with his cold eyes. "Yes, perhaps Lady Caroline conspired to take the life of the madman who had conspired to take hers. She did not know he was her son."

"She must have suspected it. Buckle certainly knew something."

He sighed and said, "She told me that she did not."

"You believed her because she is a grand lady."

"Why this sympathy for Payne? He ripped the intestines out of three women. He would have killed Amelia Brittain if you had not stopped him. He had planned to murder Lady Caroline Stearns. He had effected her return to San Francisco, he had access to the McNair mansion. She was in danger.

"As I have said before," he continued. "My concern was the murder committed by Senator Jennings. The Slashings were the proper province of the police. I only concerned myself with them to insure the indictment of Jennings."

I turned back to my desk. I was at work on an article on the Chinese slave girls but, because of Mr. Macgowan's anti-Chinese policy, *The Hornet* would probably not publish it.

Chubb had produced as a cover for *The Hornet,* a vast squid with its tentacles spread over California. Its eyes were medallions of the faces of Huntington and Stanford, so labeled. An enormous shining hatchet had chopped off one of the tentacles, labeled "Senator Jennings," with an anguished medallion face of the Senator attached. The blade of the hatchet was labeled "Crime and Punishment." The paper was full of the Jennings arrest, a long news piece by Smithers, replete with adverbs, my own sidepiece on the spite-fence. Tattle was loaded with self-congratulation and a lambasting of the Railroad so smug that if Bierce's definition of self-esteem as "an erroneous appraisement" did not occur to me, it should have.

Bierce and I were summoned to Captain Pusey's office to view the painting of Lady Godiva, which detectives had discovered in a warehouse on Sansome Street. It had been concealed by gunny-sacking until Pusey tracked it down. John Daniel was present, dressed in a neat blue suit with a white boiled shirt and four-in-hand necktie. He watched the proceedings from the corner. He didn't seem much interested.

Bierce would not speak to Captain Pusey, but he was greatly affected by the painting. "What a lovely woman," he said, mooning over Lady Caroline as a young woman like a tenor in a romantic aria. She was indeed a lovely piece, Virginia City's own grande horizontale. Her gardenia flesh illuminated Pusey's office, her hair hung in golden ringlets, parting over her breasts, her expression of pride and modesty was perfectly depicted. The veins on the neck of the white horse had been graven with artistic perfection. Sgt. Nix regarded the painting disapprovingly.

"She is Senator Jennings's property," I said.

"He will have hard times getting this beauty back," Captain Pusey said smugly. It was the writ of I-want-what-you-have-got that Nix had enunciated, and moreover Captain Pusey had the painting in his possession.

"Shake hands with the gentlemen, John Daniel," Pusey said, when it was time for us to depart, and John Daniel complied.

"How I would be gratified to puncture that gelid old efflation," Bierce said when we left police headquarters at Old City Hall, meaning Captain Isaiah Pusey.

I was working on the slave-girl piece when the natty little Railroad representative, Smith, called on Bierce again. He had a daisy in his buttonhole.

"We understand you are to be congratulated on the indictment of Senator Jennings," he said brightly to Bierce. "Congratulations from the very top, if you know what I mean."

"Tell Mr. Huntington that I could not be more gratified," Bierce said, leaning back in his chair. "The Girtcrest Corridor Giveaway will have to find a new sponsor."

"Yes, that will be some trouble." Smith snapped his fingers to show how much. He took from his pocket a folded sheet of paper, as Lawyer Curtis had done, but this was no list of philanthropies.

"The investigator investigated!" he announced. "These items!" He held up a single finger.

"The real owner of *The Hornet* was—until recently!—C. P. Gaines, who is also one of the owners of the Spring Valley Water Company. The author of Tattle castigated the water works while it was advertised and promoted in other parts of the paper. The author of Tattle—all unknowing, we are certain—with his *great* popularity, thus acted as a shill for the very aqueous corruption he purported to be exposing. Is it not true?"

Bierce looked sour. "That is not news. I forced Charley Gaines to sell out."

Smith held up a second finger. "Sold out to Robert Macgowan, whose brother Frank owns sugar plantations in the Hawaiian Islands. The funds for the purchase thus came from those very sugar planters whom Tattle has abused for their rape of the Sandwich Islands. The Hawaiian men enslaved on the plantations, the women in Mother Hubbards! Nor can we think the investment is a disinterested one.

The Hornet is and will be editorializing and promoting favorable terms for Hawaiian sugar exports in the treaty that is presently being negotiated with King Kalakaua, and denouncing the opponents of the annexation of Hawaii, which Tattle has continually opposed. Is this not true?''

Bierce did not speak.

''Thus again, the author of Tattle is shilling for the very opposite of the righteous—so righteous!—opinions he appears to hold.''

Smith smiled brightly, holding up a third finger. Bierce appeared to have sunk into his chair.

''It is reported from St. Helena that Mrs. Mollie Bierce, in her husband's protracted absences, has been conducting a liaison with an attractive—and wealthy!—Danish gentleman there!''

Smith refolded his paper and returned it to his pocket. He beamed at Bierce. ''Is it not true?''

''Get out,'' Bierce said.

Smith executed a fancy little step as he went out the door.

''Huntington!'' Bierce said, staring at his skull. ''The swine of the century has beaten me!''

Later he sighed and said, ''The bubble reputation!''

He went home to St. Helena that weekend.

On Monday he showed me the first paragraph of his final column. He had resigned his position despite Mr. Macgowan's protestations and offers.

''We retire with an unweakened conviction of the rascality of the Railroad gang, the Water Company, the *Chronicle* newspaper, and the whole saints'-calendar of disreputables, detestables, insupportables, and moral *canaille*. We trust *The Hornet* will not extend to them a general amnesty.''

I said, ''I don't think you ought to let Huntington badger you into quitting the paper.''

He sat in his chair, hands in his lap, with his cold, composed face gazing at the skull. "I have considered retiring anyway," he said. "I require the time to write some fiction."

"A novel?"

"A bastard form," he sneered. "No, I have a dozen stories in my head, short pieces. They concern ghosts for the most part."

" 'The outward and visible sign of an inward fear,' " I said, quoting him.

"They come after me in their squads and companies," he said, with a twist of his lips. "They fill my rooms. They have weight, they have demands, they pursue me until I must forge them into stories that say—" He laughed, without amusement. "That say what? That say 'Why did we die?' Did we Federals die to preserve a Union that was not worth so many lives to preserve? Did we Confederates die to preserve the obscenity of slavery, when not one in a hundred of us owned a slave? What did we die *for*? So Abe Lincoln wouldn't go down in history as having lost half the Nation? So Bobby Lee wouldn't have to admit he'd been defeated months, and *so many* lives, before he finally surrendered? The ghosts present their demands," he said.

"I have left Mollie," he added. "We are separated."

Hot wings beat in my head. "Because of some rumor—"

"It is in fact only a rumor," he interrupted. "There is no liaison. However, he has written letters to her."

"You have separated from Mrs. Bierce because someone wrote her *letters?*"

"She must have encouraged it," Bierce said.

"Does she admit that?"

"There are a thousand ways a clever woman can attract attentions."

"That is unfair!" I protested, but he turned his cold bitter face away from me.

"I do not engage in competitions," he said.

He was insisting on fulfilling Lillie Coit's prophecy.

"Unfair," I said again.

He turned. His eyes were cold as steel. "If we have come to personal judgments perhaps it is time to end this association," he said.

"Yes, sir," I said. I had already returned his revolver to him.

I went back to my new room on Bush Street and tore up the letter I had written to Amelia Brittain, likening her marriage to a wealthy man more than twice her age not only to Sarah Althea Hill's liaison with Senator Sharon, but to the transactions of Morton Street. I had even quoted Bierce on marriage: "On the offer of a woman's body: a custom as a sacrifice of virginity, to earn dowry, or as a religious service, a religious duty." I didn't want to quote Bierce any more, for he had made me ashamed of myself. Amelia had warned me against becoming like him.

My father had been right about him. Lillie Coit had been right about him. He would die a lonely and a hated man.

That night I sat down to write a letter to Amelia, addressed to her at 913 Taylor Street, expressing my hope that she would find great happiness in her marriage.

In the Alhambra Saloon the backs of the Democracy solidly lined the bar, and Chris Buckley sat in his corner, surrounded by his crowd. With him were fat Sam Rainey and skinny Mattie Mogle. I had been summoned, and I made my way through my fellow Democrats to present myself to the Boss.

"It is Tom Redmond of the True Blues," he was informed. His unblinking eyeballs fixed on me. He sat in a big chair leaning his two hands on the head of his cane. His pals, seated and standing, regarded me in a moment of silence. I had the feeling of a schoolboy brought before the headmaster.

"Your boss has quit *The Hornet,*" Buckley said, smiling. "And what will you do, Tom?"

"I will look for another position."

"Would you be interested in a job as a schoolmaster? There are positions available."

"I'll try to get work as a journalist."

"What paper?" Sam Rainey said in his gravelly voice. Seated beside Buckley he looked like a wise old frog.

"I have a friend at the *Chronicle*."

"Republican," Buckley said, shaking his head, smiling.

"We can talk to George Hearst," Mogle said. "The *Examiner*'s Democrat for sure."

I shrugged.

"Your boss was not always a reasonable man," Buckley said.

So I was to defend Bierce.

"He was not pleased by the scandals in the school directors, that was for certain," I said. Where there were jobs Buckley could pass out.

" 'A crying roguery,' I believe he put it," Sam Rainey said.

"That was mild for Bierce," I said. I was feeling a little more cheerful, all these Democrats looking at me with disfavor because I had worked with Bierce, who was as hard on Democrats as he was on Republicans.

"He especially didn't like the Board of Supervisors granting a substantial portion of Beach Street to the Spring Valley Water Company," I went on. "It reminded him of the Girtcrest Corridor giveaway."

"*That* is the Railroad, Tom," Buckley said reprovingly.

"And *this* was the water works."

"Bierce is a very negatively minded kind of fellow, Tom. You will admit that yourself, I'm sure. We are trying to ascertain if you are going to be that kind of journalist also, to the detriment of the Democracy."

"Why, Mr. Buckley, I would think the Democrats ought to be reproved as well as the Republicans, when they go in for boodle, and dummies on the payrolls and giveaways. Don't you?"

"Those things should be corrected in the Party councils, not in the newspapers."

"Oh, my!" I said. "Is that what you called me here to tell me?"

There was another silence.

"For instance," I said. "Captain Pusey has collected a deal of money from Lady Caroline Stearns for services rendered. For silence, that is. As for many years he collected the same kind of boodle from Senator Jennings. And everyone knows he has been collecting it from Mammy Pleasant's employer, Thomas Bell, for decades."

"Isaiah Pusey is a good Party man, Tom," Buckley said. He was no longer smiling.

"I suppose his tendencies to blackmail that come from his position, and from his archive of photographs, will be corrected in the Party councils?"

Silence again.

"I think 'a crying roguery' like that has to be addressed in the newspapers," I said.

"We understand you were given a beating by the Railroad ruffians," Sam Rainey said.

"Is that a threat?"

"What we are trying to understand," the Blind Boss interrupted, smiling, "is if it is your intention to carry on the same kind of warfare with the Railroad as Bierce has done."

"Why?" I asked.

"There have been some accommodations made, Tom. We are not going after the Monopoly so hard, and the SP is giving us some funds for the fall campaign."

"I see," I said. I felt as though I was dropping down a mine shaft. "Well, don't count on me, Mr. Buckley. I am Antimonopoly to the grave."

The Blind Boss turned his face away with a pinched expression, as though I had created a bad smell. I gathered that I was excused. So I left the Alhambra Saloon gathering of the party chiefs of the San Francisco Democracy.

 epilogue

FUTURE, *n.*
That period of time in which our affairs pros-
per, our friends are true and our happiness is
assured.

—THE DEVIL'S DICTIONARY

enator Jennings was found guilty of
the murder of Mrs. Hamon but appealed. He was dying from stomach
cancer, however, and during the sec-
ond trial was brought to the courtroom in a wheelchair. He did not
receive much sympathy. He was represented by Bosworth Curtis.

The Morton Street Slasher murders joined the list of San Francisco's unsolved murders. The theory that the Slasher fled to London,
where he resurfaced as Jack the Ripper, gained considerable cre-
dence.

Lady Caroline Stearns and her son also returned to London. Her
daughter was married to the son of the duke of Beltravers at Beltravers
late in August. The wedding was an immense affair, with its shocking
costs published in the *London Times.*

Amelia Brittain and Marshall Sloat were married in September, in
Trinity Episcopalian. I rented fancy duds to attend. It may not have
been as grand an affair as the Beltravers wedding, but it was too grand
for me. The fanciest turnouts with the fanciest horseflesh clogged
Post and Powell, and uniformed servants and footmen hung around
them during the ceremony. I'd never been in an Episcopalian church
before. It was pallid Roman Catholic. Amelia and her banker were

very small up toward the altar. He was bald-headed, with ginger tufts of hair peaking over his ears like a wildcat. Ramparts of flowers surrounded them. Ranked in pews were the instant aristocrats of the *Elite Directory of San Francisco*. I didn't enter in the hymns or the prayers. I felt heavy and loutish, as I had when I'd knocked down Beau McNair and received a bloody nose in return. There were fat gents in full regalia and various arrays of chin whiskers looking mighty comfortable with themselves, there were old women with embonpoints like kitchen ranges, there were young men and women admiring each other. I didn't attend the reception.

When I quit *The Hornet* I got a job at the *Chronicle,* for a slight increase in wages over what Mr. Macgowan had paid me. The *Chronicle* was as anti-Chinese as *The Hornet,* but they did publish my piece on the slave girls- which I quote because it was to become important to my career as a journalist:

> Chinese slave girls can be found in San Francisco in parlor-houses or cribs, the parlorhouses with all the Chinese trappings expected by tourists, musk, sandalwood, teak, silk wall hangi-ngs, comical ceramic gods, and scrolls. These houses are in Grant Avenue, Waverly Place and Ross Alley. There are only a few of-hem. There are cribs without number. They line Jackson and Washington Streets, and Bartlett, China and Church Alleys.
>
> In 1869 the *Chronicle* reported a cargo of nine- and ten-year-old Chinese girls as though they were any commodity arrived from the Orient. "The particularly fine portions of the cargo, the fresh and pretty females who come from the interior, are used to fill special orders from wealthy merchants and prosperous tradesmen. Less fine portions of the cargo would be 'boat-girls,' from the seaboard towns, where contact with sailors would have reduced their value."
>
> That item was published six years after Lincoln's Emancipation Proclamation.
>
> The girls are sold at about the age of five by their parents. Syndicates farm as many as eight hundred girls, bringing

them along to an acceptable age, at which time their prices might be seventy-five or eighty dollars in China. In California they are worth from two hundred to a thousand, depending upon their degree of attractiveness. Pay for their services ranges from fifteen cents to a dollar.

The crib girls on Jackson and Washington Streets, and in the alleys, are exposed like chickens in cages. The cribs are ten or twelve feet wide, containing a front room and back, divided by a curtain. Reformers claim that up to 90 percent of the girls are sick. Their indentured prostitute contracts, which are usually for eight years, add on two weeks for every sick day. If they try to escape their indenture is changed to life. If they are too sick to work they are transported to a "hospital," which they do not depart alive.

I played baseball with Elmer Nix once more, at the new baseball diamond at the Central Park at 8th and Market, both of us playing for teams to which we no longer rightfully belonged, for Nix had quit the police to become a dispatcher for the San Francisco Stock Brewery. I had the pleasure of throwing him out at second base in a double play.

The Girtcrest Corridor Bill passed in early 1886.

Captain Isaiah Pusey became San Francisco chief of police in 1891.

I continued to write occasional pieces for the *Chronicle,* on events, scandals; profiles and expositions for tourists and newcomers to the City; on Emperor Norton, on Sarah Althea Hill, Judge Terry and Senator Sharon, on King Kalakaua and Queen Liliuokalani, Lucky Baldwin, William Ralston, the Big Four, Boss Buckley and Boss Ruef. My extended piece on the Chinese slave girls was published by Bret Harte in the *Atlantic Monthly.* It caused a stir, and my journalistic fortunes were much enhanced.

I published some work that gave pain to the Democratic bosses of the City, the Republican bosses of the state, and the Southern Pacific

Railroad. If I was by no means as brilliant as Bierce, I was not as cynical either. Later I published several books and collections on San Francisco history.

I think my father eventually became as proud of me as if I had been a fire chief. He continued to distribute boodle in the legislature on behalf of Railroad issues. We met for supper about once a month at one of the better San Francisco restaurants, the Gent paying for the repast even after I became well able to do so. The Former-Spade messages to Bierce were never mentioned, my father's single act of disloyalty to his employers.

Some years after her marriage, I met Mrs. Sloat on Geary Street. Amelia was with another handsome young lady, both of them dressed to the nines with elegant hats and tight bodices with low necklines that revealed flesh as smooth as chamois, both of them laden with packages of purchases. They were up from Woodside for the day.

The friend went to the City of Paris while Amelia and I had tea. Her gloved hands fluttered. Once she touched my hand. She smiled and laughed like the Amelia I remembered. She seemed happy. Her husband was a dear man, she said. She loved him very much. She called him "Marshy."

"I think I have made my husband happy," she said.

"How could you not?" I said.

She gazed at me with her eyebrows rising up her forehead and her brown eyes filling with tears.

Looking down, she said, "Marshy is ill. It is doubtful that he can live for two more years, Doctor Byng tells me. He is very brave. I will be a very wealthy woman, Tom."

I didn't say anything to that.

"Have you read any good books lately?" she asked, changing the subject.

I said I had not had much time to read, lately.

"I have been rereading Jane Austen. She is very fine."

"I guess so," I said. I thought about the social elite at Amelia's wedding. I said I didn't much like Jane Austen.

"All the characters think about is money," I said.

Amelia looked as though I had slapped her. She rose, daubing at her eyes. "You have not yet learned irony," she said. She gathered up her packages, awkward in her haste.

"I'm so sorry," I whispered. "Please forgive me!" But I didn't know if she had heard me, for she was gone with a swish of her brown velvet skirt past the table.

I sat alone with my eyes stinging as though they had been dipped in acid.

I remembered Bierce saying that perseverance in one's principles might be praiseworthy, but obduracy in perseverance was stupidity.

I called on Senator Jennings in his room at the Grand Hotel during a court recess. An Irish maid with a face like a side of bacon let me in and went to see if the senator was sleeping. She ushered me into sickroom stink, Jennings braced sitting in a big bed with a half dozen medicine bottles on the table beside the bed. His face was gray as blotting paper.

"I remember you, you're Bierce's boy Friday," he said. He did not sound hostile. "I know your daddy. Is Clete still working for the SP?"

"Yes, sir."

"Working for the Railroad," he almost sang, as though he could make a song of it. "The Railroad dollar did exasperate those that wasn't getting it. What's that nasty son-of-a-bitch Bierce doing now?"

"He's living in Sunol, writing ghost stories about the War."

"Tell him I don't hold no grudges," he said. "We're going to beat it this time. Bos's just that much smarter than they are.

"I'll live to see it," he went on. His lips fluttered when he spoke, as though there were no muscles in them. "Sworn I'd live to see it. We'll beat that one, but there's another I'm not going to beat."

I said I was sorry to see him laid up.

"See that glass of water there? Would you measure exactly twelve drops from the brown bottle into it? Otherwise I'm going to be yowling like a catamount with a cactus up his ass in about two minutes."

I measured in the laudanum, and he swigged the water down with an explosive "Ahhhh!

"Tell Bierce it was McNair that had Gorton cold-cocked," he went on. "Al was one cadging, complaining nasty piece of work. It was Nat McNair."

"I'll tell him," I said and asked if he minded talking about George Payne.

"Don't mind talking about it if you ain't going to print it."

"I won't print anything you don't want me to."

"Promises made," he explained. "Guess who's paying Bos Curtis."

I said I expected it was Lady Caroline Stearns.

He nodded once, grinning, and wiped his damp lips with the sleeve of his nightshirt.

"The woman you hate."

"Son," he said, "when the crabs are chewing on your innards, and old man Death is standing by with his scythe pointed at *you,* you don't have time for hating. I am pleased to say I am over it. It is like shedding off your shoulder a hundred-pound sack of shit. Anyway I'd be hanged by the neck by now if it wasn't for Bos Curtis and that lady paying him. Elza's still sticking by his guns; that was her agreement with Bierce. But Bos is a kind of favor a man don't have any right to expect."

I said Bierce had figured that Mrs. Hamon had made the mistake of telling him, Senator Jennings, that she was going to see Bierce with certain information, and he had met her to dissuade her from it, which encounter had ended in Morton Street.

Jennings didn't want to talk about that.

"That is all I hear about in the courtroom, son. George Payne now, that is interesting."

He closed his eyes, his eyelids fluttering like moths. His lips twitched. "You know, I took that German fella's painting of Highgrade Carrie out of my office in Sacramento and I had it brought down to that saloon me and another chap had on Battery Street. This young fella'd come and sit at the bar half a day staring at it.

"I don't know when I figured out he was Carrie's son, *my* son. I still don't know how it works about twins. It was maybe my jism and the Englishman's swapping around inside her, and the fancy twin was his and the crazy one mine.

"He knew that painting was his mother, too. He'd bartend for me Saturday nights. It was a queer sort of coincidence. He was kind of gentle, you'd never consider he was thinking about cutting doves' guts out. There was something wrong with his peter, I guess. So whores'd made fun of him, that he didn't forget."

"Morton Street whores," I said.

"I told him about the Society of Spades, and how Eddie Macomber and me'd been choused by his mother and McNair, and Al Gorton. I was still hot under the collar—I don't deny that. But I never told him he was my son.

"Bierce was wrong about me pushing him to slash those whores, and going after Carrie. But there was maybe somebody else pushing on him, maybe the Missus Payne he'd been farmed out to, who was some kind of invalid. He knew plenty about Carrie and his brother and things in London. Isaiah Pusey'd told me about his brother in some whore-muckery over there.

"It was crazy. He loved that painting, couldn't stop looking at it, but he hated the lady, his mother. *Hated,* like Bierce said.

"Hated his brother too. That had everything he'd had took from him.

"He was fixated on that mansion of Nat's. He'd found a way to break in and he'd pretend it was his, pretend he was one of the aristocrats from up there. Steal flowers out of the vases and bring them to the saloon. I didn't realize he was even crazier than I was about getting shat on by those people."

"You and Captain Pusey were old friends," I said.

"You could call it that," Jennings said, with the floppy grin.

"I didn't think much about the boy's brother coming back and all that, but he was stone-set loony on his *dispossession,*" he went on. "I never thought of him being after Carrie—to *kill* her. I didn't think about him being the Morton Street Slasher until the second one, and by that time I had some concern of my own in the matter. And he went after that skinny daughter of Jim Brittain's, I understand."

I said that was true, although it had been kept out of the papers.

Senator Jennings shook his head in dismay.

"I guess the Morton Street slashings will never be solved," I said.

"Won't be solved because of me, I can promise you. What about Bierce?"

"He made a promise to Lady Caroline."

"She is good at that," he said, eyes still closed. "Well, I fucked her before she got to be a grand lady; got her in a family way, she told me. That was something! She wasn't so much of a fuck, but by God she was surely Be-You-Tee-full!"

He lay with his eyes closed, cheeks puffed out as he breathed. "The *best,*" he said, "was a little Chinee girl, couldn't've been twelve years old." He held up the first joints of his index and second fingers pressed together in a tight crack. "Like that," he said. "Just like that! Wonder where that little nonpareil is now?"

"Probably dead," I said. "When they come down sick they put them away."

He puffed out his cheeks some more and asked me to prepare another glass of laudanum in water. When he had drunk it, he sat there with his head sunk on his chest and his eyes closed.

"Nobody ever figured out your Daddy was Eddie Macomber," he said softly.

"No, they didn't," I said.

He snored.

The nurse came in to tell me it was time for his nap.

I called on Senator Jennings twice more, to find him lower each time. I tried to find Mrs. Payne, George Payne's adopted mother. I had no help from Mammy Pleasant, who had nothing to gain from me. I made inquiries around Battery Street, I asked so many people if they knew of her that I got tired of hearing my voice speak her name. I never found her.

Senator Jennings died before there was a judgment in the second trial.

A couple of years later Amelia Sloat telephoned me at the *Chronicle*. She sounded breathless. I sat in the dusty, noisy cubicle where the telephone was, the earpiece jammed up against one ear and my mouth close to the mechanism's mouthpiece. I closed my eyes to savor her voice in my ear.

"Will you do me a favor, Tom?"

"Anything."

"This is very difficult for me," she rushed on. "Tom, you must understand, I love Marshy very much. And he loves me very much. But I want to have a baby, and he wants me to, but he had an illness when he was a young man that left him unable to—to *father* a child. But because he loves me he has given me permission to have a child that will be someone else's child but that we will raise as our own. Do you understand, Tom?"

I was being summoned instead of Mammy Pleasant.

I didn't mention old ironies.

We made arrangements to meet in one of the private dining rooms upstairs at the Old Poodle Dog. That was of course an evening I will not forget, no more than Jimmy Fairleigh had been able to forget Caroline LaPlante—filled with wine and laughter, but more tears than laughter, and seriousness of purpose. Arrangements were made for a second meeting a month hence, if it should be necessary.

It was not necessary, and in January of the following year I received an announcement of the birth of Arthur Brittain Sloat. On it was written in a familiar bold hand, "Thank you," without a signature.

I saw the notice of Sloat's death two years later in the obituaries of the *Chronicle*. He was survived by his widow, the former Amelia Brittain, and his son, Arthur Brittain Sloat. Mr. Brittain died about a month later and I figured that Amelia might have moved to town to be with her mother.

I walked down the steep block of Taylor Street from California Street past 913 three different times before I caught a glimpse of the boy. He was playing on the porch where once the Slasher had attacked his mother, a tow-headed child in a black and white sailor jumper running and banging things together, that I finally saw were pots and their lids. He ran and banged, and was silent and invisible behind the railing for periods, until a nurse in a blue uniform with a white doily on her head came out to bring him back inside the house. I didn't catch sight of Amelia.

By then I was married myself.

So is time the lock and occasion the key that does not always fit.

In the society columns it was noted when Amelia Brittain Sloat left for New York with her son.

Belinda Barnacle was married in her eighteenth year, but not on her eighteenth birthday, to a young fellow named Haskell Green, who was a boarder at the Barnacles' establishment. Green had a job as a coal salesman for the Cedar River Coal Company. He was "a real go-getter," Mr. Barnacle assured me. I sent leather-bound, gilt-edged fine editions of *Pride and Prejudice* and *Sense and Sensibility* as a wedding present.

Senator Sharon died before *Sharon v. Sharon* came to its conclusion. Knowing he was dying, he vowed that his estate would expend every penny he owned fighting Miss Hill's outrageous fabrications. "Why, she would be the highest paid whore in history," he was reported to have said. "The grandes horizontales of Paris are cheapskates compared to her. I hear they charge a thousand francs a night. If Allie wins out, she'll be netting about a hundred and fifty thousand *dollars* per."

On hearing of Sharon's death, Bierce wrote in his column in the

Examiner: "Death is not the end; there remains the litigation over the Estate."

The State Superior Court ruled in Sarah Althea Hill's favor. Mrs. Sharon was awarded $2,500 per month as alimony, and $55,000 for counsel's fees. Mrs. Sharon promptly went on a shopping spree. Unfortunately the Federal Circuit Court was still to be heard from. There would be no more shopping sprees for Miss Hill.

I knew that Bierce had been moving from place to place. He spent some time at Larkmead with Lillie Coit. He lived briefly at the Putnam House in Auburn, and in a boardinghouse in Sunol. My wife and I called on him in Oakland, where he had taken an apartment. She was intimidated about meeting the man about whom she had heard so much, but Bierce was in a fine mood. He had a new job.

We sat on a sofa in the small, hot room, while he brought us tea and ranged before us, gesturing as he told the story of his employment, the same Ambrose Bierce, with his fair mustache like a pair of sparrow's wings, and his curly, silvering hair, and his cold eyes beneath shaggy brows. He wore a checked suit and a high collar and tie.

"This young man came to my door," he told us. "The youngest man, it seemed to me, that I have ever confronted. His appearance and manner were of the most extreme diffidence. I did not ask him to apply himself to my better chair but kept him on my doorstep.

"He said he had come from the *San Francisco Examiner.* Of course I knew that George Hearst had recently presented the *Examiner* to his son, Willie, as a plaything.

" 'Oh, you have come from Mr. Hearst,' I said.

"And he lifted his blue eyes to me and cooed, 'I am Mr. Hearst!' "

Bierce laughed and clapped his hands together. Young Hearst was assembling the finest stable of journalists in the West. Peter Bigelow and Arthur McEwen had already been employed. Hearst wanted Bierce to write a column for the Sunday *Examiner.*

"And I will do it!" Bierce said. "I am anxious for some City clamor and movement. I am tired of the scent of pine trees!"

And he said to me, "Perhaps you will come to the *Examiner* too, Tom."

I said I was very happy at the *Chronicle,* but I would look forward to seeing him in the City.

"Yes, we had a pleasant association," Bierce said. "What detectives we were!" He said to my wife, "You must persuade your husband, my dear."

She said in a small voice that she would try.

Our association was never again to be what it was. I tried to be of some comfort to Bierce when his sixteen-year-old son, Day, with whom I had participated in double-play practice in St. Helena, shot himself in a fracas over a girl that you did not have to be Ambrose Bierce to know was a piece of utter human stupidity. His second son, Leigh, died of acute alcoholism in 1901.

That same year the first "society" novel of Amelia Brittain Sloat was serialized in *Scribner's Magazine.* The title was *Shadows in the Glass.* The heroine of her novel, Clara Benbough, was forced by her husband's syphilitic sterility to beg an old friend to father her child. The novel was considered quite daring.

Amelia Brittain Sloat's novels were often compared to those of Gertrude Atherton, the most famous and daring of the California lady novelists.

A year later Sarah Althea Hill Terry was remanded to the State Insane Asylum in Stockton. *Sharon v. Hill* had gone against her, in appeal after appeal. She had married Judge Terry, who was thirty-four years her senior. In *Sharon v. Sharon* and *Sharon v. Hill* Terry was her most steadfast supporter, even including Mammy Pleasant. The last appeal of *Sharon v. Hill* was pleaded before Judge Stephan J. Field, who should have recused himself. He had been a friend of Senator Sharon's, had sat on the State Supreme Court with Judge Terry and was his implacable enemy.

When the ultimate crushing decision was read, both Sarah Althea and Judge Terry became violent. Terry was confined in jail for six months for his outbursts, Sarah Althea for three.

A year after the decision Mr. and Mrs. Terry encountered Judge Field in a railroad station. Terry assaulted the judge, striking him twice, and was shot dead by the judge's bodyguard, one Dave Neagle, who had served as a deputy sheriff with Wyatt Earp in Tombstone, Arizona.

Mrs. Terry's conduct in the following years became more and more erratic. She was destitute. She had lost her famous auburn-haired looks, and she was losing her wits as well. Mammy Pleasant took her in, at the Octavia Street mansion, but Sarah Althea became more and more pathetic, and a public nuisance.

Ambrose Bierce, never notable for his compassion, wrote of her:

"The male Californian—idolater of sex and proud of abasement at the feet of his own female—has now a fine example of the results entailed by his unnatural worship. Mrs. Terry, traipsing the streets, uncommonly civic, problematically harmless but indubitably daft, is all his own work, and he ought to be proud of her."

Mammy Pleasant signed the commitment documents.

Gertrude Atherton had an encounter with Bierce in Sunol, where, after having submitted to some savage criticism of her novels, she gained the advantage over him by laughing at his attempt to embrace her. They became fellow columnists on the *San Francisco Examiner,* but her contempt for her readership was without the wit that Bierce exercised, and she soon returned to New York and her career as a novelist. She and Bierce, however, embarked upon a long correspondence. He became a faithful admirer and critic of her work, and she regarded him as her muse.

Her one-time companion, Sibyl Sanderson, was established as an opera diva of international repute and continued to shock San Franciscans by becoming the mistress of the composer Massenet.

I encountered young Arthur Brittain Sloat at a meeting in New York of the Newspaper Guild, of which I was at that time an officer. He was a reporter working for James Gordon Bennett at the *World*. Looking at him was like seeing in a mirror not my reflection but the reflection of myself twenty-two years before. He must have thought I was drunk from the confusion of my greeting.

His mother was at that time on her third marriage and her seventh novel, which was a fictionalization of the Rose of Sharon.

Huntington remained Bierce's chief enemy. Crocker had died in 1888, Stanford in 1893, and Collis B. Huntington became the Southern Pacific Railroad. In 1884 he had been able to cross the country entirely on lines he controlled. His dislike of Leland Stanford, which had always smoldered, caught fire in the senatorial election of 1885, when Stanford doublecrossed Huntington's friend and faithful Railroad ally Aaron A. Sargent to capture the Republican nomination. In 1887 Stanford "trifled" again with Huntington, making a deal with George Hearst and San Francisco boss Chris Buckley to assist Hearst's future candidacy in return for Democratic support for a second term in the U.S. Senate.

"I don't forget those who have played me false," Huntington said.

His chance to strike back at Stanford came when Stanford had overextended financing his son's memorial, the Leland Stanford Jr. University. Huntington prevented the former governor's withdrawal of Railroad funds to balance his personal accounts. The Railroad was then under heavy investigation by the government, and Stanford would have been indicted except for the timely decisions of Justice Stephan Field of the State Supreme Court, who had never been known to let down a millionaire friend.

Huntington was to take one more swipe at his old partner. When

Stanford died the estate was immediately tied up in lawsuits, the most important of which was that filed by the federal government attaching assets until the Railroad's $57,000,000 debt was settled. It seemed that the university must close its doors. "Close the circus!" Huntington growled, and let the Stanford estate fight the battle of the Big Four's liability, which he also, in his time, would have to face.

By Mrs. Stanford's heroic efforts the university was kept in operation. A friendly judge allowed her to claim professors and staff as personal servants. Race horses were sold, Mrs. Stanford's household servants and gardeners were dismissed, her carriage let go. The university was kept open despite Huntington's malignity.

As the cold-hearted old magnate grew older, he became an easy mark for cartoonists, with his bald, double-domed skull, which he kept covered with a rabbinical skullcap. Caricaturists customarily portrayed him and his railroad lines as an octopus.

The electorate had begun to take a different view of laissez-faire capitalism, and the Railroad's rate structure, which was universally viewed as arbitrary and discriminatory, was widely blamed for the depression of the 1890s. Moreover the Railroad's second-mortgage governmental bonds were soon to fall due, and Huntington girded his forces for the fight against their payment. He employed representatives in Washington and in state capitals, whose duty it was to "explain" to legislators what was "right." He insisted on the American privilege of supporting the election of officials whose views coincided with his own. Payments were made when necessary, but he did not view this as bribery. A bribe was a voluntary purchase for personal advancement, the wrongdoing of which he had accused Stanford.

When I wrote a memorial piece on Bierce for the *Chronicle,* I was pleased to describe his final triumph over Huntington and the Railroad, which had been a long time coming:

> William Randolph Hearst sent Bierce to Washington to help
> the Hearst newspapers fight the Railroad Funding Bill. This
> Bill would have been the biggest giveaway yet to the Southern

Pacific Railroad. The $75,000,000 debt to the U.S. govern-
ment was to be fobbed off in the form of 2 percent bonds due
in 80 years. In effect it was a total gift to the Southern Pacific.
Huntington had bought up enough senators, especially those
of the Western states, to insure the Bill's passage.

Bierce immediately went into action in the *San Francisco
Examiner* and the New York *Morning Journal*, in the style of
invective he had perfected, abusing the Railroad and Collis
B. Huntington, and praising Senator John T. Morgan, chair-
man of the senate committee that had summoned Huntington to testify before it, and who embarrassed the president of
the Railroad with probing questions.

Bierce wrote, "Huntington has been able to remove his
hand from the public's pocket long enough to raise it over a
Bible. In Sacramento the Railroad's bagmen are as common
a sight as the senate pages, but instead of sending lobbyists
to Washington to accomplish his crowning achievement of
the purchase of the U.S. Senate, Huntington has packed his
own baggage full of greenbacks and come to tend to matters
himself."

In trouble in committee, Huntington produced testimo-
nial letters from prominent Californians attesting to the Railroad's benefits to the state and the extraordinary ethics of its
proprietors. Bierce pursued the authors of these testimonials
as he had pursued Aaron Jennings. He publicized them in
"Bierce's Black Book," where their names were broadcast until they recanted. Recant they did. The senate revelations,
Huntington's arrogance and ignorance as shown in the committee hearings, and Bierce's harpoonings were so shocking
that all but two of the testimonials were withdrawn. The senatorial tide turned against the Southern Pacific Railroad.

Huntington encountered Bierce on the steps of the capitol. "How much?" he growled in defeat, and he uttered his
familiar judgment, more cynical than Ambrose Bierce had
ever been: "Every man has his price!"

"Seventy-five million dollars," Bierce said in his triumph.
"Payable to the U.S. Government!"

Designer: Seventeenth Street Studios
Compositor: Binghamton Valley Composition
Text: 10/14 ITC New Baskerville
Display: ITC Ozwald
Printer and binder: Maple-Vail Book Manufacturing Group